ST. THOMAS PUBLIC LIBRARY
36278008233041

DP

D0861137

NOV - - 2016

SPECIAL MESSAGE TO READERS

THE ULVERSCROFT FOUNDATION
(registered UK charity number 264873)

was established in 1972 to provide funds for research, diagnosis and treatment of eye diseases. Examples of major projects funded by the Ulverscroft Foundation are:-

- The Children's Eye Unit at Moorfields Eye Hospital, London
- The Ulverscroft Children's Eye Unit at Great Ormond Street Hospital for Sick Children
- Funding research into eye diseases and treatment at the Department of Ophthalmology, University of Leicester
- The Ulverscroft Vision Research Group, Institute of Child Health
- Twin operating theatres at the Western Ophthalmic Hospital, London
- The Chair of Ophthalmology at the Royal Australian College of Ophthalmologists

You can help further the work of the Foundation by making a donation or leaving a legacy. Every contribution is gratefully received. If you would like to help support the Foundation or require further information, please contact:

THE ULVERSCROFT FOUNDATION
The Green, Bradgate Road, Anstey
Leicester LE7 7FU, England
Tel: (0116) 236 4325

website: www.foundation.ulverscroft.com

THE COMIC BOOK KILLER

Hobart Lindsey is a quiet man, a bachelor living with his widowed mother in the suburbs and working as an insurance claims agent. Marvia Plum is a tough, savvy, street-smart cop. Then fate throws the unlikely pair together. A burglary at a vintage comic book store leads to a huge insurance claim that Lindsey must investigate for his company — and to the brutal murder of the store owner, for which Marvia must find the killer. Lindsey and Plum, like oil and water — but working together to unravel a baffling mystery!

Books by Richard A. Lupoff
in the Linford Mystery Library:

THE UNIVERSAL HOLMES

THE CASES OF CHASE AND
DELACROIX

ONE MURDER AT A TIME

THE EVIL BELOW

ROOKIE COP

MURDERS GALORE

RICHARD A. LUPOFF

♦

THE
COMIC BOOK
KILLER

Complete and Unabridged

LINFORD
Leicester

ST. THOMAS PUBLIC LIBRARY

First published in Great Britain

First Linford Edition
published 2016

Copyright © 1988 by Richard A. Lupoff
All rights reserved

A catalogue record for this book is available
from the British Library.

ISBN 978–1–4448–2736–1

Published by
F. A. Thorpe (Publishing)
Anstey, Leicestershire

Set by Words & Graphics Ltd.
Anstey, Leicestershire
Printed and bound in Great Britain by
T. J. International Ltd., Padstow, Cornwall

This book is printed on acid-free paper

1

Hobart Lindsey put the Contra Costa *Times* on the seat beside him, and the KGO morning news on the Hyundai's radio. He waved to his mother, standing at the window, and pulled out of the driveway, headed for his office.

The news itself was the usual mix of natural disaster and human atrocity. Only in the sports headlines was there ever any talk of heroes, and even in sports it seemed there were more drug busts and paternity suits than points scored or championships won.

Not that Lindsey's own life was so exciting. But, by gosh, if he had the chance to earn the kind of money and glory those athletes had, he wouldn't stuff it up his nose or pour it down his gullet or blow it on a moment's pleasure with some cheap floozy!

But, alas, there wasn't much of a chance of money or glory settling insurance claims.

Not if you were as honest as Lindsey was. Unless . . . He permitted himself a fleeting daydream. Maybe today something would happen to lift him out of the humdrum. A crisis, an opportunity, a chance to escape the everyday round of claim forms and statistical reports and his unchanging life at home with Mother —

He hit the brakes to keep from rear-ending a Mercury Sable rolling down the ramp into the garage under his office. It looked like Eric Coffman's station wagon, so he waved, just in case Eric was looking in the rearview mirror. He parked the Hyundai and headed for the elevator.

* * *

'This is terrible! They cleaned us out, they took everything!' The upset voice was a youthful, reedy tenor. 'I'm ruined, ruined,' he sobbed. 'Oh my God, call me back right away, please!'

Lindsey hit the rewind button on the Answermate and listened to the message again. The caller had given his name at the end of his message. Lindsey jotted it down. Terry Patterson. Unfortunately he hadn't left any number.

Lindsey frowned; he shouldn't have to take the calls off the machine. That was part of Ms. Wilbur's job. But that's the way it is, the responsible executive arrives at his desk early! That had always been his philosophy throughout his eleven years of faithful service to International Surety.

He snorted in exasperation and surveyed the office. International Surety didn't believe in pampering its employees, and the furniture was functional at best. The computer was the only thing in the office that got any kind of pampering!

Lindsey wondered if he was ever going to get any recognition from management. How many years did it take to get noticed?

He would have got to the office still earlier, but he'd had to wait at home for Mrs. Hernandez. He couldn't leave Mother alone, and Mrs. Hernandez simply couldn't arrange her mornings to reach the house before seven-thirty.

Even so, Lindsey arrived before Ms.

Wilbur. He'd looked over the mail — routine — and had put six spoons of decaffeinated Maxwell House in the Mr. Coffee machine.

There was still the Contra Costa *Times* to be scanned. The usual scandals and disasters. There was an interesting piece on crime statistics that compared felony rates in various cities in the Bay Area. Oakland and San Francisco and Richmond, as usual, were in a hot race for the dubious honor of most felonies per capita. Especially murders! The little island town of Alameda, as usual, came in dead last. One homicide in the past six months: a retired navy man had apparently surprised a burglar in his living room and paid for it with his life. No clues, also as usual.

Once the coffee was brewing, Lindsey tossed aside the newspaper and sat down in front of the Answermate. The counter showed three calls overnight: Mrs. McMartin chattering and jabbering over a fender-bender; old Mr. Candliss, whose wife had passed away; and then the call from Terry Patterson.

Lindsey returned the calls in order. He phoned Mrs. McMartin and told her to

4

get three estimates and submit them to the office. The usual. Then he looked at the Candliss file. Mr. and Mrs. had full life policies in matching amounts. Mr. Candliss would get about enough to bury her if he did it on the cheap. Lindsey jotted a note to Ms. Wilbur to send Candliss a set of claim forms.

Lindsey ran the tape from Terry Patterson again. 'This is terrible! They cleaned us out, they took everything! I'm ruined, ruined. Oh, my God, call me back right away, please!'

Lindsey queried the computer but there was no household policy in Terry Patterson's name. He sighed and called up the data base. If Patterson wasn't the policyholder, it was probably a commercial policy. He told the computer to search for Patterson's name as the responsible party.

Lindsey looked up from the display screen as Ms. Wilbur arrived. 'I'm sorry I'm late, Bart. I couldn't help it.' She opened the closet, took off her jacket and hung it inside. She walked over to the Mr. Coffee and smiled faintly. 'Smells good.'

At least she called him Bart, not Hobo. His mother had named him Hobart, one of the worst names invented in the annals of man. He'd given up long ago trying to get Ms. Wilbur to call him Mr. Lindsey, but at least she used the preferred version of his first name. He hated Hobo almost as much as he hated Hobart.

Pouring herself a cup of coffee, she sat at her desk and rewound the cassette on the Answermate and started through the calls again. 'Oh, poor Mrs. Candliss died,' she said. 'Don't you want to handle this yourself, Bart?'

He told her he'd have handled it himself if he'd wanted to handle it himself. Ms. Wilbur sniffed and picked up the phone, presumably to call Mr. Candliss.

'Do you know a Terry Patterson?' he asked.

Ms. Wilbur was murmuring condolences into the phone. Good gosh, the man was going to collect. Let the relatives offer handkerchiefs — International Surety was going to send money!

Without putting down the phone, Ms. Wilbur scribbled *Comic Cavalcade* on a memo slip and shoved it toward Bart. Lindsey frowned, then realized that it must be the account that Patterson had called about.

He looked back at the glowing display. The computer had found Terry Patterson, and the account information appeared on the monitor screen. It was a store called Comic Cavalcade. Terry Patterson was listed as sole proprietor.

There was an address in Berkeley and a phone number. Berkeley! Lindsey found himself hoping he could settle this pipsqueak claim without having to go to Patterson's place of business. He hated comic books and everything to do with them. And Berkeley . . . well, everyone knows that town and what it's filled with. Drug pushers, hippies, rich university students, yuppies, homosexuals, and communists. And then there are the bad guys!

He played Patterson's message again. It sounded like an ordinary burglary. And anyway, how much could they get from a store that sold comic books? Lindsey would tell Patterson to call the police and have Ms. Wilbur send him a claim form.

In fact, he'd rather have Ms. Wilbur handle the whole thing, only she was still on the phone with Mr. Candliss and Lindsey was in no mood to wait.

He jotted down the phone number for Comic Cavalcade, then dialed. The reedy voice that matched Terry Patterson's on the tape said, 'Comic Cavalcade. The store is open from eleven a.m. to ten p.m., seven days a week. If you wish to leave a message, please wait for the signal.'

When the sound came over the line he said, 'This is Hobart Lindsey at International Surety in Walnut Creek, returning your — '

'Mr. Lindsey!' Patterson must have been monitoring calls. 'Mr. Lindsey, thank you for calling. Oh, this is terrible. I think you'd better come over here.'

'I don't know if that will be necessary,' Lindsey said. 'Have you notified the police?'

'Yes, sure. First thing. There's an officer here right now, but I think you'd better come in.'

A police officer — that was a pleasant

8

surprise. Lindsey hadn't expected that the Berkeley police would bother with something like a burglary at a comic book store. 'How great is the loss, Mr. Patterson?'

'I haven't priced everything out. I've done an inventory; I think I know everything they took. But — '

'Was this a break-in?' Lindsey asked.

'Sort of. They didn't smash the window or anything. I think they, uh, jimmied the back door lock.'

'Well, it sounds like a police matter to me. How much do you estimate your loss to be?' Lindsey looked at the display screen to check Comic Cavalcade's deductible. If it was a petty loss, it wouldn't even be worth processing the claim.

'Uh, I'll have to double-check this, Mr. Lindsey, against the price guides and such. But I figure they got some really choice items.'

Lindsey counted to five. 'Could you just give me a rough dollar estimate of the value of those comic books? Just a preliminary figure.'

'Uh, ab-about a quarter of a million,

Mr. Lindsey. A lot of the things were on consignment, you understand. So I d-d-didn't just lose my own stock, I'll have to make good to the owners. I can't pay that kind of money, M-Mr. Lindsey. International Surety has to stand by me. You have to. Please!'

Lindsey muttered something into the phone and hung up. He was trembling.

Ms. Wilbur asked if he wanted a cup of coffee.

2

Lindsey asked Ms. Wilbur to hold the fort while he took a run into Berkeley. He grabbed his briefcase and headed for the door. He got his Hyundai out of its basement parking spot and fought his way into the traffic.

For a minute Lindsey thought about telephoning Harden at Regional, but he decided against it. He'd bring Harden on board when he had some solid information the company could dig its teeth into.

Patterson had to be some kind of a wimp — a grown man who made his living selling comic books to children! Had there even been a burglary at all? Maybe Patterson had stolen those comic books himself. Maybe there had never been any comic books, and he was attempting to defraud International Surety of a quarter-million dollars.

Possible fraud, Lindsey jotted in his pocket organizer as he waited at a traffic light on Monument Boulevard. *At least contributory negligence.* Already he was coming up with some good ideas about how to save the company money.

Maybe he'd send a memo direct to Legal and copy Harden. Lindsey knew Harden wasn't above taking his ideas to Legal and presenting them as his own. Harden would get the glory, then toss a couple of crumbs to Lindsey after the fact.

Lindsey got on the freeway and headed for Berkeley. He parked in a municipal garage and walked to Comic Cavalcade on Telegraph Avenue. UC was back from semester break and foot traffic was heavy. A vagrant snap of wind stirred a flutter of newspapers and fast-food containers along the pavement.

He stood on the sidewalk in front of Comic Cavalcade and reconnoitered. The glass display window was filled with *Spider-Man* and *Batman* and *Fantastic Four* comic books, and Japanese robots and toys and greeting cards.

The kind of thing that Lindsey had loved, once upon a time. But he was a man on the shady side of thirty now, and such things were no longer part of his life. He wished they'd never been! He'd grown up surrounded by comic books and toys, and only gradually had he come to realize what those things had meant to Mother. How they had shaped her life, made her the sad creature she was now. And, at least indirectly, taken so much from him.

He tried the door but it was locked. A 'Closed' sign hung at eye level.

He checked the neighboring establishments. On one side of the comic store was a clothing shop. Through the window he saw a high-school-age girl with purple hair standing behind the counter. Lindsey thought he might want to check with the girl, find out if she was on duty when the alleged burglary took place.

On the other side of the comic store was a pizza parlor. A black man in full chef's regalia spun a circular sheet of pizza dough, threw it into the air and caught it when it spun back down.

Lindsey took his pocket organizer out of his briefcase and jotted a note. *Pizza parlor . . . clothing store . . . access to C.C. stock?*

He returned to Comic Cavalcade and pressed his nose to the glass and peered inside. A young man in a disreputable-looking shirt slouched behind the counter. He was tall and skinny and wore dark-rimmed eyeglasses. A police officer stood opposite him. A rack of comic books blocked Lindsey's line of sight, so he could see only part of the officer's back.

The young man started to wave Lindsey away, then realized who he was, came to the door and let him in. He locked the door again.

'M-Mr. Lindsey?'

'Yes.' Lindsey handed him his card. 'You Terry Patterson?'

The young man gulped and nodded, then put the card into his jeans pocket. He said, 'Off-Officer Plum, uh, M-Mr. Lindsey is here, uh, from the insurance, uh, company.'

Officer Plum turned around, picked up a clipboard holding incident report forms, and halved the distance between them. Lindsey realized simultaneously that Officer Plum was female and that she was black.

The first thing they did was exchange

cards. At least they did that right in Berkeley. Marvia Plum, Berkeley Police Department, was all that was printed on hers; in red ink she had added a telephone number.

'I was just leaving,' Officer Plum said. She was short and very dark. Her hair was cropped close to her scalp. The way she filled her form-fitting police uniform was impressive. Lindsey was momentarily distracted. He wondered if the department dressed female officers like that to distract criminals.

She picked up her uniform cap and yanked it down over her wiry hair.

'But we haven't had a chance to — '

'My work is done.' She started moving toward the back of the store and the likely rear exit. 'We can't hang around all day. I don't know where you've been since Terrence called you, but we've checked the crime scene for evidence, Terrence has filled out the forms . . . I've got a lot of other work to do.'

'Well — wait just a little minute.' He strode purposefully after her, taking in his surroundings.

The main room of the store seemed

fairly standard. The merchandise, cheap, glossy-covered comic books and other paraphernalia, stood on display in revolving wire racks, on tables, in glass cases, and mounted in clear plastic covers on the walls.

Lindsey followed Officer Plum into a back room that held more wall displays and more glass cases. Unlike the cases in the front room with their simple sliding doors, these were conspicuously locked. Lindsey couldn't resist inspecting the contents of a couple of them. He recognized some of the comic books — issues that he'd seen at home as a child.

Lindsey couldn't help blinking when he saw among them the crudely rendered cover illustration of *Gangsters at War*. A square-jawed, unshaven ruffian in a ragged set of army fatigues waved a submachine gun in one hand and a sizzling grenade in the other. His lips were drawn back in a snarl. Underneath his army fatigue jacket, through gaping holes, part of a prison-striped uniform shirt could be seen.

Lindsey squatted in front of the case to get a closer look. He scanned the glossy cover, searching for the artist's identifying mark. There it was: a circle that outlined a tiny stylized face, a heavily arched brow, a pair of mirror-image slashes that defined both the nose and eyes. The sketch, Mother had explained long ago, was really a signature. The brow line and slashes were the initials J.L., the eye dots periods. The drawing had been done by Joseph Lindsey. Lindsey's long-dead father.

He frowned. He couldn't take the time to think about Father; couldn't mix his personal life with his professional performance. Besides, he'd never even met the man. He found his way to the back door of the shop. The hasp that normally secured the door had been pried away from the doorframe and now hung loose. Other than that, there was no evidence of forceful entry, and no disarray or physical damage within the store.

At a sound from the narrow hallway Lindsey turned. Officer Plum hadn't left after all. She was standing with her clipboard in her hand. The wooden butt of a heavy revolver protruded from a small holster she wore on one hip. A pair of nickel-plated handcuffs hung from the other hip. A tiny two-way radio was clipped to one shoulder of her blouse.

Terry Patterson stood behind her, forehead creased with worry above his dark-rimmed, thick-lensed glasses.

'Mr. Lindsey, what's your opinion?' Officer Plum asked.

'I guess this is where they backed the truck up. Parking lot in the back? Loading dock?'

Officer Plum said, 'What truck?'

'The truck — I don't think they could have fit it into a station wagon, do you?'

'What are you talking about, Mr. Lindsey?'

'Mr. Patterson says they got away with $250,000 worth of merchandise. A quarter million! How many pounds, how many cubic feet of paper does that represent?' Lindsey peered over the police officer's head at the store owner.

Patterson blinked owlishly. 'I don't think th-there wasn't any truck here, Mr. Lindsey.'

'Then how did they get away with the loot?'

'Uh, I sup-suppose they could have carried it in a carton or backpack. Or — or — ' He pointed at the insurance adjuster. 'Or, uh, somebody could have carried the comics away in a briefcase like y-yours, Mr. Lindsey.' He swung round at a sudden rapping on the glass of the front door of the shop.

'Uh, Marvia, uh, Mr. Lindsey. It's Jan — Janice — and Linc. M-My staff. Can I let them in? Can I open the store now?'

'Okay with me, Terrence,' said Officer Plum.

Patterson took the distance back to the front door with huge, birdlike strides. Jan and Linc, Lindsey could see, were standing with their arms around each other's waists. Jan was Asiatic and Linc was some kind of nondescript racial mixture.

Officer Plum said, 'I don't think you understand what happened here. This wasn't a massive theft of stock. Whoever knocked this place over knew exactly what they were doing. Terrence tells me that approximately just thirty-five items were taken.'

'He just gave me a dollar value on the

phone. He said a quarter million. I figured it would take a stadium full of comic books to make that much. You'd have to haul them away in a truck.'

'No way.' She shook her head. 'Just thirty-five of them. You don't know anything about comic books, I take it.'

If only she knew! 'Not the modern ones,' Lindsey said. 'When I was a kid I read a few. *Archie*, *Richie Rich*, Disney stuff. And my father was a cartoonist. He drew for the comics.'

'Anything in the store?'

Lindsey moved his head to indicate the display case containing *Gangsters at War*. 'He wasn't very good, I'm afraid. He was just getting established. He died before I was born.'

'Oh, I'm so sorry!' She pursed her lips.

'I never knew him, so I never missed him.' Lindsey hoped she wasn't going to ask him more about it.

Officer Plum said, 'But family is so important.'

Lindsey said nothing.

After an awkward pause, Officer Plum said, 'About these stolen comic books

. . . a lot of people collect them. Sometimes they even form syndicates and buy into them, as investments.'

She knew a lot about comic books for somebody who had just come to investigate a burglary. Lindsey said so.

'I collect them myself. Just a few.'

If she hadn't been so black, Lindsey thought, she would have blushed.

'Thirty-five items, worth $250,000. That makes just over — '

'A little over seven thousand apiece,' Officer Plum interrupted. 'I have a detailed inventory here.' She tapped her fingernail against her clipboard. 'I'm sure Terrence will provide you with an inventory on his claim, but if you'd rather, I can get you a photocopy of the report. You'll probably want one anyway, to verify the insurance claim.'

Lindsey hesitated.

'Well, I have to go.' She turned around, walked to the front of the shop, spoke briefly with Terry Patterson, then left.

Patterson came back to where Lindsey was standing. 'Y-You brought me the insurance forms, Mr. Lindsey? I really need to take care of this. Those weren't my comics. I mean, some of them were and some of them weren't. I don't know what I'm going to do. I — '

Lindsey put up his hand. 'I have the forms here, don't worry. But you know, we can't just make out a check for this kind of money until there's been an investigation. We have to make sure that the claim is legitimate. And if there's any chance of recovering the loot, we have to work on that angle.'

Patterson made a low, moaning sound.

'Besides,' Lindsey said, 'there are a lot of unanswered questions. For instance, your two, ah, helpers.'

Linc and Jan were in the front room. They had opened the street door as if no crime had been committed. They might have seen Officer Plum leaving and heard the end of Lindsey's conversation with their boss. They must be boiling with curiosity.

Linc was arranging stock on the wire racks and tables. Jan was standing behind the cash register. Already several customers had gathered inside the store. A handful of what looked like elementary-school children clustered at the wire racks, and an older man with greasy-looking gray hair and a bald spot stood near the wall. The elderly man gazed up at a thirty-year-old copy of *Reform School Girls* that hung in a transparent bag. Instead of the customary colorful drawing, the cover featured a photograph of a busty female model. A cigarette hung from the corner of her mouth, smoke drifting lazily upward. She had her skirt hiked up and was adjusting the top of one sheer stocking. The top of her dress was pulled low over her shoulders.

'Look at those two,' Lindsey said. 'How do you know they didn't steal the comics? What time did the burglary take place, anyway?'

'I, uh, Linc closed last night. He phoned me at home. That's our regular procedure. This is just a small business, you see. I have to keep close watch on it. I've put everything I have into it, and everything I could borrow. It's expensive to run a store, you know.'

'Go on.'

'So, uh, I have to keep close tabs,' Patterson said, blushing slightly. 'And so Linc phoned me with the day's totals, and to tell me that he'd secured the store, deposited the receipts at the bank, and he was at home.'

'Where?'

'Uh — just a couple of blocks from here — '

'Never mind. I'll want a complete list of employees and their home addresses later on.'

'Anyway, I arrived to open this morning early — around seven o'clock, to check the stock because I was going to make the run to Hayward, to the distributors today. I saw the broken lock on the back door, but I didn't see anything obviously missing, so I checked the special collectibles and that's when I saw what was missing.'

'And you found it right away, and you know exactly how much the missing items are worth.'

'No, uh, only approximately.'

'Listen here, Mr. Patterson. I think I can get you off clean. I'll be very direct with you: I don't think there was any burglary here. I think it was an inside job.'

'You mean Linc or — or J-Jan?' He leaned against a glass display case.

'Cut the corn, sonny,' Lindsey told him with a sneer. 'I mean you.'

Terry Patterson carefully removed his glasses, laid them on the display case, and slid to the floor in a dead faint.

3

The kid was only out for a couple of seconds, if he was really out at all. While Linc Morris and Lindsey got Patterson propped up against the glass display case, Janice Chiu stayed in front to watch the store. Poor Patterson was pale and sweating. His breathing was shallow and his hands trembled visibly.

Classic shock — was it the stress of the burglary made worse by Lindsey's accusation? Or was it the knowledge that his scheme had failed and he was in deep trouble?

Patterson stirred and looked around. 'Where — where are my glasses?'

Lindsey picked them up and handed them to him. Patterson fumbled them onto his nose. Linc Morris said, 'Maybe I ought to call an ambulance, Terry.'

'I'm okay. I j-just felt a little dizzy. I didn't eat breakfast. Maybe a bite of food — '

'All right,' Lindsey told him, 'there has to be an eating joint nearby. International Surety'll buy you a Danish and coffee.'

Patterson was starting to get his color back, and he told Morris to make the Hayward run for him, pick up the new shipment of comics from the distributor and bring it back to the store. Jan Chiu could keep watch over Comic Cavalcade and take care of the customers while Morris was gone.

They crossed the street as soon as there was a break in the traffic. Lindsey led Patterson into the first eating place he saw, a black-and-white art deco café. He slid Patterson into a booth and stood in line to buy him a sweet pastry.

Patterson disappeared the Danish so fast Lindsey figured he must have missed his dinner last night as well as his breakfast this morning. Lindsey refilled his coffee cup and said, 'Well, how 'bout it, Terry? You ready to give everything back and drop it? Officer Plum there might be pretty annoyed with you for filing a false report, but I think we can still square it.'

'No, it's the truth, Mr. Lindsey.' He

held up his hand like a witness in court. 'So help me. I th-thought it was your job to be on my side, not against me.'

'I don't want to see you ruin yourself. Look, Terry, you're just a kid — '

'I'm t-twenty-six.'

'Don't mess yourself up now. You don't think we're going to pay out a quarter mil on this phony claim, do you? We'll deny the claim; it'll drag on for years. You'll never see the money. But you will see the inside of a cell, I can promise you that!'

Maybe I overplayed that a little, Lindsey thought as Patterson started to cry.

'What can I do to convince you?' the kid sobbed. 'I found the door jimmied when I came in this morning. Then I checked the stock and discovered the missing comics. I'll swear an oath. I'll take a p-polygraph test. How's that? Would you believe that if I pass it?'

'Let's leave that for now.' Lindsey decided to let up on him a little. This case might be his big chance to shine, to be noticed by the bigshots . . . 'Do you have a list of the missing items?'

'Off-Officer Plum took that. B-But I

can make another list,' he said.

'You memorized 35 items?'

'Uh, I can visualize everything that they took. Comics are my life, Mr. Lindsey. If I don't get the money for the ones they took, I'll lose my store, I'll lose everything. I'll never pay off the consignors.'

Lindsey gave him an International Surety ballpoint and a lined pad. He sat there making the list. He wrote down the first dozen or so without slowing down. Then he stopped and closed his eyes for a few seconds, opened them and wrote down the rest. Finally he scanned the list, nodded, and handed it to Lindsey. 'It — It was the whole RTS order,' Patterson said. 'I don't know what I'll do. What will George say? What about the consignors?'

Lindsey scanned the list, took his pen back and slid it into his pocket. 'Hold on,' he said. 'What order did you say?'

'Uh, Ridge Technology Systems. Ridge was my customer. They were going to buy the comics.'

'Ridge Technology? That sounds like some kind of electronics outfit.'

'Y-Yeah,' Patterson said. 'They build

computers. We even have one of them in the store, for inventory and accounting. A Circuitron 60.'

Lindsey grinned. The computer at International Surety was a Circuitron 60. He remembered the classes on how to use the thing. He had gone first, then sent Ms. Wilbur. When she came back she helped him figure the thing out.

'You often sell comic books to high-tech corporations?'

Patterson shook his head. 'No. Usually we sell to private collectors. But this guy came in one day — '

'What guy?' Lindsey had his pocket organizer in his hand, ready to jot down the name.

'George, uh, Dunn. He came from RTS and had this computer printout with a list of comic books. He said his company wanted to buy them as an investment. Something about tax shelters and needing to spend the money before the tax reform law took effect. He said they wanted exactly these comic books. He told me how much they were willing to pay for them and the prices looked about right to me, so I said we'd try to assemble the collection they wanted.'

Lindsey studied the list Patterson had handed him. 'They wanted these exact issues?'

'Well, uh, M-Mr. Dunn said if they couldn't get exactly these comics we could propose substitutes for them. Like another issue from the same era, of the same comic. Or another title in the same publisher's line, with the same artists and features.'

'And you got 'em?'

Patterson nodded. 'It was a hard job. Some of the comics were in store stock, some came out of my own collection, and some came from consignors. But I got the whole order together for them. And now everything is gone. Everything!'

Lindsey read the list again carefully. Patterson had to have an eidetic memory. He not only had the thirty-five titles, but the date and issue number for each, a one-word comment on its condition, and a price. Lindsey looked at the prices and whistled.

'Twelve grand for a comic book?' he said.

'Th-Those are Overstreet prices.'

'Overstreet?'

'Overstreet is the oldest and the most authoritative. Especially for Golden Age — that's 1940s and earlier. Thompson and Thompson is better for Silver Age — sixties. Sometimes people will pay way over guide if they want something badly enough.'

Lindsey smiled wryly. Father would turn over in his grave if he knew that. If he had a grave, that was. His Mother had told him he hadn't made twelve thousand in his entire short career.

'Give me a quick definition of Silver Age and Golden Age.' He wanted to be prepared for Harden's inevitable questions.

'Uh, the first really big boom in comics started when *Detective Comics* — DC — brought out Superman and Batman. They started their superheroes with Superman in *Action Comics* for June '38 and Batman in *Detective* for May '39. The boom lasted all through World War Two — the GIs really loved comics, see. And the comics from that period are called Golden Age.'

Lindsey nodded. 'Go on.'

'After the war the boom fizzled out. Most of the superhero comics died out. For a while there the ECs were the only bright spot, and the then censors killed them off. Comics were pretty sparse for a decade or more. Then in February '59 DC brought back the Flash and in November '61 Marvel started *Fantastic Four* with the Human Torch in it and there was another big boom. The Silver Age.'

Lindsey was trying to keep his eyes from glazing. He ran his finger down Patterson's list. 'There's one here for twenty thousand! What's this? *Science Fiction*, third issue, 1933?'

'It's too bad that's coverless. Still, it's inscribed. It's a unique item. With a cover it would be worth fifty. It's a mimeographed mag. It was put out by Jerry Siegel and Joe Shuster, the guys who invented Superman. Superman collectabilia is a whole thing of its own, Mr. Lindsey. This has a short story in it with the very first appearance of the Superman character. He wasn't anything like the final version, but it's the very first. And this copy is inscribed by both Siegel and Shuster. There are people who would kill for it!'

He seemed to hear his own words as if somebody else were speaking. He turned pale and stopped.

'You have copies of these price guides in your store?'

'We stock them. You can have a couple, c-compliments of the house.' He managed a weak smile.

Lindsey nodded. Darn, the kid was so sincere, so eager to please, Lindsey found himself starting to believe him. He decided to reserve judgment.

'I can also give you the name of an independent appraiser, if you like,' Patterson added.

'That would be very helpful.'

'Uh, Professor ben Zinowicz,' he said.

'Ben Zinowitz,' Lindsey repeated. 'Is that Zinowitz, i-t-z?'

'I-c-z. And it's ben with a small b. His full name is Nathan ben Zinowicz.'

'Okay. Lindsey jotted the name down. 'Maybe I'll pay our Professor Zinowicz a little visit. Where — '

He gave Lindsey directions to the

prof's office but warned him to phone first, as ben Zinowicz was kind of picky and he didn't like drop-ins

Lindsey studied the directions to ben Zinowicz's office. Then he said, 'Look, Patterson. If you're playing straight all you have to do is keep your nose clean. And phone me at once if you get any bright notions about who took the comic books or where they went.'

The kid nodded and blinked, eager to please.

'And,' Lindsey added, starting to feel like a tough private eye, 'don't leave town without telling me first.'

What about the police? Patterson wanted to know.

Lindsey said it would be a good idea to tell them too. They left the restaurant. Patterson went back to his shop, his shoulders slumped.

★   ★   ★

Lindsey followed Patterson's directions and found Professor ben Zinowicz's office without much trouble. It was in a classic

35

neo-Grecian building called Wheeler Hall. When Lindsey mentioned ben Zinowicz's name, the receptionist in the main office acted as if he'd asked for the president — maybe the Pope. She gave him an office number and he walked away, straightening his tie.

Lindsey knocked on ben Zinowicz's door and heard a crisp voice snap, 'Come!' Lindsey thought, *I hate people who respond to knocks or door bells or knocks with 'Come' instead of 'Come in.' You tell a dog to come; you tell a person to come in*.

The room was furnished with a thick Oriental rug, an antique desk and matching chairs. A beautiful painting hung in an ornate frame between dark-stained bookcases behind his desk. Lindsey did a double-take at the oil painting. It was a family portrait of Donald Duck, Daisy Duck, and Huey, Louie, and Dewey.

'Yes?' Professor ben Zinowicz said. He was sitting behind his desk, looking as if he were posing for a portrait himself. He could have been anywhere from fifty to sixty, with steel-gray hair, a deeply lined face, and sharp eyes the same shade as his hair.

Lindsey entered the room and closed the door. He sat in a chair which, compared to the steel furniture at International Surety, was like something out of Buckingham Palace.

Lindsey reached into his jacket, pulled out a business card and handed it to the professor. Zinowicz read the card, frowned, and dropped it into a tooled-leather waste-basket. 'You don't have an appointment with me. If you'd called, you could have saved yourself the trouble. I carry life insurance through the University of California and auto and fire through my own broker. Please close the door behind you as you leave.'

'I'm not an insurance salesman, I'm a claims adjuster,' Lindsey told him. 'I've come to ask you for help. The claim is being filed on a commercial casualty account. Stock loss, burglary. The insured indicates an intention to claim an inordinate value for the stolen merchandise, and he suggested that you might verify his valuations. Of course, we'll need an independent verification even if you do support the claim, but this is a preliminary appraisal.'

The prof looked up from his papers. 'Let me understand you, Mr. Lindsey. Are you attempting to hire me as a consultant?'

'Okay, Prof,' Lindsey said, 'let's put it on that basis. Interested?'

That brought the first smile Lindsey had seen to the professor's face. 'I might be.' He laced his fingers under his chin and leaned back in his overstuffed leather swivel chair. 'Just what, specifically, do you want me to do? Bear in mind that I charge five hundred dollars per hour.'

'For starters I just want you to look at a list of comic books and tell me what they're worth.'

'A list?' His eyebrows tried to fly away. 'Nobody can tell you what comics are worth from a list. Condition is everything. Two copies of the same comic book could be worth vastly different amounts. Then there are other variables. Is the copy inscribed by any of the artists or writers? Does it have an interesting provenance?

Has the paper been de-acidified? Is there rust around the staples? Have they been carefully removed and replaced with stainless material?'

'What about *Science Fiction*?' Lindsey asked. 'The Superman thing.' He tried to recall what Patterson had told him. 'From 1933. It's coverless. Shouldn't it be worthless?'

Now ben Zinowicz gave a real smile. 'I think I know the item you mean. It's nearly extinct — one, at most two copies survive. A cornerstone item of modern sequential narrative. As for condition — let's just say that *Science Fiction* is the exception that proves the rule.'

Lindsey nodded. 'I think you're hired.' He crossed his fingers. Harden at Regional would have to go for this, or Lindsey would have to go over his head. One way or another, he could see that these silly missing comic books were going to make or break his career with International Surety. This might be the very opportunity he'd been searching for!

4

'The Regents are very touchy about faculty doing outside work during the hours they're paid by the taxpayers. A professor is a professor, eh?' ben Zinowicz paused to preen, then said, 'I maintain an office in my home, for my consulting business. I'm in the Contra Costa directory. Please telephone for an appointment — I divide my time between the university and out-of-town engagements. If I'm not home when you call, my secretary will set up an appointment for you.' He shook Lindsey's hand, his grip chilly and stiff.

He retrieved his Hyundai from the municipal garage, obtaining a receipt so he could put the fee on his expense account along with the mileage between Walnut Creek and Berkeley and the money he'd spent on Terry Patterson's breakfast. He drove back to the International Surety office in Walnut Creek.

Ms. Wilbur looked up from her work

when Lindsey entered the office and hung up his coat. 'Call Mr. Harden at Regional. He wants to know about the Comic Cavalcade claim.'

'There's no such claim. I talked to Patterson and to the Berkeley police. Patterson has a set of claim forms but he hasn't filed them yet.

'I'm sorry,' Ms. Wilbur said. 'You know it's standard procedure to notify Regional at once of all claims above $100,000. I phoned Regional. Mr. Harden wants you to call him right away. And Mrs. Hernandez wants you to call home. Your mother is having a bad day. You might have to leave early.'

Lindsey picked up the telephone and dialed Regional and was put through to his boss. 'Listen, Lindsey, what's this about comic books?'

'It was on the overnight tape. Comic Cavalcade — it's a retail shop in Berkeley. Standard commercial account. They had a burglary.'

'Ms. Wilbur says it's a claim for a quarter million. A quarter-million dollars' worth of comic books? My kid has stacks of the things; they cost him a buck apiece. What the hell are they trying to pull? What are you doing about it?'

That was just like Harden — excitable, always ready to assume the worst, always ready to think Lindsey hadn't been on the ball. But this time Hobart Lindsey was ready for him!

'They're collectibles, Mr. Harden. They're worth prices into five figures, according to the insured. He referred me to the standard price guides and to a consultant at the University of California. I've already had one meeting with the consultant, and I'll need Regional's authorization to pay his fee.'

Harden cleared his throat. 'What does this big dome charge?'

Lindsey told him.

'And how many hours will it take?'

'I don't think it should take more than half a day. Or a day at most.' He expected Harden to hit the ceiling, but all Harden did was grunt.

'That doesn't sound so bad, but what's your plan? Do you think the claim is sound?'

'I don't know yet. I've already visited the store, interrogated the proprietor, consulted the police and contacted an outside consultant. I'll keep you posted on my progress, Mr. Harden.'

Lindsey could hear him snort. 'Look, we don't want to pay out any quarter million bucks. If you can pin this on the insured and disallow the claim, that's great. If you can't, you're to recover the stolen property. You know what I'm talking about?'

'You want me to play detective?' Harden didn't respond. 'Do you want me to try and get the comics back through a fence?'

'I'm not telling you what to do. You know the way this industry operates. We'll offer a reward for the stolen goods if that's what it takes. Insurers have been known to buy items back from third parties, no questions asked. Do you understand me? If it's going to cost us a quarter mil one way or a fraction of that the other, which do you think the company will go for? This is a big claim and we don't want it botched. Do you understand me? If you don't think you can handle it, just say so and I'll send somebody out there who can.'

You bet he would! Somebody named C. C. Harden.

'I can handle it, sir! I've never let you down before and I'm not going to start now.'

As Lindsey hung up he looked at the back of Ms. Wilbur's head. Whose side was she on? he wondered. At International Surety it wasn't uncommon for spies to be planted in other people's offices.

Lindsey cleared his throat. 'Ms. Wilbur, would you phone for a sandwich for me? Have the deli send up a ham and cheese.'

She said, 'Huh.' He knew she didn't like performing tasks like that; she considered them unprofessional. But she picked up her phone and dialed.

Lindsey punched the other line and dialled home. With hardly a syllable of greeting, Mrs. Hernandez launched into a diatribe. 'You better come home, Meester Leensley. Your mama, she's not having such a good day. She been talking about

44

bad things. She threaten me. Maybe you can do something with her, Meester Leensley.'

He sighed. Maybe a little butter would help. 'You know you're wonderful with her, Mrs. Hernandez. Maybe because you're a woman, you understand her better than I do. Don't you think you can handle it?'

Mrs. Hernandez mumbled.

'Maybe a cup of tea,' he suggested. 'And you know how she loves the old movies on TV. Maybe you could find one for her.'

Mrs. Hernandez said, 'I guess so. I guess I give it a try. Maybe she take a nap for me, even.'

Lindsey said, 'You're a gem, Mrs. Hernandez.'

'But Meester Leensley, are you sure you really wanna go on like thees? Don' you think your mama might be better off — you know — in a home?'

Maybe she would be, he thought. He'd miss her, but it would certainly give him more freedom. There was no way he could invite any young ladies over to the

45

house, the way things stood. And that put an awful crimp on his social life, such as it was. He enjoyed a drink now and then with friends, and he did get invited to an occasional party. He liked women, he liked talking with the ones he met, he liked being near them. But it seemed never to go anywhere beyond that.

Still, she was his mother.

'You keep things under control, okay, Mrs. Hernandez? Call me if it's a real emergency. I'll be home at the usual time.'

* * *

Over the next couple of days the case of the comic books moved along in routine fashion. Terry Patterson filed his claim forms. Lindsey looked them over and phoned Comic Cavalcade.

Patterson answered the phone. 'Did I fill everything in right, Mr. Lindsey?'

'You did 'em just fine, Terry. You really going to push on with this? I warn you, there's a stiff penalty for insurance fraud. Ask that cop, that what's-her-name.'

'Officer Plum, sir. I don't have to ask. I

believe you, Mr. Linsdey. But this is an honest claim.'

'Well . . . ' Lindsey let that hang for a while, then: 'You understand contributory negligence, Patterson, don't you? A rusty hasp and a two-bit padlock don't constitute exercising reasonable care and responsibility.'

'Your company inspected the store when they issued the policy, Mr. Lindsey.'

Damn! 'All right,' Lindsey sighed. 'We'll process the paper, Patterson. But don't hold your breath till you see a check. There's a lot of investigating that needs to be done.'

He hung up, then called Officer Plum at the number on her card. He got Berkeley police headquarters. It took him four tries to reach her, and even then she couldn't take the call and promised to get back to him. Later, she told him she'd been out on cases. He felt stupid. Had he expected her to be assigned to the Comic Cavalcade burglary full-time?

Lindsey checked his pocket organizer, found his note concerning Ridge Technology Systems. He decided against telephoning

George Dunn. An unannounced visit might be more productive than an appointment.

As far as Lindsey was concerned, he knew all he wanted to know about Berkeley. But when Officer Plum returned his phone call she responded to his demand for effective service with a lecture on the city and its problems. Mainly she told him that she wasn't putting too much time or effort into solving the Comic Cavalcade burglary. She made it very clear that some eighty-year-old dowager, who happened to be the widow of a distinguished ex-chancellor of the University of California, had higher priority with the burglary squad than a comic book store run by a twenty-six-year-old ex-hippie dropout.

In a way Lindsey could sympathize, but that wasn't going to save International Surety's quarter million bucks — nor would it make the name Hobart Lindsey shine at Regional. He hung up in disgust and redialed, asking for the commander of the felony squad, one Lieutenant O'Hara. Now there was a cop! Who could ask for anyone better than Lieutenant Joseph Francis Xavier O'Hara?

48

O'Hara invited Lindsey to come into his office for a little chat, so Lindsey drove to Berkeley for the second time in a week. O'Hara's office was upstairs in the old building that housed the Berkeley Police Department. He looked up and grunted. 'Understand you're dissatisfied with the conduct of one of our officers. Is that right?' O'Hara was in civilian garb. He had his coat off and his revolver on his hip.

Lindsey said, 'Not exactly. Officer Plum seems to be a conscientious worker. I just don't think she's very interested in this case, Lieutenant.'

O'Hara already had a file folder on his desk. He opened it, pulled a pair of rimless glasses out of his pocket, and slipped them onto his nose. 'Officer Plum seems to have conducted a correct investigation of this crime.'

'What about fingerprints?'

O'Hara turned a couple of sheets of paper. 'They found plenty. Some of them were even clear enough to use. Let's see, we found Terrence Patterson's, Janice Chiu's, A. Lincoln Morris's — that's the staff of Comic Cavalcade. They were very cooperative in giving us samples for comparison.' He gave Lindsey a deep look. 'We found a great many others, presumably belonging to customers. We found several belonging to Professor Nathan ben Zinowicz from U.C. Those were on file with the state, you know. They're printed when they get a teaching credential — part of the old loyalty check. Law's still on the books. And we even found a couple of yours, Mr. Lindsey. Checked them with your company's bonding people. You aren't the burglar, are you?'

Lindsey's jaw dropped, then he realized that O'Hara had been jibing at him — as well as establishing his subordinates' efficiency.

O'Hara raised his face from the papers. 'We found a lot of others, but none that seem to lead us anywhere. So . . . ' He tossed the folder back onto his desk. 'It's an open case,' he said.

'What does that mean?'

'It means we keep the case on our open list, and if anything further develops, we pursue it.'

'That sounds like hooey to me. This is going to cost International Surety a quarter of a million dollars if those comic books don't show up! What are we paying taxes for?' Lindsey was angry. 'Why do we have police?'

Lieutenant O'Hara leaned forward and poked a blunt finger toward Lindsey's face. 'This town has one of the most highly trained and hardest-working police forces in the United States. We are also one of the busiest, and I would say the most constrained by rules and political interference.

'I'm a fairly high-ranking officer on this police force, Mr. Lindsey, and in another four years I plan to retire on what you would call my nice fat pension. In my years of service I've been run down by a maniac, shot twice, I've saved a child from drowning and delivered eleven babies, and if you want to see my medals and certificates of commendation I keep 'em in this drawer in my desk along with my lunch box.

'Now, this town has a large transient population because of the university and the street people, and we've got very serious problems with murders, rapes, and drug-pushing all the way from the schoolyards and the flatlands to the rich people in the hills. I am not going to pull an officer off residential burglary investigations with their potential for violence and death, to have her chase down a box of comic books to save your company paying off an insurance claim!'

Lindsey felt his face getting hot and red. 'These aren't just comic books, Lieutenant O'Hara! There's a lot of money involved. Have you read that folder? Have you talked to Officer Plum? We're talking about a quarter of a million dollars!'

O'Hara said, 'If anybody tries to fence those comic books, we'll hear about it and you'll get them back. If the burglar wanted 'em for himself, I'm afraid they're gone forever.' He shrugged. 'You're free to try and track 'em down yourself, provided you don't overstep your rights as a citizen.

'And now I'm goin' to sit here on me fat Irish duff and eat me lunch. Don't let the door smack you on the ass on your way out!'

Lindsey picked up his briefcase and stamped out of O'Hara's office.

On the staircase outside he came face to face with Officer Plum. She looked up at him, startled. 'Mr. Lindsey! Were you looking for me? Did you get some new information on that Comic Cavalcade case?'

Lindsey said, 'Never mind! One thing I'm learning, if you want something done around here, you have to do it yourself!'

He shoved past her and headed for the street.

5

The RTS offices were in the Rockridge
section that straddled the Berkeley-Oakland
city line. Ridge Technology turned out to
be a standard California yuppie operation. A receptionist dressed in up-to-the
minute casual chic smiled helpfully when
he walked in.

'I'm looking for George Dunn,' he told
her.

'Is Mr. Dunn expecting you, sir?'

'No.' Let her stew on that.

'And the purpose of your visit is . . . ?'

'I'll take that up with Mr. Dunn.'

Frowning, the receptionist picked up a
telephone handset and murmured briefly.
Lindsey could see her appraising him all
the while. Business suit, briefcase, neatly
groomed.

'Mr. Dunn is very busy but he says he'll
take your call.' She pointed. 'Please use
the visitors' telephone.'

Lindsey sat down on a chrome and

cushion settee and picked up the phone.

'George Dunn here. Can I help you?'

Lindsey gave his name and affiliation. 'Perhaps you were aware of the burglary at Comic Cavalcade in Berkeley. Terry Patterson gave me your name, Mr. Dunn. I think you'd better speak to me. In your own interest . . . '

'*Burglary?*' Dunn's voice suddenly escalated an octave. 'Uh, I'll be right out.'

A door swung open and a thirtyish well-dressed man hustled through. Beneath razor-cut hair his face showed stress.

'I didn't know anything about any burglary. Patterson said he was just about finished assembling the collection. Are the comic books safe? When did all this happen? You'd better come with me.' He nodded at the receptionist.

The receptionist came forward and handed Lindsey a plastic badge with a monogrammed RTS on it and a superimposed word, 'Guest'. 'Please be sure to return this to me on your way out.'

Lindsey clipped the badge to his lapel. Dunn led him into an office containing two desks. One was Dunn's. At the other

55

a woman was working at a computer terminal. She looked up at Lindsey and Dunn as they entered.

George Dunn said, 'Lindsey, this is Selena Mabry. She's Marty Saxon's technical aide. I'm his admin aide. We share this office. Marty's through there.' He pointed at a door to an inner office. He also sent a high sign to Selena.

She logged off her computer and stood up. 'I'm heading for that meeting at the Marriott as the official RTS rep. Marty doesn't want to go. I hate meetings. I don't see why we can't just teleconference. Some of those old geezers don't think it's real if they can't spill their martinis down your cleavage.'

She headed out the door.

Dunn indicated a visitor's chair beside his desk. He hit a couple of buttons on a keypad. 'Hope you don't mind my recording this?'

Lindsey said, 'Uh, I guess not.'

'Now, tell me about this burglary.'

'Someone broke into Comic Cavalcade last night and stole thirty-five comic books, according to Terry Patterson.'

'Our collection,' Dunn said.

'That's what he says. Did you own the comic books?'

'Not yet, thank heaven! We made a contract and we had to put down a deposit — it was our lawyer's idea, not Patterson's. If he doesn't deliver, we get the deposit back.'

Lindsey jotted a note in his pocket organizer.

Dunn resumed. 'Look, Mr. Lindsey, I don't see why you insurance people came to RTS. Comic Cavalcade suffered the loss, so you have to pay. Are the Berkeley cops in on the act?'

'Officially, yes,' Lindsey said. 'But they don't seem to be doing much. Too busy with muggers.'

Dunn spread his hands. 'Whatever. That's your problem and Terry's. RTS will just have to get back its deposit and look for another supplier.' He rubbed his eyes. 'Patterson said he'd completed the order?'

Lindsey extracted Terry Patterson's list from his pocket organizer and laid it before Dunn. Dunn read it and shoved the paper back to Lindsey. 'Yes, that's our order.' He frowned. 'Now the scarcity factors will all change and the values will jump. Circuitron will probably change the whole list around. What a nuisance! Selena will blow her program when she hears about this.'

Lindsey glanced at the Curcuitron computer on Selena Mabry's desk.

'But I still want to know what you need from RTS,' Dunn said.

'If I can track down those comic books, I stand to save my company a great deal of money. If I know who wanted them, and why, then there's a good chance I can find them, isn't there?'

Dunn frowned. 'You think somebody from RTS stole them? Somebody in-house, or somebody we hired? You think maybe Marty Saxon has them stashed in the president's office?'

'I don't think so,' Lindsey said. 'But it's possible.'

Dunn smiled thinly. 'If you had any inkling of what this is about, you'd know that we didn't steal those comic books. If somebody walked in and offered them to us for nothing, we wouldn't want them. If we don't pay for them we don't have any use for them. This is a tax situation. We have to convert surplus cash into hard assets or we get taxed on it.'

Lindsey nodded. That fitted with the things he'd been told. 'Tell me a little more about how you selected the comics for your list.'

'Well, we started with some standard investment portfolio software. It wasn't hard to change the parameters from earnings-to-cost ratio, long-term value accrual, product-line performance projections and so on, to characteristics of comic books. Things like scarcity, age, condition, theme category, artists and writers. In fact, we came up with a piece of plug-in software that we've been marketing to collectibles dealers and collectors for the past few months. Very profitably, I might add.'

'I suppose you can account for your whereabouts last night?'

Dunn stood up. 'If you're trying to weasel out of paying the claim by saying we stole the comics Patterson was assembling for us, you'd better haul back to the cops and get them to do it for you. Don't come around here making wild accusations.'

He glared at Lindsey, who stood up and slipped his pocket organizer inside his jacket.

'Don't forget to give back your guest badge on the way out,' Dunn told him.

★ ★ ★

Lindsey headed back toward Telegraph Avenue and Comic Cavalcade. Patterson agreed to Lindsey's suggestion that they find a restaurant together so they could talk without interruption.

While the waitress was filling their orders, Patterson asked Lindsey when he could expect his check from International Surety.

'Don't get eager, Patterson. I told you once, it's going to take a while.'

'But — but the consignors! Th-They still think their comics are safe. I-I suppose they'll have to know eventually. I was hoping we could either get the comics back or the money in time to pay them. What should I tell them?'

Lindsey said, 'Before you tell anybody anything, get up a list of the owners and give it to me. Maybe one of them stole his own merchandise back. That way he'll have both the comic book and the money. Plus all the other comics!'

'Oh, no,' said Patterson. His sandwich arrived and he began to devour it. 'The consignors are all serious, honest collectors. Nobody would do a thing like that!'

'That's what you think, kid,' Lindsey said. 'Get me the list. Now, you said you had an idea for getting the comics back. Spill it.'

'Well, I just th-thought that whoever took them might try to sell them again to other comic store owners, who all know each other. If anybody brings in the stolen comics they could get in touch with us right away, or maybe call the police.'

Lindsey agreed that was a very good idea. He asked him who his chief competitor was.

'Uh, Jack Glessner. He owns Cape 'n' Dagger, a comics and mystery bookstore.

He's on Diamond Street in the city, and he has branches in Los Angeles, Sacramento, Modesto, and Santa Barbara. Are you going to call him?'

'I'm going to visit him.'

'Uh, don't tell him I gave you his name, okay? I used to work for him before I opened my own store and he's kind of, uh, annoyed about that.'

Lindsey said, 'Okay, kid. I'll tell him I got his name out of the Yellow Pages.'

* * *

Mother was a lot better that night. In fact she cooked supper for them, just like the old days. While they ate, Lindsey asked her about Father.

'Don't you remember him, Hobo?'

'He died before I was born, Mother. You remember that.'

She looked vague. 'Died?'

Maybe it had been a mistake for Lindsey to raise the subject, but here he was involved with comic books, and Father had been a comics illustrator.

He reached across the table and put his

hand on Mother's. She came back into focus and said, 'We met at art school. I wasn't very talented; I just enjoyed the atmosphere. The boys used to wear berets and little beards, the girls wore baggy sweaters and big skirts and black stockings, and we'd take the Key train across the bridge on Saturdays and drink wine in North Beach and listen to jazz and talk and talk until morning. They were fighting in Korea, but we didn't care much about it; we had our own little world. And then — '

She started to cry. Mother's hand was still in his and she clutched him tightly, then picked up her paper napkin in her other hand and started to wipe her eyes.

Lindsey prompted, 'Was Father drawing comic books then?'

She sniffed and nodded. 'It was hard for him to get work. Most of the publishers were in New York. They didn't like out-of-town artists. He did a few stories and he got to draw one cover. I've never seen him so excited as when he got that assignment. You'd think it was for *Collier's* or *The American Magazine!*'

Lindsey knew about that cover. *Gangsters at War* number 26, April 1953. A framed copy of it hung in the living room. He had also seen a copy of it in the display case at Comic Cavalcade. Puzzling, because the drawing was crude, and there were no superheroes in the book or drawings by famous artists.

'Joseph never saw that book. He drew the picture while he was still at school. Then he got drafted. We got married when he came home on leave. It was just before Halloween, I remember. Then Joseph had to report to his ship, and he was killed three months later, on January eighteenth, 1953. Killed when a MiG crashed into his destroyer. They sent me a medal and his insurance money and an American flag. His commanding officer came to see me. And I have you to remember him by, my little Hobo. Joseph will be proud of you when he gets back. And he'll have lots of work. They have lots of publishers out here now. You'll see.'

Sometimes Mother got confused. She was easy enough to handle then, provided you didn't quarrel with her. If Mrs.

Hernandez would just remember that, she'd get along all right. Lindsey didn't really want to put her away. She just needed someone to stay with her so she didn't wander off or get into trouble.

After supper she seemed happy washing the dishes. Lindsey sat down and made two phone calls.

First he tried Cape 'n' Dagger in San Francisco. 'This is Hobart Lindsey, International Surety calling. I'm trying to reach a Mr. Jack Glessner.'

'That's me.' There was an odd intonation about the voice, as if the man had a limited amount of breath and was rationing the syllables.

'This concerns an insurance claim. I'll need to discuss it with you, Mr. Glessner.'

'Let me have your number,' Glessner said. 'I'll have to call you back.'

Lindsey gave him the number.

'Aren't you working awfully late?' Glessner asked.

'Ah, I brought some work home with me. There's so much paperwork, you see, and — ' He heard the receiver click down.

Maybe Glessner thought he was investigating a claim against Cape 'n' Dagger. International Surety wasn't Cape 'n' Dagger's carrier, but half of their accounts came through agencies, and the insureds didn't know or care who the carrier was, they just dealt with the agent.

Was Glessner, or somebody working for him, the burglar? Patterson had implied that he bore a grudge against him for opening his own shop. He'd have the double motive of picking up a batch of highly valuable merchandise and ruining his ex-employee, now his rival. And Glessner could act as his own fence. He had connections, customers, even owned stores in other cities. Fanatical collectors had been known to buy stolen goods even though they knew they were getting hot merchandise. That would explain why he had sounded spooked . . .

The phone rang. 'Sorry to hold you up,' Jack Glessner said. 'What's the problem, Mr. Lindsey? I thought my insurance was in good shape.'

'There's nothing to worry about, Mr. Glessner. International Surety needs some information and cooperation with a little problem. Could I come and have a chat with you some time soon?'

'It's getting late, and you're at an East Bay exchange . . . '

'Walnut Creek.'

'That's a long trip. Would tomorrow be okay?'

Lindsey arranged to meet in the morning. Then he looked in the Contra Costa book and found Professor Nathan ben Zinowicz. The book listed a number, but no address. He rang the number.

A cultured contralto voice said, 'Ben Zinowicz, ye-es?' It didn't sound anything like the professor.

Lindsey said, 'Is he there, please?'

'This is Francis speaking. May I be of assistance?'

'The prof told me to call for an appointment. So I'm calling.'

'The professor is traveling right now. Perhaps if you will just tell me about it . . . '

Lindsey explained the reason for his call.

Francis said, 'Stand by please, Mr.

Lindsey.' He put him on hold and the sound of a string quartet came across the line. From the kitchen Lindsey heard the sounds of Mother putting away the china and glasses.

'I've been in communication with Dr. ben Zinowicz,' Francis resumed, 'and he will see you tomorrow evening.'

'Okay. Just give me directions to the address, and the time. I'll be there.'

'We are located in Point Richmond. Take Canal Boulevard west from Highway 17. Follow that until you pass the municipal pool and cross the Santa Fe tracks. Turn right on Railroad Avenue. Park halfway up the block and cross the street. You'll find the Baltic Restaurant. I'll meet you in the cocktail lounge. Wear a white snap-brim hat and carry your briefcase so I'll recognize you. Tomorrow, eight-thirty p.m.'

And he hung up.

6

In the morning Lindsey went to see Jack Glessner. All the way to Diamond Street he seethed over that last phone call. He felt like dropping ben Zinowicz from the case and hiring some other expert to work on the comics.

If ben Zinowicz had stolen the comics, the smartest thing for him to do would be to play it absolutely straight with International Surety, evaluate Patterson's list, collect his consulting fee and then butt out. He only drew attention to himself by acting the way he did, and by letting Francis act the way he did.

But maybe he was smart enough to know how to behave to avoid suspicion — by behaving the opposite way he had to be showing that he was not guilty . . .

The computer wizard who'd come to explain the Circuitron 60 software at the company seminar would call it 'infinitely recursive.' A hopeless case, not worth pursuing.

Most of the buildings on Diamond Street were old, either pre-earthquake or part of the reconstruction that had followed the disaster. Lindsey enjoyed the walk until he came to the store. There was a broad display window divided into sections for the cartoon fans and the mystery readers. The comic side had a display of recent and older comic books, posters, robots, and toys like the ones Lindsey had seen at Comic Cavalcade. The mystery side featured an array of books and a sign identifying the authors as Bay Area residents. Half the whodunit writers in the country must live in San Francisco or nearby towns! The center-piece of the display was a stack of copies of a police procedural written by the head of the San Jose Police Department.

The store was busy. Two or three clerks were helping customers while a cash register kept up a steady electronic din. The comic book buyers were young, mostly scruffy, dressed in T-shirts and jeans or old army fatigues. The mystery fans tended to be older, better dressed, more conservative. The store itself looked prosperous and well-kept.

Lindsey went inside and asked the young woman behind the cash register if Mr. Glessner was in, giving his name.

She consulted a note taped to her side of the register, nodded, and directed him to an office that doubled as a stockroom.

Jack Glessner looked ten years older than Terry Patterson, which made him just a little older than Lindsey. But he hadn't aged well. He looked up as Lindsey entered, put down a coffee mug he was holding, then pushed himself upright to shake hands. His handshake was cold and clammy, his movements slow and cautious.

Lindsey wondered if Glessner was sick, or disabled by some old injury.

'What's this insurance problem?' Glessner asked. 'Who made a claim against us?'

'Mr. Glessner,' Lindsey asked, 'what's your take on Terrence Patterson?'

'Terry? He can't possibly have a claim against Cape 'n' Dagger after so long.'

'Mr. Patterson has filed a very large claim with our company, and it's my job to evaluate its validity.'

If Glessner wanted to assume that the claim was against him, that wasn't Lindsey's fault. It seemed to have put Glessner off balance. That might push him into spilling something useful.

Lindsey opened his briefcase and pulled out a leather folder. He rattled a sheaf of forms that had nothing to do with Glessner but would look impressive as all get-out, and limbered up his pen.

Glessner had begun to sweat. He lifted his mug carefully, holding it in both hands, and sipped. Lindsey wondered what was in there besides coffee. Maybe Glessner was suffering from malaria or drug withdrawal. Both conditions produced cold sweats.

'Terrence Patterson is an ungrateful bum,' Glessner said at length. 'I taught him this business. When he came to work for me he was just a college kid. A nerdy fan.' He reached into a desk drawer, took out a thermos bottle and poured himself a refill. 'Can't offer you none. That's the end of it.' He took another sip.

Lindsey wiggled his pen some more.

'Oh, Terry. Yeah, he used to hang around my shop all the time. Had a little place down on Valencia then. He used to come in after school, buy a few comics, trade a few. He didn't know a thing about 'em. Kept asking for a job, said he'd work for minimum. I said no way, but he was persistent. He said, 'Okay, I'll take my wages in trade, no cash.' So I let him work for trade, taught him everything, built up the business, got this place, started opening branches. I brought Terry along with me, put him on salary, made him manager here. He learned all the contacts, all the prices, everything. From me. Then when he gets good and ready, he walks out on me and opens his own store. Been building up his stock out of my stock for a year. He can rot in Berkeley for my money. So what's his claim, mister investigator?'

Lindsey said, 'Do you have a problem with stock shrinkage?'

Glessner grinned. 'You know some of the lingo, insurance man. All retailers suffer shoplifters. We try to keep an eye out for 'em. The few we recognize, we kick out. The rest, as long as they stick to the small-ticket items, we can eat the loss.'

He stopped talking, opened his desk and took out a brown prescription bottle. He swallowed a pill with a sip of coffee. 'Vietnam. Goddamn VA medicine.' He rubbed his face with his bandana. 'I don't get it. What would shoplifting have to do with Terry Patterson?'

'What about big-ticket items? You do carry the older comics — collectibles — don't you?'

'Sure. Golden Age stuff gets up into five figures nowadays. Even the Silver Age stuff runs into high three, sometimes four. So do some of the early undergrounds — any first edition Crumb, Wilson, Irons, Bodé, they go nuts for it. All the regular collectors, they've been onto it for years. Now the libraries and universities are jumping on the bandwagon. Twenty years late — as per usual!'

Lindsey nodded. 'What about shrinkage?'

'Very rare.' He wasn't sweating now and his skin had lost its grayish tinge. 'We keep the valuable stuff locked up. Anybody wants a look at it, we know who it is and we keep close watch over 'em.'

'But it does happen?'

'Once in a while. Especially at conventions. All the fans come out; they invite some professionals as special guests. Mainly they go for the artists. Then there's always a dealers' room. Then the stock can get pretty messy. Things disappear.'

'What do you do about that?'

He laughed. 'Somebody steals a book and takes it home and hides it under his bed, there ain't much we can do, is there?

'But there's no wholesale action in stolen comics if that's what you mean. All the dealers know each other. If somebody turned up with a *Thunder* number one or some early *Marvel Mysteries* or — '

Lindsey said, 'I get the idea.'

'Yeah. If that happened, word would spread real fast. And if somebody was missing that issue, he'd know. The seller would have some tall explaining to do. If he was a collector, he'd be blacklisted by all the dealers and all the other collectors.

If he was a dealer himself, he'd be out of business in six months.'

Lindsey pondered that. What impact would this have on the Comic Cavalcade situation? Whoever stole those comic books probably intended to sell them. But it was possible that the thief was a collector himself. Possible, but unlikely. The burglar would almost certainly try to dispose of his loot; and when he did, there would be a chance to catch him.

'But look, Jack.' Another idea had struck Lindsey. 'Let's take that hypothetical case of yours. Somebody walks into Cape 'n' Dagger carrying a valuable comic. Give me an example.'

'*Sensation* one. First Wonder Woman outside the Justice Society.'

Lindsey shook his head. 'You got me. I know who Wonder Woman is, but what's the rest of that?'

Glessner nodded and launched into his explanation. 'Okay, back in 1940 M. C. Gaines started *All-Star Comics* as a regular anthology-type book — separate stories, separate characters. With number three they put all the characters together to make the Justice Society of America. Very important issue, very valuable. Had the Flash, Green Lantern, Hawkman, the Atom. Then with number eight they decided to add this female character to be the secretary of the society. Talk about sex roles, eh?' He laughed, then coughed until he caught his breath again.

'Okay, what was odd, see — all the other characters had come from other comic books. Green Lantern from *All-American*, Flash and Hawkman from *Flash Comics*. But Wonder Woman didn't come from anywhere. Her origin story started in *All-Star* eight. It was a sort of tryout. Well, the kids ate her up. All those little girls who didn't feel comfortable with Superman or Batman, they could make-believe they were Wonder Woman. Gaines must have known it would go over big. He had this new book in the works already, that he could feature her on the cover of. That was *Sensation*. So the first issue of *Sensation* was the first really separate Wonder Woman story, even though it was really a continuation of the origin story in *All-Star* eight. It was the first Wonder Woman story separate from the Justice Society.' He stopped again and mopped his brow.

Under his breath Lindsey said, 'Maybe you've told me more than I really wanted to know.' Aloud he asked, 'And what's this *Sensation* number one worth?'

'Mint, a grand easy. Lesser condition, lower price.'

That agreed with ben Zinowicz's lecture. Lindsey went on, 'Now, somebody who owns this book was robbed a few weeks ago. Word is out. The dealer who's offered the book knows it. He suspects he's being offered hot merchandise. So the dealer asks the seller for a provenance.'

Glessner burst out laughing. He pushed himself up, walked around his desk and lifted Lindsey by the elbow. 'C'mon. I'll show you some stuff.'

He walked Lindsey to the front of his store, then edged behind a glass display case and fished a heavy key ring from his pocket. He opened the back of the case and pulled out a copy of *Sensation Comics* for January 1942. The cover featured a crude drawing of Wonder Woman leaping across the front of the United States Capitol.

'You know where I got this comic?' Glessner asked. 'At a flea market!'

'I thought there wasn't that much trading in the expensive comics. That mostly it's done through dealers.'

'That's right. What you get at flea markets is mostly junk. Lots of recent comics, kids who decide at the age of fifteen that they're more interested in computers or dope or girls; all of a sudden they're too grown-up for comics, so they dump their collections for a few bucks and invest in software instead. Or marijuana.'

'But then . . . ' Lindsey indicated the *Sensation*.

'Once in a while Grandpa will die and the kiddies decide to clean out the old man's room. Junior and the missus are in their forties or fifties themselves. They see all this old junk that Grandpa saved, comic books and pulp magazines — and they dump it. Give it to their own kids, or throw it in the garbage, or haul it down to the Salvation Army.' He paused and drew a breath. 'Or they sell it at the flea market. They clear fifty bucks and think they've made a killing. I won't tell you what I paid for this *Sensation*,' he said, 'but a provenance? That's nothing but a joke.'

Lindsey was crestfallen. 'It's a hopeless case, then. The seller claims he bought the comic book in a flea market. The dealer says he stole it from another store. Nobody can prove anything.'

Glessner said, 'Look, I've given you a course in the comic book business. Now, you got to tell me what this is all about. What about Patterson's claim against me?'

'Well,' Lindsey admitted, 'it really isn't against you. It's against International Surety. You see, he was burgled. And if I can't recover the stolen comics, the company is going to have to pay out a quarter of a million dollars.'

Glessner stared blankly.

'And I'm going to ask you and all the other dealers I can reach to help me recover those comics,' Lindsey said. 'Of course, International Surety will pay a reward for any stolen merchandise we get back. We might even . . . ' Lindsey lowered his voice. ' . . . buy them back ourselves, no questions asked. If the price is right.'

7

Feeling like a total fool, Lindsey stopped on the way back to Walnut Creek and bought a white snap-brim hat for his appointment with Francis. He was playing detective now, with a vengeance, and he didn't like it.

He left the hat in his car and rode the elevator up to his office. The first thing he did when he got back to his desk was telephone Harden at Regional with his report on Comic Cavalcade.

Harden said he wanted a daily report on the case and he wanted to see progress. 'What about Patterson?' he asked.

'I'm not going to pay him the quarter million,' Lindsey said. 'I'm going to recommend that we sit on the claim. Disallow it if he insists on a quick response. But I can talk to him. Let him know that he only has a chance if he waits.'

Harden grumbled some more and hung up with a reminder to call him again the next day.

Lindsey phoned home and asked Mrs. Hernandez to stop next door and ask little Joanie Schorr to come over and spend the evening with Mother. He had an appointment in Point Richmond and he didn't know what time he'd be home. Joanie had done it often enough; her parents were glad to see her taking care of an older person, and the girl was happy to make the money.

Mother hadn't always been like this. Lindsey remembered the days when he was a kid, when she'd seemed calm and normal. Every once in a while she'd get upset, but he'd figured she was just like everybody else's mom.

Then he remembered that day in the summer of 1963, when he pushed open the door to Mother's room and found her lying on her bed, surrounded by souvenirs, wearing clothes that were years out of date, talking on the telephone.

He'd asked who she was talking to and she said, 'It's your daddy, my little Hobo.

Want to say hello to your dad?'

Then he had pressed the receiver to his ear. There was a man on the other end reciting the weather forecast.

His mom was dressed up in the clothes she'd worn when Dad was alive, and she was calling the weather forecast number and listening to the man talk and making herself believe it was Dad.

That was how young Lindsey had found out his mother was seriously crazy.

Once in a while Lindsey would stop in an old bookshop and bring home a copy of *Life* or *Collier's* from thirty years ago, and Mother would think it was the latest issue and sit for hours turning the pages, looking at pictures of Grace Kelly and John Foster Dulles, ads for De Soto cars and Dumont televisions and looking happy.

Lindsey lost himself deliberately in the numbing routine of paperwork until it was time to retrieve his Hyundai and leave for Point Richmond.

As far as Lindsey knew, Richmond was a mostly black, mostly poor, rundown city with one prosperous shopping mall that catered to suburbanites rather than locals, and one major employer, a huge oil refinery and office complex near the San Rafael Bridge. He'd never been to Richmond himself, and was surprised to hear that somebody like Professor ben Zinowicz would live in such a town. But Point Richmond, it turned out, was on what used to be called the right side of the tracks. The rest of the city was on the wrong side.

To get there he followed Francis's complicated instructions to meet at the Baltic Restaurant. The back of the Baltic opened on to Railroad Avenue, the front on to Park Place.

The bar was furnished with polished mahogany and old brick, and lighted by polished brass fixtures. A huge mirror behind rows of bottles seemed to double the size of the room. The place was bustling with socializers, a few serious drinkers, and couples waiting for service in the restaurant.

Lindsey slid onto a bar stool. He kept his hat on and laid his briefcase across his lap. He ordered a white wine cooler. It seemed the correct drink to order here. The female bartender served it up without comment.

He turned on his stool, surveying the occupants of the bar. Which of them was the mysterious Francis? The hat and briefcase, he thought, were conspicuous enough. It was the appointed hour. There was a campy nude painting on the long wall opposite the bar. He looked at it, then spotted a young woman sitting alone at a table beneath it.

She was wearing a loose blouse that set off her skin and her long, jet-black hair. She was spectacular. He thought she exchanged a look with the bartender, but he wasn't sure.

She noticed Lindsey at the same moment that he noticed her. She lowered her glass and smiled. She was watching him.

Lindsey swallowed hard and tried to smile back. He took a breath, picked up his glass, and made himself cross the room to her table. He managed to say, 'Are you Francis?'

She laughed. 'That beats what's your sign. No, I'm Margarita. Just like my drink.' She held up her nearly empty glass. 'Who are you?'

He said, 'Never mind. I, ah, it was a little, ah, mistake.' He should go back to his bar stool and wait for Francis, for the real Francis.

But he couldn't walk away from Margarita. It had been hard for him to approach her and strike up a conversation. And she had smiled and responded, even if the smile had contained something peculiar. He felt an interest in this woman, and that feeling was not a familiar one these days. If Francis didn't show up, that was his fault, not Bart Lindsey's.

He felt a tap on his shoulder. It was the manager or owner.

'Hobart Lindsey?'

'Yes.'

'Phone call for you.' The manager pointed to the desk.

Lindsey left Margarita, half-hoping that it was Francis calling to cancel out. It was Francis, but he wasn't canceling. 'Are you alone?' he asked.

Hobart hesitated a millisecond, then said he was.

'Good. Now this is important. Leave the Baltic at once. Someone is watching you. Go back to your car. I'll meet you there and take you to Dr. ben Zinowicz.' He hung up.

Lindsey went back to the table where he'd left Margarita and told her he had to leave but that he hoped to see her again. She said, 'Sure,' and looked away. Was she laughing at him? His face felt hot.

Lindsey left the bar and made his way back to Railroad Avenue. As he started between his Hyundai and a new Audi, he heard the crunch of footsteps on gravel. Before he could turn to look for the source he was dazzled by a brilliant light. Then he heard a thump that seemed to come from inside his head and he was spiraling downward in the center of a swirl of sparklers. He never even felt it when he hit the ground.

★   ★   ★

He knew he was dreaming. He was James Bond for real, a prisoner in Dr. No's laboratory. He was strapped to a moving

88

table and Dr. No was laughing as he sent the table toward a laser beam that would cut Hobart Lindsey in half. He could feel himself moving toward the deadly beam. The laser was a brilliant color that blinded him even as he squeezed his eyelids shut against it.

Dr. No's laughter was a monstrous hooting that blared in Lindsey's ears.

Somewhere a timekeeper was pounding a bell as if Bart were a boxer who had been counted out.

Lindsey woke up.

The dream was real.

The laser was a flashing light that swept brilliantly across Lindsey's face every couple of seconds.

Dr. No's hooting laughter was the blare of a diesel horn.

The timekeeper's gong was the crossing bell a hundred yards away, where Canal Boulevard crossed the Santa Fe tracks.

Lindsey struggled to move. He wasn't tied up, thank heaven. Every muscle in his body ached. He strained, trying to drag himself off the tracks before the massive train reached him.

Sweat slicked onto his face and hands. He was lying in coarse gravel and dry dirt. The sound of the train was a roar that threatened to burst his head. The earth shook with its vibration.

Lindsey made a supreme effort to drag himself back — too late! The train roared above him — and passed. He watched the cars as they clattered past; felt the cold wind that they stirred and the sting of pebbles and dirt the wind threw at him.

Then the train was gone.

He pulled himself to his feet. He staggered around until he spotted the Hyundai, then lurched to it. He stood trembling against the door and lifted his arm to his face. His Timex read nearly midnight. What in hell had happened?

How could the engineer have seen him lying across the tracks and just kept on going? But that wasn't what had happened. If it had, Lindsey would have been killed. He must have regained consciousness, at least partial consciousness, at least long enough to drag himself off the tracks before passing out again. To the engineer, he must have looked like a drunk. Once he was safely off the tracks, the incident was closed: just a near-tragedy that hadn't quite happened.

Or had the engineer never seen him at all?

His briefcase — where was it?

Lindsey wandered around until he found it under one of the Hyundai's tires.

There was a pounding in his ears, a monstrous ache and soreness at the side of his neck, and his entire head throbbed. He felt his skull gingerly and found the source of the throbbing: a huge, tender swelling. When he brought his hand away it was sticky with blood.

His new white hat was gone. Probably it had been shredded and dragged away by the train. He felt a sudden, absurd sense of loss. The hat had surely absorbed part of the blow that had produced the swelling — and knocked him unconscious. If not for that, he might never have awakened.

And his neck — he touched the sore spot and a bolt of pain lanced all the way to his fingertips.

He felt through his pockets. He still

had his keys. He opened the Hyundai, laid his briefcase on the passenger seat, then climbed in and leaned his head against the wheel.

Suddenly the laser was back. Someone was shining a flashlight in his eyes. The door of the Hyundai was being opened — he hadn't thought to lock it when he got in.

A voice said, 'I sure hope you're not planning to drive that car anywhere.'

The newcomer lowered his flashlight and shined it around the inside of the car. Lindsey could see now that the person behind the flashlight was wearing a police uniform.

'Someone,' Lindsey gasped, 'someone . . . '

The police officer took him by the elbow. He said, 'Would you get out of the car please, sir?'

Lindsey climbed unsteadily from the Hyundai.

The policeman stepped back and played his flashlight around the car, then back at Lindsey. He started to say something else, then he changed his mind. He said, 'Turn around.' Lindsey did.

He heard the officer whistle. 'What happened to you? You have your wallet?'

Lindsey patted himself, found the wallet and took it out of his pocket.

'Don't hand it to me, sir,' the officer said. 'Just see if everything is in it. Your money there? Credit cards? Driver's license?'

Everything was there.

'Do you know what happened to you?' the police officer asked.

'I think somebody hit me. I was coming out of the Baltic, and this is my car, and the next thing I knew the train was coming and I couldn't get off the tracks in time. And then the train went past and I was off the tracks. I don't understand.'

'You weren't in a fight? You don't know who hit you?'

Lindsey tried to shake his head. His neck felt the way Linda Blair's must have when she made *The Exorcist*.

The officer said, 'You want to come to the station with me and file a report, sir?'

Lindsey tried to think. Francis had

mousetrapped him into this, that much was certain. Had he actually intended to kill him? Was all the cloak-and-dagger stuff just a blind?

But why? Lindsey kept coming back to that. If ben Zinowicz had stolen the comics and was afraid that Lindsey could trace them to him, that would explain his wanting to put Lindsey out of the way. But these draconian measures were stupid and unnecessary. He could just breeze through the case, even pick up a fat consulting fee as icing on the cake.

Maybe Francis was acting on his own. Or . . . what if an ordinary mugger had bopped him? Somebody who'd been waiting outside the Baltic to slug the first tipsy customer to emerge, and grab his wallet? But if this were a simple mugging the criminal would have stolen his money and credit cards, and he wouldn't have thrown him on the Santa Fe tracks. And who was the person Francis claimed had been watching him? Was that all a false lead, or had Francis actually been trying to help him?

'Did you hear me, sir? Do you want me

to call an ambulance?' The policeman's voice startled Lindsey back to the present.

In that moment he made his decision. He'd already had his fill of trying to deal with the police in Berkeley. He wasn't going to drag the Richmond police into this too. This case was going to be his making in International Surety. If the Richmond police got involved, he'd find himself back in the office all day with Ms. Wilbur, and kowtowing to Harden at Regional.

That wasn't for Hobart Lindsey. Not anymore.

'Just . . . if you could help me back to the Baltic, officer. Let me get a cup of coffee inside of me and I'll be all right.'

'You're sure?

'There's no way you'd find the person who hit me, is there?'

The policeman hesitated. 'We'll do our best.'

'That's what I thought.'

8

Back in the Baltic, Lindsey stumbled into the bathroom and washed up. He took a long, hard look at himself in the mirror. His face was streaked with dirt and there was a reddish bruise on one cheek — probably the result of landing face down when he was slugged. The only mark on his neck was a red bruise just above the shirt collar. He wiped his face with a paper towel and attempted, gingerly, to put his hair in a semblance of order.

He found a pay phone and dialed Nathan ben Zinowicz's home number. The damned answering machine asked him, in Francis's plummy contralto, to leave his name, number, and message. Lindsey could imagine the professor and his secretary sipping brandy, monitoring incoming messages and waiting to hear from him.

He hung up.

Lindsey returned to the bathroom and

rubbed a wet paper towel on the back of his neck. He felt totally lousy but he didn't think he was seriously injured. He wriggled his fingers and moved his arm carefully. Everything was working, despite the blow on the side of his neck. He didn't need medical treatment.

He left the Baltic a second time, peering over his shoulder. No one approached him. He drove home, left his car in the driveway, and let himself into the house.

Mother had gone to bed. Joanie Schorr was watching a late movie. She looked away from the screen and gave a yelp as she saw him clearly.

'What happened to you?' She jumped to her feet.

'I got mugged coming out of a saloon,' Lindsey said. 'Somebody thought I was easy pickings. I'm all right and they didn't get anything.'

Joanie relaxed. She said, 'Something I've been meaning to tell you, Mr Lindsey. Your mother loves the old shows and movies so much, she could get a lot of them on tapes or disks and never have to watch anything new.'

'I'll give that serious consideration. Do you want me to walk you home now, Joanie?'

'No, I'll be all right.'

* * *

The next morning at nine-thirty Lindsey phoned his office. Ms. Wilbur had just arrived, but she assured him that she could take care of everything if he wanted to go straight into Berkeley.

Lindsey considered that the best way to approach Nathan ben Zinowicz was to do the opposite of what the professor had requested: just barge in and face him down. Lindsey decided to take a chance on catching ben Zinowicz in his office. He left his car in Walnut Creek and rode into Berkeley with the rest of the commuters.

Lindsey opened the professor's office door without knocking. Ben Zinowicz was seated behind his desk, and for the first time since Lindsey had met him, the professor did not look totally in control of the situation.

Lindsey marched across the room,

thumped his fist on ben Zinowicz's desk, and said, 'All right, I want to know what the hell is going on!'

Ben Zinowicz made a quick recovery. 'I would ask you the same question. I thought I'd asked you to make an appointment.'

'I did. I phoned your home and your secretary made an appointment to meet me at a saloon in Point Richmond and I got mugged for my trouble. You're fortunate I haven't blown the whistle on you. Or would you like to talk to the police about it?'

'I'm sorry for your misfortune, Mr. Lindsey. But you can hardly lay it at my doorstep. And as for an appointment, I don't know of your ever having made one.'

'Well I did, too.' Lindsey had burst in here full of righteous indignation and now he found himself acting like a naughty child trying to wriggle out of trouble. 'Anyway, I talked to my regional office and they've authorized me to pay your consulting fee.'

'Well, that's very nice to learn. I'll tell

you what. I'll be traveling tomorrow
. . . Why don't we arrange this for . . . '
He flipped the pages of a desk calendar.
' . . . Sunday afternoon. Is that all right
with you?'

Lindsey said it was okay.

'And you say you've been in Point
Richmond?'

'Oh, yes.' The knot on Lindsey's head
throbbed and the side of his neck ached.

Ben Zinowicz gave him directions to
his house, on up the hill beyond the town
square. 'Turn left on Marine Street, down
the slope to Ocean Avenue. Make sure
you turn left on Marine. That's the bay
side. The other way leads to the refinery
side of town.' Lindsey could see the look
of distaste as ben Zinowicz said the
words. He gave Lindsey the number of
his house on Ocean Avenue, and named
the hour he was to arrive. 'Please be
punctual,' he repeated.

Lindsey made one more effort. 'You're
sure you don't want to do this work right
here and now?'

'I explained that on your previous visit.
Please try to understand that I mean what

100

I say. Until Sunday, then, Mister . . . '

Lindsey took his briefcase and left.

★   ★   ★

Back at the office Ms. Wilbur told him that Jack Glessner had called. 'He said to tell you that '*Wow nothing*' had turned up in Sacramento and you could have it back for ten percent of the price guide. He said it was the finest copy he'd ever seen and if you didn't want it, he'd have no trouble unloading it on a collector.' As Lindsey sat down, she added: 'I don't suppose you want to tell me what that means, by any chance?'

'Just comic book business.' In fact he had no idea what '*Wow nothing*' meant. Trouble, probably. He held his head in his hands. 'Get me Regional, would you, Ms. Wilbur? See if Harden is in.'

He told Harden what had happened. Harden said, 'Ten percent of the price guide? What does the price guide say?'

Lindsey was ready for the question. 'Four thousand for mint, two thousand for good, a grand for fair.' He fished around for his copy of Patterson's original list. 'The insured says the copy is near-mint.'

Harden said, 'Huh! They don't expect retail, do they? Patterson knows that we only insure up to his cost. Glessner has to understand that too.'

Lindsey said he was sure they understood. Harden said to go ahead and negotiate with Glessner. If International Surety got the book back, eventually it would be returned to Comic Cavalcade. In the meanwhile, they'd already come down heavy on Patterson and he had got rid of his flimsy hasp-and-padlock arrangement and invested in some sensible protection for his store. They always did that after the horse was gone.

Lindsey phoned Cape 'n' Dagger. A clerk there said that Glessner had left early, and gave his home number.

'Sorry I sounded grumpy,' Glessner told Lindsey after he'd identified himself. 'I was trying to take a nap.'

'You all right?' The man really sounded rotten.

'I'm okay. Listen, you want to talk about that *Wow*, you can come over and look at it. Give me a while to rest up first.'

'How about a couple of hours?'

'Sure. See you later.' Glessner hung up. Lindsey phoned the Schorrs to hire Joanie for the evening. Then he called home and asked Mrs. Hernandez if she'd stay with Mother until Joanie showed up.

'Sure, Meester Leensley. Er, I was wondering. You think you could buy one of those machines to show movies on your TV? I think Meesus Leensley, she really enjoy that. You know how your mama loves the old movies.'

'Maybe. I'll look into it, Mrs. Hernandez. Joanie will be over in a little while. I'll see you tomorrow. Yes. Thank you. Goodbye.'

After work he stopped at Max's Opera Plaza for a sandwich and a Manhattan. At this hour Max's catered to working people who stopped on their way home from the office, people Lindsey felt he could relate to.

Lindsey felt a hand on his shoulder. He turned and recognized the broad-shouldered, red-bearded man in a three-piece suit. It was Eric Coffman. The lawyer had once been involved in a case that Lindsey was adjusting for International Surety and they had become friendly in a casual way.

'Bart Lindsey! Remember me — Eric Coffman?' The bearded man transferred a martini to his left hand and crushed Lindsey's in his right. 'Still up to your old tricks?'

'Sure. Trying to keep International Surety afloat, Eric. Didn't I see you yesterday, in our building?'

'Could be,' Coffman said with a shrug. 'A lot of offices in that building. Listen, Bart, I'm glad I ran into you.' He took a sip of his martini and placed the glass on the bar. 'Listen, is it true? What I've heard about International? You guys really about to go belly up?'

Lindsey blanched. 'Not a chance.'

Coffman said, 'That isn't what the scuttlebutt says. The sharks are circling, Lindsey old friend. I think they smell blood. You have your parachute ready, don't you? Man with your record shouldn't have any trouble landing on his feet.'

'You're wrong, Eric. International Surety is in good shape. Look, I'd like to stay and chat.' Lindsey made a conspicuous point of looking at his wristwatch. 'But I have an appointment in the city. Working on a big case. Recovering stolen goods. Going to save the company a bundle, and it'll be a feather in my cap.'

*　*　*

Glessner lived in an attached house with an old wooden porch. Lindsey rang the bell and stood with his back to the front door, taking in the view of Golden Gate Park down the hill and downtown San Francisco off to the right. The city's lights were blurred by the evening fog.

He heard the door open behind him and turned. He found himself face to face with a pudgy stranger who said, 'Lindsey?'

Lindsey said, 'Is Jack Glessner, uh . . . ?'

The man nodded him into the hallway. 'I'm Alvin Olsen. Jack's in the TV room.'

Lindsey followed Olsen down the hallway. Glessner was slouched in a soft chair, a quilt thrown over him, his forehead beaded with sweat. On the huge TV screen a black and white image showed a china-doll blonde throwing her arms around a nonplussed businessman type.

'*I Married a Witch*,' Jack Glessner said. 'Wonderful little flick. You know it, Lindsey?'

'No, but don't miss it on my account.'

Glessner punched a remote control button and the TV screen went dark. 'We've seen it a lot of times; we can always watch it again. Would you put the disk away, Alvin?'

Lindsey said, 'You really recovered the stolen comics, Glessner?'

He smiled. 'Just the one. *Wow* nothing. Alvin deserves the credit for that. I doubt we'd have ever seen it if anyone else had got it back.

'Have a seat. I'm sorry I'm not a better host, but my body's kind of down tonight. Do you want a beer? Soft drink?'

Lindsey shook his head.

Olsen rejoined them. He had a large-size manila envelope in his hand. Glessner said, 'Alvin here manages the Sacramento store for me. He found the comic today, and drove in with it after he called me.'

Lindsey said, 'He *found* it?'

Olsen grunted, 'That's right.' He shook his head in disbelief. 'People come in all the time. Sometimes they'll buy a comic for a buck and never come back. Sometimes they drop a bundle and become regulars. You try and keep an eye on 'em but there's too many.'

Lindsey said, 'What happened?'

'We'd had a little flurry of customers, maybe eight or nine people in the store. I was busy talking to a regular collector type, and out of the corner of my eye I thought I saw something funny going on by the cash register — so I shoot over there fast. The guy's gone by then, but instead of swiping anything, he left something.' He picked up the manila envelope. 'This.' He opened the clasp on the envelope and gingerly slid a plastic bag from it. '*Wow* nothing.' Olsen looked at the comic book as if it were an original da Vinci.

To Lindsey it looked like an ordinary comic book. The cover featured a drawing of a typical superhero wearing red tights. He sported an Adolphe Menjou moustache and a floppy little rooster's crest on top of his hood. He had a slightly effeminate look. 'What's so special about this?' Lindsey asked.

Olsen said, 'It's called *Wow* nothing because they didn't put a number on the cover. It was the first issue; the next was called number two.'

Lindsey reached for the comic book but Olsen's hand shot out like a rattlesnake and grabbed his wrist. 'Some of these old comics get very fragile. The paper acidifies; it gets very brittle. We're trying to save the paper with various chemical treatments, but there's a long way to go. This one . . . ' He pointed at the comic book. 'This one, somebody must have got a bargain on the cover stock. It looked good when the comic came out. Ralph Daigh, the production chief at Fawcett back then, said so in an interview a couple of years ago. Daigh's retired now but this fan got word to him through Fawcett and went and taped an interview with him. Daigh told him there was a chemical impurity in the paper. They almost all crumble. This is the best *Wow* nothing I've ever seen. Not that I've seen very many.'

'And that's the only reason it's so expensive?'

Glessner said, 'It's a nice comic too. The rarity is just for starters. First issues are always in demand. Mr. Scarlet's origin story — he was a sort of Batman clone. Simon and Kirby work — that adds value too.' Obviously, Mr. Scarlet was the prancing superhero in the red hood.

Glessner picked up a glass of clear, sparkling liquid and sipped through a straw. 'Still, it's that cover that does it. Mainly. Yes. I doubt that there are three copies this good in the world.'

Lindsey told Glessner that International Surety could pay ten percent for the comic, but ten percent of wholesale, not the guide.

Glessner exchanged looks with Olsen. Lindsey could see that he would get the comic after a little haggling. But he was very worried about its provenance. Who was the unidentified person who had left the comic book in Cape 'n' Dagger's Sacramento store? Why had he done it? And how had he got the comic book? Was he the burglar?

He closed the deal with Glessner, wrote out a voucher and receipt in behalf of

International Surety, and accepted the heavy envelope from Olsen. He laid it gingerly in his briefcase. Glessner agreed to contact Lindsey again if any word on the comics reached him through the dealers' grapevine. Or if another mysterious stranger returned any of the other missing comics to his stores.

9

Lindsey traveled home through the San Francisco night, clutching his briefcase. On arrival he put his briefcase safely away. It still contained the fragile copy of *Wow* comics — his first major prize in the case. He felt weary and sore and was glad to go to bed.

The next morning, Saturday, Mother was up and dressed early, eager for an outing with her Hobo. Lindsey got her into the Hyundai and drove to the video store, where they bought a VCR and took it home. He spent the rest of the morning struggling with the VCR. It didn't seem too complicated, but the manual that came with the machine had apparently been written in Korean — and translated by somebody who was out to get revenge for America's role in the Korean War.

But eventually he thought he'd got it right. He'd picked up an old Bowery Boys movie and popped the cassette into the

VCR — it worked! Mother sat in the easy chair with her legs folded under her like a young girl and grinned at Leo Gorcey and Huntz Hall. Lindsey stayed for a few minutes, then went outside to mow the lawn.

* * *

Joanie Schorr came over Sunday after lunch to stay with Mother while Lindsey went to Point Richmond. Before leaving the house, he decided to try the Berkeley police one more time. He dialed headquarters and found himself apologizing to Officer Plum for their brief encounter outside Lieutenant O'Hara's office.

Officer Plum had not taken offense. Lindsey couldn't tell if she was doing public relations work or just being friendly.

'Have you got anything more on those comic books?' he asked. He almost told her about Jack Glessner and Alvin Olsen and the recovery of *Wow* nothing, but something made him hold it back.

'Nothing. I'm really sorry.'

'But you are pursuing it? I'm sure you

appreciate this is very important.'

'Believe me, Mr. Lindsey, I understand. I'll let you know. Enjoy your Sunday, now. We're not all lucky enough to have it off.' That ended the conversation.

Maybe she wasn't a total ogress after all. She did have a pleasant phone manner and an appealing voice. Hadn't she sounded almost friendly — even sexy? Huh. On the other hand, she hadn't really been any help.

He left the house and drove to Point Richmond. The Hyundai labored a little getting up Golden Gate Avenue, but Lindsey kept his eye out for the right street and turned left as he'd been instructed.

Ben Zinowicz's house had the look of a Cape Cod colonial. There was a BMW in the driveway. Powder blue. License NBZ-PHD. The professor did not suffer from any lack of self-esteem. The lawn was immaculately trimmed. The house was a sparkling white with shutters and trim the exact shade of the lawn.

The driveway was wide enough for two cars, so he pulled in next to the BMW. He strode up the flagstone walk, and using the glittering brass knocker, rapped on the door. Suddenly it was pulled open and an enormous figure filled its frame. Looking down at Lindsey, it asked, 'Mr. Lindsey?' The plummy contralto voice confirmed that this was the professor's elusive and irritating secretary.

'That's correct,' Lindsey said.

Francis led him inside the cottage. He was wearing a purple tank top cut like an old-fashioned man's undershirt that revealed neck muscles slanting down into his shoulders. His arms were muscular like a weight-lifter's and his shoulders broad, his waist narrow. And he was barefoot.

Inside the house Nathan ben Zinowicz sat in a captain's chair behind an antique desk. The room in which he greeted his guest was furnished in a nautical motif, with a ship's capstan set out for decoration and a binnacle converted into a cocktail table. Behind ben Zinowicz the small-paned windows offered a view of the bay.

'Clear view this afternoon,' ben Zinowicz said. 'Later on the fog will come in and this will all disappear.' He turned toward Lindsey. 'Then we draw the drapes and light the fire and our snug little home could be anywhere we choose in all of space or time.' He smiled almost shyly. 'I'm being romantic,' he said. 'I was in the navy when I was a youngster. Once you get the sea in your blood, you never get it out again.'

Lindsey wasn't distracted by ben Zinowicz's unexpected show of civility. He and his friend Francis, who had suddenly made himself scarce, still had a lot of explaining to do.

'Well, then,' ben Zinowicz said, rubbing his hands together, 'may I offer you a drink, or shall we get right to work? I was just correcting some proofs.' He gestured deprecatingly at a bundle of long paper sheets on his desk. 'A little review piece for the Proceedings.'

'No drink for me,' Lindsey said. 'And before we start to work, I want to know what that was all about the other night.'

Ben Zinowicz raised his eyebrows. In the gap of silence that followed, Lindsey thought he heard a door drawn shut, and a moment later the sound of an engine starting.

'The other night, Mr. Lindsey?' the professor said.

'Yes. Somebody slugged me on Railroad Avenue, behind the Baltic Restaurant, as I've already told you. Whoever did it left me on the Santa Fe tracks. I think I was actually on the tracks, but somehow I managed to pull myself off them. I was knocked out. If I hadn't woken up, I would have been killed by a train.'

Ben Zinowicz shook his head and made the tsk-tsk sound. Lindsey said, 'I had an appointment to come here. Your friend Francis phoned me at the restaurant and said he'd meet me outside. Some fantastic cock-and-bull story about spies. He was going to wait for me at my car. When I got there somebody let me have it on the side of the neck.' He touched his aching neck at the recollection and winced.

Ben Zinowicz leaned forward. 'You think Francis was responsible for this attack? Did you see your assailant? Report it to the Richmond police?'

'I talked to a police officer about it. He

didn't hold out much encouragement. There was no way I could prove anything. But now I want an explanation. From you or from Arnold Schwarzenegger there.' Lindsey jerked a thumb toward the front of the house.

'Are you sure it was Francis? I really didn't know anything about this, and if it was he I surely apologize.'

'Thanks,' Lindsey said, 'but I still want to know what it was all about. Besides, I lost a brand-new hat.'

'Please,' ben Zinowicz sighed, 'I'll pay for your hat, Mr. Lindsey. How much?' He reached for a checkbook. 'As for Francis, let's see what he has to say for himself.' He pressed a button on the telephone on his desk. A minute passed but there was no response. 'Excuse me,' he said.

He inconspicuously picked up a cane and limped out of the room. Lindsey realized that this was the first time he'd seen ben Zinowicz walk. Either the professor hadn't heard Francis leave — or he was feigning innocence.

As ben Zinowicz left the room Lindsey

caught a glimpse of his cane. It was almost a piece of minimalist sculpture with its ornate metal head, smooth black polished shaft and plain metal tip. Involuntarily he raised his hand to the knot on his skull. Maybe Francis hadn't slugged him after all. Maybe he was the decoy while his boss did the job.

What a perfect cover for a pair of master criminals — a university professor and his secretary/valet/houseman. The supreme intellect and the fantastic physique. Ben Zinowicz could travel around the world, attending academic convocations, making contact with his control, getting his assignments, delivering reports and documents. What were those proofs he had been correcting? Some innocent piece of scholarship, or something else?

Maybe ben Zinowicz didn't have a control; he *was* the control. And he used his job to contact the people who worked for him. What did they call it in the le Carré TV series — ? Running a mole? And Francis . . . exactly how did he fit in?

Lindsey stood up and walked around the room. There were nautical prints on the walls and a naval officer's commission in an ornate frame. Another frame held three medals. Lindsey recognized two of them because Mother had received the same ones from the Navy Department for Father. One was a Purple Heart, the other a Korean Campaign Medal. Mother kept Father's medals in her dresser. Lindsey had seen her take them out and hold them for hours on end. The third trinket on ben Zinowicz's wall looked like an ornate bronzed crucifix suspended from a multicolored silk ribbon. A Navy Cross.

The rest of the room was lined with dark, richly grained bookshelves filled with academic-looking tomes and bound volumes of scholarly journals. A single shelf held a row of fiction that looked like the complete works of Ernest Hemingway in first editions.

A single oil painting hung over a brass-studded leather couch. It showed two officers in tropical whites framed against the gray of a ship's heavy gun turret. Behind them a tropical sun blazed from a cloudless sky. One of the officers was tall and dark-haired and immaculately decked out; the other was a pudgy redhead in a slightly overstuffed uniform.

The professor limped back into the room. 'One of my treasures,' he said. 'Don Winslow and Red Pennington — painted by Frank Martinek himself!'

'Where's Francis?' Lindsey demanded.

'He seems to have left the house. I'm sorry, Mr. Lindsey. He isn't a child. He doesn't need my permission to go for a drive.'

Lindsey returned to his chair and opened his briefcase, vaguely relieved that *Wow* nothing was safely locked away in Walnut Creek. The matter of the assault outside the Baltic was not settled, but there seemed nothing he could do about it now. He handed ben Zinowicz a copy of the inventory typed up by Ms. Wilbur.

'This is the list of items that our insured reports stolen. He gave us an alleged value for each item, and we've now researched several price guides — Overstreet, Resnick, Thompson and Thompson. But we'd like your independent evaluation.'

Ben Zinowicz limped to a chair near Lindsey's and spread the list on the ship's binnacle. He produced a pair of half-sized reading glasses and slipped them on, the graceful earpieces disappearing into his silvery hair. He examined the list, nodding occasionally and making little sounds.

He looked up at Lindsey over the tops of his glasses. 'Well, the first thing I can tell you, even though it isn't part of my assignment, is that the thief is very knowledgeable. An expert. For the most part he picked very desirable, very expensive items. The early *Actions* and *Detectives* and *Marvel Mysteries* are obvious, of course. But he took *Wow* nothing; he'd have to be well informed to know what that is worth. I'm also very surprised to hear that there was a copy in the area — near-mint, was it? And since you mentioned the Siegel and Shuster mimeographed item, I am not surprised to find it listed here.'

He bent over the list again, like a bloodhound snuffling over a trail. 'Some nice selections for sheer merit also. This

Baseball Comics, for instance. Not much interest in sports comics, so this is only worth a hundred dollars mint. Still, it was Eisner's work, and it's lovely and bright, unlike most of his other productions, which tend to have a noir atmosphere.' He put his glasses away. 'A very nice collection. One that I wouldn't mind obtaining for myself, if it were available. And if I had the money, of course.'

Lindsey said, 'Can you give me your valuations, then?'

Ben Zinowicz slipped his glasses back on and looked over the list once more. 'Just so, just so. Still, one man's mint is another man's near-mint — or even fine.' He eased out a sigh. 'Still . . . I shall give you values based on the condition as indicated.' He pushed himself up on his cane and carried the list over to his desk.

Lindsey said, 'There's one other thing that I meant to ask you about. There's a book on the list that kind of puzzles me. You see there, *Gangsters at War* number 26.'

'Undistinguished. Worth maybe three and half dollars mint. Really the only

122

stupid choice in the catalog.'

'Well, ah, you see, my father was a cartoonist. He was just a young cartoonist, just getting started in '53. But he did have a cover drawing on one issue of *Gangsters at War*.'

Ben Zinowicz sat watching Lindsey.

'It wasn't that issue.' Lindsey pointed at the professor's desk, at Patterson's list. 'In fact, it was on the issue before. Mother has a copy at home, and I saw another at Comic Cavalcade. It didn't look like a great comic to me, but of course it's very important to Mother. She thinks about Father a lot.'

'Of course, I understand. He is no longer living?' ben Zinowicz asked.

'He was killed. In Korea. He was in the navy.' He looked at ben Zinowicz's framed medals. 'Maybe you knew him.'

'It might be possible, I suppose, but there were so many thousands of us. And it was so very long ago ... About *Gangsters at War* — I didn't mean to deprecate your father's work.'

'Why would the burglar take *Gangsters at War* if it wasn't worth a lot of money,

like most of the comics that he took? And
it has no artistic merit — you said that
the thief was well informed and had good
taste. Why would he take this worthless
comic book?'

Ben Zinowicz shrugged. 'One of the
mysteries, Mr. Lindsey. Catch the thief
and ask him.'

'Maybe if we recover the comic book
there will be a clue in it. Uh, in fact,
maybe we could get another copy. Would
you say that *Gangsters at War* is a rare
comic?'

'Extremely. Scarcity does not necessarily correspond with value, you see. There
seems to be no demand for *Gangsters
at War*. Consequently, the shortness of
the supply doesn't really matter. Thus, the
book is almost impossible to locate, but
should you find a copy, it won't cost you
very much. For instance, we see two
copies of number 26, one of them in your
own home. If it were a sought-after item,
this would be a startling find. As it is . . . '
He spread his fingers as if he letting
worthless sand dribble away.

'Why would the thief take number 27

and leave behind 26?'

'You spoke of a definite collection. Was one issue part of that collection and the other not?'

'Terry Patterson has it on his list. But in any case, why would the thief want number 27?'

'Frankly, Mr. Lindsey, that quite intrigues me.' Ben Zinowicz shuffled the papers on his desk. 'By happenstance, I was just correcting the proofs of a review paper I've done for the Proceedings of the Institute for the Study of Mass Culture on the subject of literary extinction.'

Lindsey bit. 'What's that?'

'When a book — in this case a comic book, hence more correctly a magazine — is published, it is in a cultural sense alive. There are so many copies printed — thousands, even hundreds of thousands. Within a month or so those that remain unsold are destroyed, recycled into paper pulp. Of the rest, the majority are read and thrown away.

'Some thousands are saved, of course. Boys with precious piles of comics under their beds or on the shelves of their closets. But time passes and they gather dust and boys outgrow them and then they're thrown out. Or little brothers or sisters color in them, or the dog eats them, or they get carried to a picnic and rained on or taken on vacation and left behind. And in the so-called Golden Age, when they held wartime paper drives . . . good heavens!'

Lindsey said, 'I see where you're going. You mean a time comes when there are no copies left at all. Not one.'

'It happens,' he said.

'But — the publisher's file copies?'

'Publishers go out of business.'

'The Library of Congress?'

'Copyright registration copies? A joke! The Library of Congress used to keep its comic books in bales, like animal fodder. When the basement got too crowded they disposed of them.'

Lindsey gave it one more try. 'What about the people who worked on those comics? Didn't they keep files? What about collectors?'

'Alas! Many of the artists and writers were ashamed of working in comics. The field hasn't always been the highly respected art form it is today. Many of those workers — some of the most talented — thought they were just eking out a living while they prepared themselves for greater achievements. The pencillers and inkers had plans of becoming gallery artists, or at least commercial illustrators. The scripters, novelists.' He laughed softly. 'You know,' he added as he turned confidentially toward Lindsey, 'I even toyed with the notion of becoming a comic book writer myself at one time. Hah! I was much too literate for the job. So I became a professor. Is that amusing? Them as can . . .

'No. Many publications have become extinct over the years. Books, newspapers, magazines. Thousands of them, I suspect. And I had thought that *Gangsters at War* number 27 was one of those that just disappeared. I researched and wrote a major piece on the gangster image in Golden Age comic books for the Journal not long ago. I spent a great deal of effort and funds in collecting crime comics. I did manage to compile a run of the first 26 issues of *Gangsters at War*, but I had to give up on 27 because I thought it was extinct.

'But unless this is an error on Terry Patterson's list, there's a copy floating around out there somewhere. If anybody cares.'

★ ★ ★

In the dark, on the way out of ben Zinowicz's house, Lindsey brushed past Francis, who had just pulled his BMW into the driveway. Lindsey felt a momentary impulse to stop the man and demand an explanation from him. But before Lindsey could act, Francis had disappeared inside the house.

Another day, then. Another time.

Dense fog had swept off the bay, surrounding the house and filling Ocean Avenue like cold, damp smoke. Lindsey shivered and drove away toward Walnut Creek.

10

At home Lindsey found Mother and Joanie Schorr happily watching *The Gay Divorcee* on the VCR. Joanie left and Lindsey sat with Mother while she hummed along with the soundtrack for 'The Continental' and smiled at Ginger and Fred.

When the movie was over she said, 'They're such a nice couple. Don't they just look lovely together! I hope they make more movies like this one; I just love romances.'

Lindsey was beginning to realize that Mother had a rare ability to move with ease from one era to another. She'd slipped her moorings in time, just as ben Zinowicz claimed he could slip his moorings in space. But to ben Zinowicz it was nothing more than a make-believe game. To Mother it was real.

He persuaded her to eat a little and then got her to bed. He fixed himself a snack and sat down with a light brew.

He'd been worried about keeping up with his daily office work, but everything was going smoothly enough without him. Thank heaven for Ms. Wilbur! The comic book case was taking most of his time and talent. He'd have to update Harden at Regional in the morning.

He now had hopes that International Surety was going to save its quarter million, or at least most of it. The facts in the case were like pieces of a jigsaw puzzle, and they were starting to come together. The only problem was, he didn't have the box cover with the picture on it. All he had were a handful of fragments.

One piece of the puzzle looked a lot like Ridge Technology Systems. Somehow it was RTS's order for a specified list of comic books that had started the whole case off. But was Ridge merely a catalyst, or was the computer firm — or one of its employees — involved in some more profound manner?

A second piece was the tie-in between the proprietors Comic Cavalcade and Cape 'n' Dagger. The comics had been stolen from Terry Patterson's shop, Patterson had previously worked for Jack Glessner, and the notorious *Wow* nothing had mysteriously reappeared at the Cape 'n' Dagger branch store in Sacramento.

As long as he continued to think of these disparate elements as pieces of a jigsaw puzzle, he knew he would keep moving them around, trying to fit them together, trying to see the big picture, until it finally became clear.

Hobart Lindsey — detective!

★　★　★

He was wakened by the clock radio at 6:45 a.m. The radio was tuned to KGO, a San Francisco news-talk station. He was halfway through shaving when KGO went to the ABC network news. Lindsey wasn't paying much attention, when he heard something about a great comic book caper. In Berkeley, California, capital of world craziness.

He dropped his razor and almost cut off two toes. Before he could even get back to the bedroom to turn up the news, the telephone began to ring. He picked up the phone and said, 'Lindsey here.'

The voice was unfamiliar, cold and cruel. 'This is Johanssen at National.'

Lindsey felt his skin shrivel. It was rumored that what the legendary Harden at Regional was to ordinary mortals in the field, Johanssen at National was to Harden. The woman was more than a legend; she was practically a myth. Lindsey knew adjusters in other offices who at least had seen Harden face to face. But the executioner, Johanssen!

'Y-Yes, Ms. Johanssen.'

In words that froze his ear she asked, 'Lindsey, is it true?'

'W-Well, ah, Ms. Johanssen, I only heard a little of, ah, the report.'

'Harden tells me that it's true.'

'I, ah, then I'm sure that it is true, Ms. Johanssen. I'll have to, ah, listen to the next broadcast. And, uh, I can assure you that — '

'Don't you have newspapers out there in crazyland? It's all over the wire services. Did you really lose International Surety a quarter of a million dollars on a box of comic books? Tell me it isn't so, Lindsey. Please tell me it isn't so. And don't lie to me or you'll regret it!'

'Well, uh, I got one of the comic books back Friday night. For just four hundred dollars.'

'*Just* four hundred dollars for a comic book? Tell me, Lindsey, why is it that four hundred dollars for a comic book doesn't sound like a great bargain? You are talking about International Surety's money, aren't you?'

'Yes, Ms. Johanssen. M-Mr. Harden — '

'Don't tell me about Harden, Lindsey. I've already talked with him this morning. I'll tell you this, though. You continue your close reporting to Harden, and he'll stay off your back as long as you're handling this correctly. We're already a laughing stock in the industry and we stand to lose a bundle. You know that International Surety isn't one of those gargantuan outfits that laughs at anything under seven figures. A quarter of a million dollars is a lot of money to us! You save our neck on this and you're the newest fair-haired boy. You screw it up and

Harden will lop off your head and I'll stand by and applaud when it tumbles into the basket. Can you see the picture, Lindsey? Good, I thought you would.' She hung up.

The phone call left him too nervous to eat breakfast or talk to Mother. Johanssen must have known the truth about the takeover rumors. Even Eric Coffman seemed to know more about the takeover than Lindsey did — after all, Lindsey was just an employee. What if the possible quarter-million loss to the company put a crimp in some top-level negotiations?

He had planned to ask Mother about Father and *Gangsters at War*, about Father's brief career as a comic book illustrator and his death on a destroyer off the coast of Korea, but after this telephone call Lindsey was in no condition to deal with his disoriented mother. He settled her in front of the TV, watching game shows with the controls set on black and white, and drank his coffee.

He glanced through the Contra Costa *Times* and waited for Mrs. Hernandez to arrive. The paper had picked up the burglary story and played it for its *What next?* value. Fortunately there was no mention of International Surety in the article, and consequently no mention of Hobart Lindsey's name.

There wasn't much else in the *Times*. There was the expected follow-up on the crime statistics story of a few days ago. Every sheriff and police chief and city councillor in the area was either bragging or making excuses, depending on the statistics for his jurisdiction. Even the police chief of Alameda was claiming that his minions hadn't given up on their town's solitary homicide.

Then the phone did ring again. It was Officer Plum of the Berkeley Police Department. 'You want to keep up with your comic book caper, you better get over here to the Alta Bates Hospital. Ashby at Florence. That's halfway between Telegraph and College. You can't miss it.'

'Why a hospital?'

'Your friend Terrence Patterson is here,' she said. 'I'll be here a little longer. You'll want to talk to me, and I need to talk with you. You're going to meet Detective

Sergeant Yamura too. Don't delay, Mr. Lindsey. Patterson will be out of the recovery room in a little while and you'll want to be here when we question him. Assuming that he doesn't object.' She gave him a room number and rang off.

Lindsey called the office and left a message for Ms. Wilbur asking her to handle routine matters while he hurried in to Berkeley.

He found the hospital without too much trouble. When he got to Patterson's room, Marvia Plum, in full uniform, met him at the door. He felt his face flush when she approached him. Her spectacular figure seemed to send one signal, while the gun on her hip and her no-nonsense manner sent another one altogether. He felt something when he was around her, something that he didn't remember feeling since high school.

He snapped himself out of that with an effort of will. The last thing he needed, on top of everything that was going on, was to have his head spin and his blood race every time he saw this female cop!

'What happened?' he asked.

'Chiu and Morris found him when they reported for work this morning. Chiu rode in the ambulance with him.'

Jan Chiu came out into the corridor to join them.

'What happened?' Lindsey asked again.

'We'd better get Sergeant Yamura into this.' Marvia Plum led him and Jan Chiu to the floor's central desk. An older Asian woman was talking with a gray-haired man in surgical greens.

Plum said, 'Sergeant, this is Mr. Lindsey. He represents the company that insures Comic Cavalcade. He's been trying to recover the stolen comic books.'

'Hobart Lindsey,' he said. 'International Surety.' He handed her a business card.

The older woman said, 'Patterson didn't make it.'

The surgeon said, 'I'm sorry. That back wound — I've never seen anything like it.'

The Asian woman looked at Lindsey. 'Mr. Patterson was attacked outside his store. He was apparently beaten over the head, knocked to the ground, then stabbed in the back.'

She turned away. 'I'm sorry, Doctor. We'll need some paperwork from you but you can tend to that later if you're too busy now. The medical examiner will also need to spend some time with the body.'

The surgeon mumbled a few words and left.

Sergeant Yamura rapped lightly on the duty nurse's desk. 'We'll need a conference room.'

The nurse got them one. Janice Chiu dabbed at her eyes. Lindsey waited for one of the police officers to speak. Yamura nodded to Marvia Plum, who began the discussion.

'Chiu gave me her statement while Patterson was in the O.R. Do you want to run over it again for Sergeant Yamura, Ms. Chiu? Do you object to Mr. Lindsey being present?'

Jan Chiu looked at Lindsey. 'I recognize you.'

'I was at the store.'

She wiped her nose, nodded. 'Linc and I came to work this morning. The front door was locked but that's normal. We went in and we couldn't find Terry. He's usually the first one in. He works harder than the two of us put together and always comes in early unless he's making the Hayward run.

'Following the burglary last week, I thought maybe there would be something at the back door. We were always afraid there would be another break-in.'

Lindsey was watching Sergeant Yamura. She had a thin face and graying hair pulled into a bun at the back of her head. She wore a two-piece business suit and a white high-necked blouse. She was listening closely to Chiu, paying no visible attention to him or to Marvia Plum.

'What about the back door?' Sergeant Yamura asked.

Janice Chiu said, 'The door was locked from the inside. Everything looked okay. I don't know what made me think of looking outside, but I opened up the back and there was poor Terry. He was lying on his face and the back of his head was all bloody.'

'You didn't notice a wound in his back?' Sergeant Yamura asked.

Jan Chiu shook her head. 'I just saw the

blood on his head. We tried to help him. We didn't know how badly he was hurt. We couldn't do anything with him. I thought he was knocked out but I didn't know anything else. I ran back into the store and called 911. Then we just waited with Terry until the ambulance came.'

Lindsey subconsciously reached up and rubbed the lump on his head. Should he say anything about getting slugged in Richmond? A week ago he would have done it without a second thought. But the way things were going, and especially after getting the heave-ho by Lieutenant O'Hara, he wasn't so sure of that. But Sergeant Yamura seemed different. Maybe he should speak up. Still — he was starting to feel a little bit edgy about giving away information. He was after the stolen goods. He was a businessman, not a crusader.

Stolen comic books were one thing . . . but murder?

Yamura asked, 'Do you think this is connected with the burglary, Mr. Lindsey?'

'Was anything taken this time?'

Jan Chiu put in, 'I don't think so. Linc

140

is checking now. I'm going back to the store after I leave here, and then we'll open up.' Her hands were trembling and her eyes were red.

'No you won't,' Yamura said. 'Plum, get down there. Get a seal on the place. Somebody should have done that automatically.'

'The paramedics were there, Sergeant,' Plum replied.

Yamura said, 'Never mind. And take care of Ms. Chiu. If you don't need her any longer, see to it that she gets home safely. And get a statement from Morris. Move.'

Plum obeyed.

Sergeant Yamura suddenly had a small notebook in one hand and a pen in the other.

'I don't suppose you were in Berkeley early this morning, Mr. Lindsey?'

'Of course not. Why would I be — why would I — kill Patterson? I didn't! I was home in Walnut Creek. I've lived there all my life. I wish I'd never heard of Berkeley.'

Sergeant Yamura smiled thinly. 'A lot of

141

people say that. I suppose your wife and kiddies will all confirm that you were tucked up in your cozy bed at, say, seven a.m.?'

'I have no wife and kiddies. I live with my mother.'

'And she saw you this morning, knows you were home all night and knows what time you left the house?'

'Please, Sergeant Yamura. Officer Plum phoned me at home. How could I be in Berkeley and Walnut Creek at the same time?'

'I don't suppose you could have come to Berkeley, performed an errand, and gone back home again, all in time to receive a phone call from Officer Plum?'

'You're crazy!' Lindsey's voice cracked. 'I'm just trying to do my job. Call International Surety. Call Harden. Call Johanssen. You'll see.'

Sergeant Yamura folded her notebook and put it away. 'We'll do a little checking. But, Mr. Lindsey, you certainly seem upset for someone who's just doing a job. Aren't there standards of professionalism you adhere to in the insurance business?'

'You don't know what it's like,' Lindsey managed. 'Just trying to do an honest job, and suddenly one of the people you're trying to serve gets murdered, and the next thing, you're accused of uh, of killing him!'

'You're not accused of killing Terry Patterson. I don't think you did it. It's possible, but I don't think so. Come with me.'

He felt his eyes widen.

'Relax, Mr. Lindsey. We're not going to headquarters. We're going back to Comic Cavalcade. I want to look it over and you might be able to offer some helpful information. You might even learn something that will help you.'

As they climbed into the police cruiser she said, 'You never answered my question. I asked if you thought the killing was connected with the burglary.'

'I didn't know Patterson that well. I really don't know why anybody would want to kill him.'

'I don't see any connection yet either. That's what I hope you'll be able to provide. It might be a coincidence, but I don't like coincidences. They make me uncomfortable. They offend my sense of order, Mr. Lindsey.'

11

Sergeant Yamura pulled the white police cruiser to the curb in front of Comic Cavalcade and waited for Lindsey to climb out. She took a clipboard from the car, secured the cruiser, and joined him on the sidewalk. A crowd of Telegraph Avenue types, a mixture of U.C. students, new-style yuppies and scraggly street people stranded by the receding waves of earlier decades, milled on the sidewalk outside the store.

Yamura and Lindsey were admitted to the store by Officer Plum. Inside, Linc Morris and Jan Chiu sat side by side on tall stools, looking like a pair of schoolchildren in a Norman Rockwell painting. Officer Plum had sealed off the alleyway behind the store, the scene of the actual crime. Nothing had been touched.

'We'll get someone up here from Forensics,' Yamura said. 'Right now I want to take a look back there. You're the two who found Patterson?' She directed her question to Morris and Chiu. They both nodded. 'All right. I want a look at the area in back. Come with me. Keep your hands in your pockets. That's the safest way to avoid messing up the scene.'

'How about me?' Lindsey asked. 'I won't touch anything. And I might spot something important. I'm a kind of detective, too, you know, in my own work.'

She offered a barely perceptible nod.

Linc Morris said, 'Lieutenant, can I open the store now? We're losing business. We have competitors and the customers will just go there instead.'

Yamura shook her head. 'No, you can't reopen the store. Not until Forensics have been through everything. You come along with me and remember what I said about your hands.'

They halted at the back door. 'You've got a crash bar,' Yamura said.

'For fire safety. There was an incident a few weeks ago. Nothing happened really, but Terry was worried. We don't allow customers in or out this back way, but if there was a fire . . . 'Yamura nodded.

They went outside. The alleyway behind Comic Cavalcade was a typically cluttered passage serving the rear exits of the retail establishments on the block.

'This the fire incident you meant?' Yamura pointed to a blackened area on the wall between the back exits of Comic Cavalcade and the pizza parlor next door.

'That's it,' Jan Chiu said.

Yamura squatted for a closer look at the charred area. 'Why wasn't this reported?'

'Uh, Terry talked it over with the owners of the pizza place and they decided that it was just some street person trying to get warm at night. So they agreed not to put any inflammable trash out in the back and figured it wouldn't happen again. And it hasn't.'

'And they might have had problems over their insurance rates if they'd reported it. Is that right, Mr. Lindsey?' Yamura asked.

'Yes, it's more than possible.'

Yamura walked back to the rear door of Comic Cavalcade. Lindsey could see Officer Plum standing at the entrance to the alley, watching them. Yamura asked, 'You have the same lock system front and back? Takes a key and a code number?'

'We put 'em in just a couple of days ago. Mr. Lindsey's company made us. You have to punch a number into the keypad like an ATM machine,' Morris added. 'And you have to have a key too.'

Yamura said, 'Where was the body?'

Blanching, Morris pointed to the spot. There was no blood there; no evidence that a man had been knocked to the ground then stabbed fatally as he lay face down.

Yamura said, 'No more trash back here since the fire? Is that right?'

Where Patterson had lain and through most of the alley lay a filthy scattering of newspaper sections, food cartons, a couple of empty wine bottles and a ruined man's shoe. The shoe was marked with tiny tooth marks.

Morris said, 'Uh, we take turns with the other stores sweeping out back here. I, ah, guess we haven't kept up very well.'

Yamura squatted at the place where Terry Patterson had fallen. She picked up a corner of a *San Francisco Chronicle* sports page. Underneath it lay a large manila envelope. Yamura had a quizzical look. 'What do you think this is?'

Morris shook his head. 'Uh . . . I, uh, don't know.'

Yamura looked once more around the alley. 'Let's go back,' she said. She nodded to Morris and he punched a number into the keypad, unlocked the door and led them inside again. The police sergeant laid the envelope on a glass display counter and started gingerly to open it.

Lindsey said, 'Aren't you afraid of destroying fingerprints?'

She looked at him with a degree of respect. 'Good. This will end up in the evidence room if it looks as if it's anything at all. But right now let's be very careful and take a little peek inside.' She carefully undid the envelope's clasp and reached inside to pull out a mylar bag of the type Lindsey was starting to find disturbingly familiar. She laid it on the counter.

The mylar was clean and undamaged — protected by the outer manila envelope. Through the clear plastic

Lindsey could see not a comic book but a magazine the size of *Newsweek*. The cover was printed in two colors. The drawing showed a standard scene of a gangster and his moll, a body lying across a desk and a smoking .45 in the thug's hand. The title was *Shock Illustrated*. Linc Morris and Jan Chiu gasped.

Lindsey found the magazine thoroughly unremarkable. But then, he asked himself, what did he know about these collectors? He opened his pocket organizer, where he now carried a copy of the stolen items list. There it was: *Shock Illustrated* number 3, $1500 mint. He leaned over the mylar envelope to see if the issue number was correct. It was. That price made it one of the lesser items on the list, but he couldn't see how it was worth even fifteen cents.

Before anybody could say a word, Yamura reached into the manila envelope and withdrew a second mylar bag. This time Officer Plum and Lindsey gasped simultaneously.

Inside the transparent mylar, backed by a stiff sheet of cardboard, lay a slim pile of yellowed sheets. The top sheet was the contents page of a crudely mimeographed magazine bearing a date in 1933. The logotype read *Science Fiction*, volume one number 3. In blue ink the page was inscribed by Jerry Siegel and Joe Shuster.

'That's it, isn't it?' Lindsey whispered. 'The crown jewel!'

'The cornerstone of the RTS collection,' Jan Chiu said.

Sergeant Yamura said, 'I'm going to have to impound these as evidence.'

'I — I understand,' Morris murmured. 'They'll be safe, though? And the store will get them back eventually?'

'Definitely.' She produced a receipt form and started to fill it out. 'We'll need statements from both of you.' She looked from Morris to Chiu. 'You can take care of that down at headquarters. Make it this morning. You'll be back here by this afternoon. People forget things. You can open the store then, if you decide to.'

Morris looked puzzled. He said, 'Wh-why wouldn't we reopen the store?'

'Terry Patterson is dead, young man. What happens next is a business problem.

A legal problem. A decision will have to be made as to the best course of action to pursue.'

Morris and Chiu exchanged looks. They both appeared stunned. There was a stir outside as a second police car pulled up behind Sergeant Yamura's cruiser.

Yamura looked up from her clipboard. 'Okay. That's Forensics. You two will cooperate with them. Mr. Lindsey, I don't think there's any justification for your remaining here any longer.'

'Those comics,' Lindsey said. 'The magazines, I mean. They're worth thousands of dollars.'

'Evidence. Once they're returned, it's between your company and the store. Or the estate of the deceased. You heard what I just told Ms. Chiu and Mr. Morris. This is more of the same. You'll have to work that out among yourselves; it's not my problem. I have other work to do. Officer Plum will be in charge of this site until Forensics finishes. Once they're done you can open the store again, not one second before. Understood?' Morris and Chiu nodded. 'Officer Plum headed up this case when it was a simple burglary. I'll see to it that she remains in charge now. Phone her if you want to discuss anything. That applies to all three of you. Call me directly if there's an emergency and you can't reach Plum. But please try not to bother me.'

Lindsey found himself nodding with Morris and Chiu like a hypnotist's subject. He allowed himself to be ushered out of the store, through a small crowd of pedestrians still clustered on the sidewalk. Whatever thrill they had hoped to find was obviously not going to appear, so one by one the gawkers began to disperse.

Lindsey crossed the street and got a window table in a student café. Feeling mildly out of place, he nursed a coffee and Danish and picked up an Oakland *Tribune* that someone had abandoned. The paper was opened to the comics page. The former owner had made a few entries on the crossword puzzle, then stopped work. Lindsey took out his pocket organizer and laid it on the paper. Keeping one eye peeled in case anything happened at the comic store, he leafed through his notes.

Three items recovered out of thirty-five. Less than ten percent. The old mimeographed magazine represented a fat chunk of the insured value, and International Surety wouldn't even have to pay a finder's fee or buy-back. So far so good.

Lindsey sipped his coffee. Wait a minute! With Patterson dead, the whole claim might lapse. No, there was too much money involved. There would be an estate to contend with. And there were the consignors of the comics that hadn't come from store stock.

Lindsey groaned. He hadn't got the list of consignors from Patterson! He'd asked for it, Patterson had agreed to provide it, but the document hadn't actually changed hands.

Across the street he saw the front door of Comic Cavalcade swing open. Officer Plum, Chiu, Morris and a couple of plainclothes types hefting their equipment emerged together. Yamura had already left. The police car drove off, carrying Chiu and Morris as well as the other cops. Marvia Plum stood on the sidewalk, looking around. She caught sight of Lindsey, waved and crossed the street to join him at his table.

'You want to talk this business over?' she asked.

'Uh, h-here? Right in public?'

'Would you rather go down to Grove Street? Lots of room in a police station, but most people don't like them.'

'It's just . . . no offense, but I thought Sergeant Yamura was in charge now. Isn't she?'

Plum smiled. Lindsey found himself noticing that it was an attractive smile.

'Dorothy's a good detective, Mr. Lindsey, but she doesn't have time to pursue every case personally. This is still my job.'

'Yes. Then I'd like to help. It would be good for International Surety. What can I do?'

'Good,' she said. 'I want your professional opinion, as an investigator, of this situation.'

'Well,' he said, 'I think the murder and the burglary are connected. It's too much

155

of a coincidence otherwise. Uh, how was Patterson killed?' he went on. 'They said he was hit on the head and then stabbed. But . . . how? I mean . . . '

'We'll have to wait for the medical report, but from what they said at the hospital he was hit with something smooth. The blow to the head — there were no jagged edges, no dirt in it. Could have been anything smooth and rounded. A bottle. A baseball bat.'

'And the stab wound? Was it done with a knife?'

She reached forward and Lindsey involuntarily flinched. She laughed and tapped a fingertip on the comics page of the *Oakland Tribune*. 'You do a lot of crossword puzzles, Mr. Lindsey?'

'No. I just found the paper open to that page.'

'I do lots of them. They keep your wits sharp after too much routine. Good for concentration. The wound was deep, narrow, and round. Tapered slightly from the point of entry. The weapon passed between Patterson's ribs and penetrated his heart. It was amazing that he lived as long as he did. A strong young man. Too bad.'

Lindsey said, 'What does that have to do with crossword puzzles?'

Marvia Plum said, 'I think he was stabbed with a ferrule. That's a word you only find in crossword puzzles anymore. Used to apply to a stick specially designed for beating children. Isn't that a lovely idea? Later came to apply to a walking stick or cane, and then specifically to the tapered metal tip on a cane.' She leaned back in her chair. 'Do you think Patterson might have been killed by a dandy with a walking stick? Not many of those in Berkeley. Or by a person using a cane?'

'How?'

'Patterson comes to the store early this morning. Opens the front door using both his key and the number code. He walks to the back of the store, opens the back door, maybe by hitting the crash bar. Now, let's say that there's somebody there with a manila envelope containing those two valuable magazines. And carrying a walking stick or cane. He's surprised by Terry. He drops the envelope. Terry bends over to pick it up. *Whap!* Terry goes down.'

'Wait a minute,' Lindsey interrupted. 'What about the *Chronicle*?'

'Jesus, I don't know! Maybe he was going to use it to pick up doggie doo-doo. He had it in his hand; he dropped it when he went down. That's why nobody saw the envelope until Dorothy Yamura picked up the green sheet. What I'm saying is, maybe the killer didn't come there to kill Terry Patterson. Maybe he came there for some other purpose, like to drop off the manila envelope. Terry surprised him. He didn't want Terry to identify him. Maybe they knew each other and maybe not. But when Terry bent over to pick up the envelope, the killer responded on impulse. One hard shot.

'Then — imagine you're this person — not only has Patterson seen our walking-stick man here, where he doesn't want to be seen, but now he's knocked him out with his stick. He's getting in deeper than ever. He picks up his stick and positions it carefully on Terry's back. Maybe he has another heavy object, a rock, at hand. Or he picks up a conveniently abandoned wine bottle. Or maybe he's just a very powerful man. He pounds the ferrule between Terry's ribs and it's all over.'

Lindsey's face went cold. He put his hand to his forehead and brought it away slippery with sweat. He wiped his hands and face with a handkerchief and stuffed it back into his pocket. 'And the killer was there,' he said, 'why?'

Marvia Plum said, 'I think he was delivering those two magazines.'

Lindsey nearly dropped his cup. 'The professor!'

She looked her question at him.

'Nathan ben Zinowicz. He's a U.C. prof, a big noise in popular culture studies. Terry Patterson recommended him to verify the values of the stolen comics. I went to his house in Richmond. He walks with a cane. A war wound, he said.'

Marvia said, 'You think he did it?'

'I've been to his office and his home. He — I don't like the man. There's something not right about him.'

'You think that makes him a murderer?'

Lindsey reddened. 'Of course not,' he admitted. 'But there *is* a connection. You remember what Sergeant Yamura said about coincidences.'

Office Plum gave her beautiful smile. 'Yes. Dorothy's a good cop. But you can carry even a sound idea too far. Still, it won't hurt to check him out.' She stood up. 'Can I give you a lift?'

'Oh. Ah, no thanks. I have my car. And I want to talk to Morris and Chiu again. I'll leave a message on the tape at Comic Cavalcade. They'll get it when they come back.'

12

Back at International Surety Lindsey found a message from Jack Glessner at Cape 'n' Dagger. He jotted a note in his pocket organizer. He didn't want to talk with Glessner quite yet, so he dialed the number for Comic Cavalcade and left a message asking Morris or Chiu to phone him. For the next hour he left behind the ugly business of a burglary turned murder and caught up on office routine.

And then Officer Plum called. 'Ben Zinowicz is in the clear,' she said without preamble. 'He had an early-morning seminar today. He couldn't possibly be our man.'

Lindsey said, 'Hold on. How can you be so sure?'

'Patterson was still alive when he got to the hospital. We've got a preliminary medical report. The full one will take a while. But the pathologist says with that wound he could have only lived *a few minutes*. Time it backwards, the whole sequence couldn't have taken much more than a quarter of an hour, from the moment he opened the back door of Comic Cavalcade to the time of death. In fact, the killer couldn't have been gone more than a couple of minutes when Chiu and Morris arrived. Maybe less.'

'About ben Zinowicz,' Lindsey said. 'How do you know he's clean?'

'He was teaching his early-morning graduate seminar in mass culture. Get ready for this. It's called 'Sublimated and Expressed Hostility in the Domestic Constellation from Herriman to McManus: Ignatz and Krazy, Maggie and Jiggs.''

'He was actually there? That early in the morning?'

'He said hello to a couple of other profs, a campus cop saw him going into the building, and he has eleven grad students who were with him for an hour and a half. If he were any cleaner he'd be a Laundromat.'

'Okay.' Lindsey studied his notes. 'Look, uh, Marvia. I'd like to talk about this some more. Do you think we could get together? Maybe for dinner?' The last sentences came out in a rush.

She hesitated, then: 'All right. Provided you promise that you didn't kill Terry Patterson!'

'No,' he said. 'I didn't do it.'

Now she was laughing and he was suddenly light-headed. He thanked her and hung up. He felt his pulse racing as it hadn't since high school. He saw Ms. Wilbur watching him, a knowing and amused look in her eyes. She made a little sound and turned back to her work.

Lindsey reached for the phone again. Now he was ready to talk to Jack Glessner. Before he could dial, another call came in. It was Linc Morris.

'I got your message, Mr. Lindsey. About the consignor list. About those stolen comic books.'

'Good. And you found the list?'

'Uh, not exactly. I couldn't find it written down anywhere. We keep paper records, some, mainly 'cause we need 'em for billing and payments. But most of our records are on disks now.'

'And?'

'We all know how to use the computer for routine stuff. Mainly for inventory and ordering. But Jan and I don't know what else Terry might have had on disk.'

'Aren't there labels on them?' Lindsey asked.

'Well, Terry wrote things on the envelopes and put little sticker labels on the disks themselves. So we can see what it says. None of them say anything about consignors, but I'm not sure if that means none of them have that list. You see what I mean?'

Lindsey counted to ten. 'Okay, Morris. Whatever you do, don't let anything happen to those disks. If the list is hidden there, we'll have to find a way to get the information. Protect the disks whatever happens. Stay in touch.'

He was thinking about Ridge Technology Systems. George Dunn and Selena Mabry and her Circuitron 95. He'd got the heave-ho from Dunn last time he was at Ridge. He'd have to make a new approach, maybe bypass Dunn and try and get to Mabry instead. Or their boss, Marty Saxon. Mabry was the better idea.

Dunn had said she was the technical whiz. He scribbled more notes in his pocket organizer.

Then he picked up his phone and put through a call to Cape 'n' Dagger in San Francisco. Glessner wasn't in. Lindsey used his finger to disconnect, then flipped his organizer to Glessner's home number and dialed. Alvin Olsen answered the phone.

'This is Hobart Lindsey, International Surety. Mr. Glessner called my office this morning. I'm returning his call.'

Olsen grunted. 'Look, Mr. Lindsey, he's really feeling lousy today.'

'You mean he's too sick to talk even for a minute? Maybe he belongs in the hospital.' Malaria? Drug overdose? Glessner had said it was something he picked up in Vietnam.'

'He wants to stay home, Lindsey. But I'll ask him.'

At length Olsen came back on the line. 'He says he'd rather talk to you in person. Can you come here?'

Lindsey didn't feel like making a long journey to have a two-minute conversation with a comic book dealer who didn't

165

feel like talking on the phone. But he decided it might be important.

★ ★ ★

Olsen greeted Lindsey tersely at the door of Jack Glessner's house and admitted him. Glessner was propped in front of his TV again, watching a thriller about an aviator in a weird sort of flying wing. '*Spy Smasher*,' he greeted Lindsey. He clicked off the picture and said, 'Listen, about those stolen comics of Patterson's . . . I've got a line on some more of 'em.'

'How many?'

'Three or four, I think. I don't have the comics here.'

'Where are they — Cape 'n' Dagger?'

He gave Lindsey a wan smile. 'You're not far off. Somebody's selling hot comic books.'

Lindsey didn't say anything about the murder of Terry Patterson. Or about the return of *Shock Illustrated* and *Science Fiction*.

'Look,' Glessner said, 'these books aren't exactly legitimate merchandise right now, are they? Any trading in them that takes

166

place now is questionable. You know the law of bailments?'

'In my business, sure.' Lindsey grew impatient. 'Will you just tell me what happened?

Olsen brought a glass of mineral water for him and a couple of pills. Glessner took the pills, swigged some bubbling water, and rested for a minute. Then he said, 'All I want is a finder's fee.'

Lindsey had to think fast. Clear it with Harden or go over his head and consult Johanssen? The heck with it; he was in this for the big prize, win or lose.

Glessner said, 'Look, you paid ten percent of price-guide value for *Wow* nothing. Since I don't actually have the new ones, I'll settle for half that for the information. I'll point you to the comics. You have to cut your own deal with the seller.'

'Is the seller the thief?'

Glessner shrugged. 'I don't know. Your problem, not mine.'

Lindsey took a deep breath. 'All right. What's the dope?'

Glessner nodded to Olsen, who held the mineral water for him while he drank again. 'You know we have branches in four cities,' he said. 'Each manager has the right to buy and sell comics up to a certain price. Above that price they have to clear all deals with me.

'This morning Jerry Hayakawa called from our Santa Barbara store. Jerry said that he'd been offered a batch of high-priced comics. He started to describe 'em and I immediately figured they were part of the Comic Cavalcade haul. His supplier started off asking guide price minus trade courtesy.'

'Another dealer?'

'Yeah. But everybody knows about the burglary now. So Jerry stalled, saying he had to clear any deal this big with me. The seller said, 'Okay, but I need an answer quick.' Then he offered to drop the price, even before Jerry called me. So Jerry figured these were definitely hot comics, and warned the seller to wait until he'd heard from me what to do.

'By now the seller is real scared, and I don't know what's going on down there. If I were you I'd hop on a jet pronto and go talk to Jerry.'

Lindsey said, 'Who's this mysterious seller?'

'Ask Jerry.'

For once, Lindsey realized, he was about to get a good break. He asked Glessner if he could use his phone. He used his International Surety calling card number to try and phone Harden at Regional, but for the first time in human memory Harden was away from his desk and couldn't take the call. Harden's secretary tried to get Lindsey to call back or leave a number. He was about to comply when he had another thought.

'I can't do that. I'm on my way now. Tell Mr. Harden that I'm going to Santa Barbara. I'll file my expenses and they'll require his signature. Mr. Harden can phone his approval back to Ms. Wilbur in Walnut Creek. I'll be in touch in a day or two.'

He hung up. He'd enjoyed that conversation.

Lindsey thanked Glessner and gathered up his briefcase to leave for the airport. He stopped and slipped back into his chair. 'Can I ask you both a question?' he said. 'Why do you bother with comic books? I can understand the 'Dagger' part of your store. People like to read mystery stories. But why the 'Cape' part? Why should adults care about comics? They're garbage!'

Alvin Olsen said, 'It's a buck, Lindsey. That's all. Some people sell soap powder. We sell comic books.'

'I don't buy that,' Lindsey said. 'You don't make that much money, and you work too hard at what you do. Jack does, anyhow. There's something else going on that I don't understand.'

Glessner shoved himself up on his elbows. 'I guess it only matters if you grew up on comics like I did. Jesus, I used to wait for the new *Justice League* and *X-Men* like they were the word of God. I knew every story; I could tell you who wrote and drew every adventure.'

He laughed. The laugh turned into a cough, and he breathed slowly, deeply. 'They're my past, do you see that, Lindsey? I have some customers, the mystery side of the store, pulp collectors. They're the same way. They grew up on

Black Mask and *Dime Detective* and *Spicy Mystery*. It's the same for them. Those books are just garbage to me, but they're their past. They're their lives.'

He reached for his glass and sipped some more mineral water. 'Younger kids, they grew up on TV. I guess they'll collect their favorite stuff on video tapes. They save the toys and action figures. You know that's what we have to call 'em now? For a hundred years nobody could figure out how to sell dolls to boys. So some genius got the idea of calling 'em action figures instead of dolls, and all of a sudden it's a new billion-dollar industry. I love it, Lindsey.'

Lindsey said, 'You love comic books because they're your past.'

Glessner said, 'Yeah. I don't want those old comics to go on the junk heap. If they do, my past is gone. Dead.' He paused for a labored breath. 'And my past is all I've got. I sure as hell don't have any future.'

Olsen whispered, 'Jack.' And shot a withering look at Lindsey.

Lindsey stood up. 'I'll let myself out.'

He found his way to the door, and from Glessner's house he headed for the airport.

13

Lindsey caught a PSA jet from SFO to Santa Barbara. After the chill of San Francisco, the transition to Santa Barbara's sunshine was like a flight from winter to summer. He rented a Renault Encore on International Surety and drove it into town.

He found Cape 'n' Dagger on State Street, the town's main thoroughfare. It was a miniature of the one in San Francisco. There were three people working in the store. One was at the cash register, while another was engaged in an animated discussion with a couple of intense and unappetizing comics fans. The third worker, an Oriental, was at the end of the counter working on something, but kept looking up nervously every time a shadow fell across the glass.

Lindsey guessed this was Jerry Hayakawa. He said, 'I'm Hobart Lindsey. Jack Glessner said I ought to talk to you.'

An expression of relief crossed the man's face. 'You're the insurance man? Jack told me to expect you.' He gathered up his papers and led Lindsey to a tiny back office. 'Look, Helly Balter was in this morning. She has the comics and you better see her fast if you want to get them back.'

'Who's Helly Balter?'

'Helena Balter. She runs the Goddess Funnybook Emporium. Styles herself as the only feminist comic book shop in the world.'

'A competitor.'

'In part. Mainly, we help each other. She sends us customers who wander in looking for comic books, who don't know about Cape 'n' Dagger. We send her customers who're looking for women's comics. We carry some ourselves, but it's a specialty and she does it a whole lot better than we do. It doesn't really hurt our business, and it helps Helena. She's a great old soul.'

'Okay. I definitely want to see her. But first I want to know what happened here.'

'She walked in here this morning with

some very nice items. Said she'd love to stock 'em in her own store, but most of her trade is for low-priced items and she didn't think her customers could afford them. I took one look at what she had and immediately copped to the Comic Cavalcade burglary. Your company's taking a deep bath on this job, huh?'

'What were the comics she had for sale?' Lindsey, pocket organizer already in his hand, turned to his copy of the Patterson inventory.

Hayakawa said, 'They were all comics either by female artists or featuring female characters or themes. Marge's *Little Lulu* for June '45. *Miss Fury* by Tarpé Mills for winter '42–'43. And the first issue of *Wonder Woman*, summer '42. All in great shape. The three of 'em must have been worth a couple of grand. Even at guide prices.' He looked at Lindsey. 'They have to be Comic Cavalcade stock. You know, the word's out; nobody's going to touch that stuff now.'

'What did Helly do when you wouldn't buy?'

'She just went back to her shop to

pout. She's probably still there now. Want directions?'

'Did she say how she got the comics?'

'Nope. The more I said, the less she wanted to talk. Look, her shop is just around the corner and down the block on de la Vina. Just look for the sign. Big cutout of an Egyptian goddess type, you can't miss it.'

Lindsey jotted down the information. 'Look, if I manage to get those comics back, do you think you could look them over for me?'

Hayakawa said, 'You mean, to authenticate 'em?'

'That, and to estimate their value. I had a man back in Berkeley doing that for me.' He paused, then added, 'Of course, International Surety will pay a small fee.'

Hayakawa looked thoughtful. 'I'd rather send you to a man who can do a better job than I can — he really could use the money. A fine Golden Age artist named Sullivan Winston. Retired now, lives here in town. I know he needs the money pretty badly.'

Lindsey agreed, and Hayakawa scribbled

Winston's address and directions on a piece of paper. Lindsey took the information and headed for the door.

Finding the Goddess Funnybook Emporium took him two minutes flat.

★ ★ ★

Helena Balter sat inside with a very fat tomcat on her lap. The cat was no competition whatsoever for his mistress.

Helena Balter's nostrils twitched. She talked to her cat in a stage whisper: 'Look at that, Bubastis. I told you I smelled a flatfoot coming.' To Lindsey she said, 'Come in, officer, and let's hear what you've got to say.'

Would there be an advantage to letting her think he was the police? He said, 'I've just had a little chat with Jerry Hayakawa, Ms. Balter. About some comic books.'

'You bring a warrant, or what?'

'No, I didn't bring any warrant. I'd appreciate your voluntary cooperation.'

She sneered. 'Yeah, well?'

'Jerry says you were trying to sell him some comic books this morning. Where did you get them?'

'That's confidential information. Any dealer has scouts out all the time, scouring flea markets and thrift shops and garage sales. I can't tell you who my scouts are.'

Lindsey sighed. 'Please don't play games. I've had a long, hard day and I'm just looking for some information. You do know what those comics are, don't you?'

She shoved Bubastis off her lap and started to lever herself out of her chair. She made it to her feet, gave Lindsey a dirty look, and waddled over to the refrigerator.

Lindsey glanced around the tiny store. The walls were decorated with a few posters for comic books featuring women on their covers, and her meager stock seemed to consist mainly of adventure comics portraying jungle queens in leopard-skin scanties, romance comics featuring close-ups of vapid young girls with bright blue tears rolling down their cheeks, and gangster or jail comics with snarling gun molls on the covers.

'Yeah, have a good look, buster. That's

what the industry thinks of women.' She'd taken a huge torpedo sandwich from the refrigerator and was tearing at it with her teeth even as she spoke. She'd also set a dish of cat food on the floor and Bubastis was attacking it with equal relish. 'What do *you* read — Mickey Spillane? The Executioner? Or do you just look at centerfolds and play with yourself?'

Lindsey counted to ten. 'Ms. Balter, I will ask you once more: How did you obtain possession of — ' He consulted his pocket organizer and read out the titles. He added: 'You realize that receiving stolen property is a felony. Further, if you are found to be in possession of stolen property and refuse to divulge the method by which you obtained it, there is a legal presumption that you yourself were the perpetrator.' Gobbledegook, of course. But he figured she would believe what a 'cop' told her during an investigation.

'I bought 'em.'

'From whom?' Lindsey asked eagerly.

'I don't know.'

'Come on, Ms. Balter. You don't want

to impede an investigation, too, do you?'

Helena Balter waddled back to her easy chair and lowered herself into it. Bubastis had finished his little snack and jumped onto her lap.

'I opened up this morning and about ten minutes later this kid comes in with a manila envelope. 'Wanna buy some comic books, lady?' the kid asks me. I look at her, I look in the envelope. I'm expecting dreck.

'Instead, here are good comics. Well cared for, too. I say to her, 'Honey, where did you get these comic books?'

'She says, 'The nice man give 'em to me. He said you'd give me ten dollars for 'em.'

'I say, 'What nice man? Anybody you know? Did he ask you to do anything? Did he touch you? Is he waiting for you somewhere?'

'She says she doesn't know who he is. She doesn't remember what he looks like. Will I really give her ten dollars for the comic books?'

'Did you?' Lindsey asked.

'Listen, I may be crazy but I ain't stupid. Of course I gave her the ten dollars. So now the comics are mine, and that means they're mine to sell, too, if I want to.'

'Not if they're stolen, they're not.'

'You prove they're stolen.'

'They came from Comic Cavalcade in Berkeley. They were consigned there by their rightful owners. Both the staff of Comic Cavalcade and the consignors will identify the comics by their fingerprints — nicks in the covers, marks made by former owners and so forth.'

'Go get your warrant, then, mister detective. I don't have the comic books and I don't know where they are and you'll never find them.'

Time for a quick shift of strategy. Lindsey said, 'All right, I'm going to tell you something. I'm not really a police officer. I'm an insurance adjuster.' He handed her his card. 'But those comic books are still stolen property. I'm prepared to make you a generous offer for finding and returning the comics. If you won't return them, then I'll have to head straight for police headquarters and I'll blow the whistle on you. Also, we seriously want to track down the thief. There are plenty more comics missing — thousands of dollars' worth.'

'I know. I listen to the news.'

'We need to find the kid and get a full description, then find the man who gave her the comics.'

'Forget it. The kid was someone I don't know. There's no way we'll find that kid, unless she happens to come in here again. But I'll bet you she won't be able to describe the nice man anyhow. She was too little. So just forget about it.'

Lindsey groaned inwardly. She was right. He could try checking with Amtrak and the airlines to see if he could get access to passenger lists for the past twenty-four hours, but that would be a long shot. As soon as he'd cut his deal with Helena Balter he'd get some more comics back, but he wasn't making any progress toward catching the thief.

★　★　★

Lindsey walked out of the Goddess Funnybook Emporium with a recycled manila envelope containing three comic books tucked into his briefcase. Six of the thirty-five stolen items had been recovered. He was halfway pleased with that.

But there was the murder of Terry Patterson to consider. It was a police matter, none of International Surety's business, and he'd hardly known the kid. But could he just walk away once the insurance file was closed? He didn't think so. He wanted to keep Harden off his neck and to score points with Johanssen. And he wanted to know who the thief was and why he was giving the comics back. Was there something hidden somewhere in the pages of these particular comic books? Something that would have escaped the notice of Terry Patterson as he assembled the collection for Ridge Technology Systems? But that made Patterson look like a suspect again, and that didn't make sense because he was a victim.

Lindsey walked back to the free municipal garage where he'd left his rented Renault. He found a pay phone and looked at the slip of paper Jerry Hayakawa had given him. Winston lived at a motel. He looked up the number, dialed it, and asked for Sullivan Winston, who agreed to see him immediately.

The motel was located on Cabrillo Boulevard south of the town. It was near a white beach where college boy and girl volleyball games seemed to occupy every square foot of sand. The building itself was shabby, weatherworn and faded.

Lindsey made his way to Sullivan Winston's room and knocked. Winston pulled the door open. His face was hideously scarred. He leered up from a wheelchair.

'Come on in,' Winston said in a strong resonant voice. 'What about those comic books? They're all I have left, mister. I really need that money. Are you going to pay me off for them, or what?'

14

'Well, ah, it isn't quite that simple,' Lindsey managed. 'Could I come in and sit down, Mr. Winston? There are several things that we need to discuss.'

But inside, Lindsey was quivering. Whether he would ever find Terry Patterson's list of consignors was still an open question. But he knew that he had walked in on the first of the consignors, sitting in a wheelchair in a seedy motel room in Santa Barbara!

Winston rolled himself away from the door. 'Close it behind yourself,' he said. 'Pull up a seat and let's get to it. You said on the phone your name was Lindsey. Lindsey with an e, right? You any kin to Joe Lindsey?'

'He was my father. Did you know him? He was a comic book artist for a little while. He was killed in the Korean War.'

Lindsey watched the thoughtful, far-away look struggle to make its way through the heavy scar tissue on Winston's face. 'I know,' Winston grunted, 'I know. First I want to hear about Comic Cavalcade. I trusted those comics to Terry Patterson. He was going to sell 'em for me. I was counting on that money. I get a little veteran's pension and social security, but it's hard. If my sister hadn't taken me in I'd be a welfare case. Now the radio says Patterson's lost the comics.'

He was getting excited, and Lindsey tried to calm him down. 'He didn't exactly lose the comics, Mr. Winston. There was a burglary at his store. It wasn't his fault.' He didn't say anything about Patterson's murder.

'You're the insurance man, right?' Winston had simmered down a little. 'If Terry lost my comics, you have to pay me for them. They're worth a lot of money. They're all comics that I drew, you know. I worked in the field for forty years. I worked from the time I was a teenager. I worked until I got drafted in World War Two and then I worked again when I got out in '45.' He was getting that faraway look that Lindsey sometimes saw in his mother's eyes. 'When the Korean War started up they took me back into service. That's when I got this.' He made a gesture that indicated both the scar tissue on his face and the wheelchair he sat in. Lindsey saw now that his hands were deformed and covered with scar tissue.

'Yeah, I got pretty messed up. But I was determined. I learned to hold a pencil again, and a pen, and a brush. I learned to draw again and I went back to work and I worked until they told me I had to retire. But I need those comic books!' He started to cry. 'I need those comic books. I drew every one of 'em — they're my best work. But I need the money for 'em even more. And if Terry Patterson's lost the comics, I want the money from the insurance company!'

If one of the consignors was also the burglar, Lindsey thought, it surely wasn't Sullivan Winston. 'Things may not be so bad, Mr. Winston. Some of the stolen comics have already been recovered. I can't tell you if any of them are yours, though, because we don't have a break-down by consignor. Do you think you could provide a list of the titles you consigned to Comic Cavalcade?'

'You bet I could!' Winston rolled his wheelchair to a low dresser and pulled open the top drawer. He extracted a sheet of paper and shoved it at Lindsey. 'Here!'

Bingo! The sheet showed the perforated edges of inexpensive computer paper, and the printing revealed the fine dot-matrix pattern of a computer printer like International Surety's Circuitrons. Patterson had used his Circuitron 60 to print up a receipt for Sullivan Winston's comic books. That meant that the consignors' receipts were on disks as outgoing correspondence, if Patterson hadn't deliberately erased them, which was unlikely. Lindsey made a note of Winston's comics and the date of his receipt.

Winston's voice was rambling again. 'I can't draw no more so I got to sell my brag copies to get the money 'cause Uncle don't send me enough and that bastard killed him and somebody stole my comics so you gotta pay me 'cause my sister's a poor woman and we need the money and the bills keep coming and I — '

188

'Mr. Winston!' Lindsey took him by the shoulders. Winston came back to focus, but his shoulders continued to shake. Winston rolled away and picked up a bottle and a couple of glasses. He rolled back to where Lindsey was sitting.

'You'll really pay, Mr. Lindsey? Your company won't stiff me? I won't lose out?'

'I'm sure. Really. You'll either get back your comics or you'll get the money from us, through the insured. And in the meanwhile I'll show you a few comics that we have recovered, and if you can authenticate and appraise them for me you'll pick up a fee today.'

Winston held the bottle, trying painstakingly to work it open. Lindsey looked away from the crippled hands. 'After the war,' Winston rasped, 'after I got out of the hospital, I went back to drawing, like I said. It hurt like anything and I couldn't do really fine work, but I could still draw some. But then I started stiffening up. The docs couldn't do nothing for me, so then I really had to stop.'

Lindsey opened his briefcase. He

showed Winston the comics he'd retrieved from Helena Balter. It only took a few minutes for Winston to authenticate the comics and place a value on them that ran just a little over Patterson's own valuation.

Lindsey got Winston to write out a statement regarding the comics and sign it. Winston moved his scarred hands slowly but he wrote with precision. Lindsey made out a check for Winston — on the spot — in behalf of International Surety. It was a marvelous feeling.

Finally Winston got to open his bottle. He poured two glasses of whiskey without asking if Lindsey wanted any, handed one to him and raised the other to his lips. 'Joey Lindsey's boy,' he said. 'The poor bastard. Here's to his soul, Hobart.'

Lindsey said, 'Were you in Korea together, Mr. Winston?'

'You can call me Sully,' Winston said. 'Sure, we were on the *Lewiston*, we were on the same gun crew. Joe Lindsey thought I was some kind of hero.' He smiled faintly. 'Not a military kind of

hero. I was a big-time comic artist. I'd
worked for Victor Fox, I'd worked for
Charlie Biro, I'd worked for old man
Gaines.

'I was just putting in my time in the
damned Sea of Japan, off Chongjin. There
was a big enemy air base a little ways over
the border in Manchuria. The enemy
pilots used to come zooming down across
the border. We called it MiG Alley,
and our guys would go up in Sabres and
sometimes in those weird F-82 Twin
Mustangs and they'd have dogfights over
the Chongjin reservoir. We had a battle
group standing off the coast to bombard
enemy ground installations and to pick
up any American pilots who had to ditch.'
He sipped his whiskey.

Lindsey sat quietly. He didn't want to
stop the flow of information. This was the
answer to the question that Mother
always evaded, even when she was at her
most lucid. He'd been robbed of a father,
had never seen him, had never felt his
touch. He'd been robbed of his father's
life, but now, at least, Sullivan Winston
was giving him his father's death. An icy

shiver ran down his spine.

'Once in a while the MiGs would come out and attack us too. You know, the whole idea of the privileged sanctuary — our guys were only allowed to chase 'em back to the Manchurian border. They couldn't follow 'em home, couldn't hit the Chinese airfield.

'Anyhow, this flight of MiGs got through and they were hammering us pretty hard. Joe Lindsey and I were feeding this battery of anti-aircraft guns, and we score a direct hit on this MiG. Christ, I can see the guy's kisser as clear as if you were him, Hobart.

'This MiG blows up right in midair. I could see the poor bastard's face. Pieces of MiG flying all over the place. The pilot goes flying through the air. He must have been dead by then, but I kept thinking that he was really flying; I expected him to stretch out his arms like Bulletman and fly away.

'And the fuselage comes crashing down on the *Lewiston*'s deck, huge pieces of metal swerving and slamming around and flaming jet fuel going up, our ammunition going up, the MiG's ammunition going up.' He drained his glass, rolled away in his wheelchair, filled up his glass and drained half of it before he came back.

'Joe Lindsey and me, we both get drenched with jet fuel. We're down on all fours, screaming at the top of our lungs, trying to scramble away, crawl away, anything, trying to get away from there.

'And here comes this gunnery officer we both know, and he's got this foam thrower and he's throwing foam on the flames. And he comes running up to the two of us, all hell has broken loose on deck, and I swear I saw what happened next. It's been in my soul for thirty years, Hobart.

'This lieutenant comes throwing foam in front of him, Lindsey and me are trying to get to him, to get to the foam. And this lieutenant makes this funny kind of half-turn and he lifts his leg like a dog going to piss.

'He throws foam all over me. He saved my life. But that funny half-turn, he put his foot right in Joe Lindsey's face and Joe falls back into the flaming jet fuel and he dies. I don't think anybody else saw it. The lieutenant saved my life; they gave him a medal for it. I got my ticket home and I spent a long time in sick bay and finally I got my discharge and my pension.

'That lieutenant saved my life, but I swear, Hobart, he killed your father. The jealous bastard killed him. He killed your father.'

For a long time neither of them said anything. With a trembling hand Sullivan Winston lifted his whiskey glass and took a big swig. Shaking harder than Winston, Lindsey lifted his own glass and gulped down its contents. He put the glass on the floor so he wouldn't spill whiskey all over Winston's rug. Finally he said, 'He couldn't have slipped on something on the deck? He couldn't have been turning to get a better shot at you with the foam?'

'Mr. Lindsey, I'm certain of it. Your father was murdered. *He was murdered.*' He drained his glass and rolled his wheelchair over to the sink and washed it out. Then he rolled back to the dresser and stood the glass carefully upside down on a towel. He said, 'Take your time with that liquor. I'm in no hurry. I owe you a debt now anyway. I've been carrying that around with me for thirty years. Now that I've told you, I feel like somebody has lifted a heavy sandbag off my shoulders.'

There was another long silence, and then Lindsey asked him the gunnery officer's name.

'Lieutenant ben Zinowicz,' he said.

'Nathan ben Zinowicz?'

'That's the man.'

Somehow Lindsey wasn't surprised. It was something he had sensed, maybe even known, deep inside, all along. He felt depressed, and angry, and despondent, but not the least bit surprised. After a while he said, 'Why, Sully?'

'Envy. Resentment.'

But to Lindsey it failed to make sense. 'A gunnery officer. A lieutenant. You and my father were just crewmen.'

'I was going 'round the second time,' Sullivan Winston said. 'So I was a rating by then. But Joe was just an AB, yes.'

'Even so. Why would an officer envy you? Why would he resent my dad? Why did he hate him? It couldn't be anything minor. Not to — to kill for!'

'He wasn't a career officer, you see.' Winston seemed to be talking to his stiff, scarred, skilled hands. 'He was hardly older than your dad. I was older than the lieutenant.

'He was a college boy, Lieutenant ben Zinowicz was. He got his commission that way; he'd bucked from ensign to JG to full lieutenant in quick time. That happens in wartime. In combat zones where there are high casualty rates.

'But he really wanted to be a comic book man. Isn't that something? He studied art and creative writing in college and he wanted to do comic books. Everybody else in the business wanted to get out. Lieutenant ben Zinowicz wanted to get in. Ain't that the way it always is?' He gave a short, bitter laugh.

'Nobody thought of comic books as a real profession in those days. At the very least you'd graduate to a newspaper strip. Ham Fisher, Alex Raymond, Chester Gould, they were the idols. Once in a while somebody actually made it. Wayne

196

Boring got to do *Superman*, syndicated. Cripes, Mickey Spillane used to write *Sub-Mariner* scripts for Bill Everett. Look at him today!

'But Lieutenant ben Zinowicz wanted to be a comic book man. He used to show us his stuff. He'd invite us up to officers' country and get us in his compartment and show us these drawings and these story sketches he'd done. He knew who I was, you see.

'I was a kind of minor celebrity on the *Lewiston*; some of the men had comics that I drew, you know, stuff I'd done before I went back in service, and it was just coming out. They were always begging me to draw caricatures of them to send home, or to do nudes of Wonder Woman or Sheena for pin-ups.

'So Zinowicz looked me up, and I figured an invitation to officers' country was a nice break from the job. I told him that your dad was a comer, a bright young guy who'd started selling stuff, and after the war he was going to be a star. So Zinowicz invited us both up to his compartment and he asked us what we thought of his stuff.'

There was a screech of brakes and the blare of a car horn from outside.

'He had no talent,' Winston said. 'His drawing was hopeless. He'd had training, I could see that, but he had no aptitude at all. No life, no feeling. He knew some technique but he hadn't really absorbed anything. Anatomy all wrong, that was the killer. Bad perspective, bad composition.

'Your dad told him straight out what he thought of his work. Zinowicz said he appreciated the honest opinion, but you could tell it was burning him up. I tried to let him down easy. What the hell, maybe I was just toadying; but I was a little older, and I'd made some compromises that your dad hadn't made yet.

'So I told the lieutenant that some of his story ideas looked pretty interesting; maybe he should concentrate on being a scripter. Or even try to break in by doing some of the little text stories in the comics. Hell, nobody read the things. The scripters used to do 'em for a few extra bucks. Otto Binder did 'em, Carl Formes and Spillane did 'em. I told the lieutenant if he was interested I'd give him the names of the editors to send his scripts to; I said he could use my name to get them to pay attention.' Winston looked up at Lindsey. His eyes were watering. 'I guess that was why he saved me. And killed Joe Lindsey.'

Hobart Lindsey stood up and paced around the suddenly cramped and stuffy motel room. He wanted desperately to leave but he had to ask one more question before he did. 'Sully, didn't you do anything about it? You saw a murder committed. Didn't you do anything?'

'I did. I swear I did, Hobart. I mean, I was in sick bay. In the hospital. I was burned all over. I mean, look at me, even now.' He held his hands toward Lindsey. Lindsey turned his face away from them.

Winston said, 'I tried to tell 'em. Even in the hospital. I was yelling. You don't know what it's like, being burned. You ever put your hand on a hotplate by mistake, it's like that only a million times worse and it's all over your body and it never stops and you scream and it never stops. They give you shots and you get doped up and everything is like a dream but the pain never stops.'

But he stopped, and the room was silent. Lindsey dropped into his seat. 'How long were you in the burn ward?'

'A long time,' Winston resumed. 'I got to tell you the truth, Hobart. I guess I went nuts for a while. I mean, from the pain. But I kept trying to tell 'em what happened, and they must have thought I was hallucinating. Between the pain, the drugs, the painkillers, I guess I was. I kept seeing that MiG and the pilot like Bulletman and the lieutenant kicking Joey and — I guess I was crazy for a while, Hobart.'

He looked at Lindsey pleadingly.

'Anybody would have been crazy. You understand that, don't you?'

15

Lindsey sat there in a fugue for what might have been thirty seconds or thirty minutes. Sullivan Winston brought him out of it by shaking his shoulder with one scarred, stiff, powerful hand.

'I guess what I said was a shock to you. But I really tried to do right, Hobart. After the navy wouldn't believe me, I even called your mom about it. Did she ever tell you?'

'I don't remember. I must have been just a little kid.'

'A baby. Yeah. I couldn't travel, I couldn't go see her, but I called up and tried to tell her what happened, but she kept getting mixed up about your dad, about Joey. She couldn't understand that he was dead. She kept saying he was coming home soon. I guess I got her real upset, 'cause she just hung up on me. I never tried again. Maybe I should have, but I never did.'

He took a deep breath and said, 'I usually eat with my widowed sister. We kind of keep each other company — two relics watching the world go by. I'll ask her to add some water to the soup if you want.'

Lindsey shook his head. 'No, thanks. I appreciate it, Sully, but I need to get on.'

After thanking him again and leaving his card, Lindsey pulled away in his rented Renault and found a motel in another part of the city, on upper State Street, way out beyond what passes for bustle in sleepy Santa Barbara.

From his room he phoned Walnut Creek and made arrangements for Joanie to stay over with Mother until Mrs. Hernandez came in the morning. Lindsey went out and bought a sandwich and a bottle of whiskey and brought them back to his room. He ate the sandwich without tasting it. Then he sat on the bed with his feet up, the bottle and a plastic motel cup and a Styrofoam bucket full of complimentary ice cubes on the night table beside him.

Well, he was really a private eye now,

wasn't he? A motel room and a bottle of whiskey! Probably he should have a smoldering blonde there, too — if he'd known how to obtain one.

He thought of all the women he did know — most of them only casually. There was Mother, of course. He wouldn't want her with him, not now. He lay back and for a moment the dark image of Marvia Plum's face flashed through his mind. He smiled. He'd like to . . . what? Talk with Marvia, anyway. He'd never had a black friend in his life, let alone a black girlfriend. What would it be like to . . .

How much credence could he give to Sully Winston's story?

Mother had told him that Father had been killed while serving on a destroyer off Korea, without going into details. Lindsey had seen his father's Purple Heart and his Korean Service Medal. Why hadn't he ever pressed Mother for details of Father's death? Because, he told himself, Mother was a half-crazed old woman. But maybe he'd never really wanted to learn. He just didn't like violence. In his business he had to deal with death frequently, but death was always abstract . . . Little pieces of paper, life insurance claims, death certificates from the State of California. A safe little piece of paper.

Lindsey had never known his father and he'd never particularly wanted to find out about him. Shouldn't he have wanted to learn? In Sullivan Winston's room he had realized that he did want to know. And Winston had told him, maybe told him too much.

He kept seeing that scene as Sullivan Winston had described it as a series of comic book panels, everything outlined in sharp black lines and colored in with bright inks, reds and yellows and blues. The exploding plane, and the dead pilot flying through the air like Bulletman, and the pieces of the plane bursting into flames. The two crewmen covered with flaming jet fuel, and the lieutenant with the foam thrower saving one and murdering the other.

Sullivan Winston in a wheelchair for life. Joseph Lindsey, deceased.

Nathan ben Zinowicz, war hero, college professor, contributing editor of the Proceedings of the Institute for the Study of Mass Culture.

Everything got mixed up. The cartoon panels got transferred to the screen of the TV set he'd unconsciously switched on. Lindsey lay on his back watching them, filling and emptying the plastic motel cup with whiskey, until he passed out.

*   *   *

The morning sun came through venetian blinds and punched him in the eyeballs. Lindsey sat up and his head felt as if Professor ben Zinowicz or his pal Francis had worked him over with that polished walking stick. There was a fiery, sour taste in his mouth, he felt sick, and the room stank of spilled whiskey.

He'd never been thoroughly drunk before, not even in high school when drinking was an illicit thrill and getting stinko and throwing up and passing out was a male rite of passage.

Early in the spring of '68, he'd

thumbed a ride in a hippie van with a teenage girl he knew slightly from his economics class. They found their way to a free concert in Golden Gate Park, and danced to the music, sampled a marijuana cigarette that was passed from hand to hand, wandered barefoot in warm grass.

The girl — Lindsey couldn't remember her name — had wandered away in the crowd. She stayed in San Francisco almost a year before returning to Walnut Creek, and would never talk about what she had done during those months.

Lindsey had found a ride home the same night. He'd felt a mixture of euphoria and panic there at the concert. When he got home his mother was nearly hysterical and demanded that he promise never to leave her like that again. Guilt-stricken, he had given his word.

Now he sat on the side of his bed in a motel room in Santa Barbara, suffering the first hangover of his life. It took him an hour to get himself cleaned up and checked out. The desk clerk still gave him a dirty look. Maybe he just smelled bad.

He turned in the rental car, poured himself onto an airplane, and somehow managed to get home without further disaster.

Mrs. Hernandez gave him a nasty look. He didn't say anything to her. He looked in on Mother, saw that she was all right, and climbed into bed.

He slept till noon, woke up and had a shower and shave, got some coffee and a couple of muffins inside him, and slept some more.

He drove down to his office and added the newly recovered comics to those already in the International Surety safe. Then he went to the video store and asked if they had anything about the Korean War. It seemed to be a forgotten era. They had exactly one movie about the Korean War: *Pork Chop Hill* with Gregory Peck. He pressed the clerk behind the counter for more, and was told that there were others around — but nobody ever asked for them so they didn't bother to stock them.

Lindsey rented the one they had and brought it home to watch. Mother wandered into the room and sat down beside him, a cup of tea in her hand. She was wearing a housedress and fluffy slippers. Her hair was gray and tangled. She was fifty-two years old and she looked like eighty.

She watched the movie for a while. She said, 'Your father will be home one day, little Hobo. Does it make you sad, not having him here? He'd be so proud of you. When the war ends he'll come home and we'll both have him with us.'

He didn't say anything. When the movie ended he put the tape away, went to bed and cried himself to sleep.

The next day he returned the tape on his way to International Surety. Ms. Wilbur took a long look at him but said nothing.

He studied the mail, answered phone calls, took his lunch at the Japanese place downstairs. He called Harden and told him that he was making good progress. He'd recovered three more comics in Santa Barbara and he'd found one of the consignors. He had an idea about finding the rest of the consignors and he might even have a lead on the thief. If Lindsey was right, he'd find the rest of the comics when he had the burglar at bay.

Harden wanted details and Lindsey fenced with him and finally told him that he was very busy and had to get on to other things. He hung up the phone and told Ms. Wilbur if Harden called back he was out of the office.

Harden didn't call back.

When he arrived home later, Lindsey got Mother to drink a glass of wine with her evening meal. Then he sat with her while she ate. Lindsey himself had no appetite.

He said, 'Mother, how did my father die? I know he was killed in Korea. How much do you know about it?'

She looked at her plate for a minute. 'You know, he was in the navy, on a destroyer. His commanding officer came to see me about it. He was a very young man, hardly older than your father. And I was such a young woman then, really a girl. A bride. I was carrying you; you weren't even born yet.

'The lieutenant came to see me. He was wearing his uniform with medals on his chest. He'd been wounded along with your father; he was walking with a cane. He told me about it.'

She looked at him, and Lindsey could see the light fade from her eyes, could see her losing her focus, losing her grasp on the moment. She wandered into the past, smiling. 'When the war ends he'll be coming home. He's going to finish going to school and then we'll move to New York if we have to, and he's going to be a famous cartoonist, like Milton Caniff or Chester Gould. You'll see.'

Lindsey walked behind her chair and gave her a kiss on the top of her head. She turned around and smiled at him. 'What a sweet thing to do, Hobart. Sometimes you're just like your father.'

Lindsey called Joanie and asked her to come over. He was spending half his salary on Mrs. Hernandez and Joanie Schorr. Maybe he should do something with Mother after all. But he couldn't just stick her in a home.

He checked his pocket organizer, then double-checked with the telephone directory. He took a deep breath and dialed

Marvia Plum's home number. She answered the phone herself. Did that mean no husband, no live-in boyfriend, no parents?

'Uh, this is Hobart Lindsey. I need to talk to you. About, ah, about . . . some things.'

She said, 'All right.'

He said, 'Did you eat dinner yet?'

'No, I haven't eaten.'

'Can I take you to dinner?' He got it out in one rush, conscious of his rapid pulse and breathing, feeling like a fool. He'd never been much of a lady's man. In school he hadn't been much for dating and parties.

Marvia hesitated, then: 'Dutch. I'll meet you at Plearn, okay? That's the Thai place by the U.C. theater on University.'

'Great! What time — '

'How about an hour?'

He got there first. He found a parking place and walked up and down in front of the restaurant, watching college students milling in line, waiting to get into a Hindi language double bill at the U.C.

Marvia Plum walked up the street, past

211

the swirling students. It was the first time Lindsey had seen her out of uniform. She drew admiring stares and a couple of comments from young males standing in line. A black man near the end of the line said something rude. Marvia ignored him. Lindsey found himself feeling angry and jealous.

She smiled when she saw him. She took his hand and a jolt of electricity shot up his arm. He looked into her face to see if she'd felt anything, but he couldn't tell.

The restaurant wasn't too busy. Standing at the wine bar, Marvia made small talk and Lindsey clutched his glass to keep it from shaking. During their meal he found himself staring at Marvia and feeling the eyes of others, even in Berkeley, appraising a white man and a black woman eating dinner together.

He said, 'Anything I tell you, does that have to become official information?'

She gave him a funny look. 'I thought this was social.'

He reddened. 'It is. I mean, I called you up because I, uh, really wanted to see you.' He looked away. 'I mean, can I talk to you about my work too? You won't mind?'

'No.'

'You're still working on the burglary at Comic Cavalcade?'

She frowned. 'It's a murder case, Bart. I'm much more interested in Terry Patterson's death than I am in those comic books. I can understand it if your company has a different viewpoint.'

'Have you got any more information?'

'Patterson's parents drove up from Modesto. They'll take the body for disposition as soon as the medical examiner releases it. They want Chiu and Morris to run the store until they figure out what they're going to do.'

Lindsey caught himself rubbing his head. The swelling was almost gone now. There was still a scab there. Patterson might not have been hit any harder than he had been when he'd been left on the Santa Fe tracks to die; only by luck had he escaped being crushed by a locomotive. In Patterson's case, the attacker had been more careful. He hadn't left it for an outside agency to complete his work.

'Marvia, what if I knew about another murder?'

'Then you'd better report it. Right away.'

'Well, I'm not sure it happened. I can't prove it.'

'This has something to do with the comic book case in Berkeley?'

'No. In Korea. Actually, on board a ship during the Korean War.'

She shrugged her shoulders. 'Forget it,' she said.

He said, 'I can't. I think I know who the killer was, and it's somebody I've met. What I want to know is, can I do anything about it? If I report this, can the police do anything?'

'Let me get this straight. The alleged murder took place in wartime on a U.S. navy ship? Military personnel involved — both killer and victim?'

'Yes.'

She said, 'I don't think there's much you can do. There's no statute of limitations on murder, but after this much time I don't think anybody's going to be interested in prosecuting the case.

214

Anyway, that would be federal jurisdiction. Maybe Justice Department, more likely the navy itself. You could call the U.S. Justice attorney's office, but I don't think you'll get very far. You don't want to tell me any more about it?'

'I'm sorry,' he said. He felt like a shy teenager on his first date. Worse. He felt like a virgin who had worked up the nerve to go to a singles bar and didn't know what to do once he got there.

He said, 'Uh, what's your sign?'

She thought that was very, very funny.

The evening took a turn for the better.

He tried to tell her about himself. Marvia seemed interested in his life in the suburbs. It was another world to her. He told her the story of his single experience with the flower children, and laughed when she said she'd gone to more than one such celebration herself.

She talked about her family. They sounded like warm, ordinary people, and he kept forgetting that they were black, that Marvia Plum was black. He kept thinking that her family was what families were supposed to be like. She loved her mother but she worshiped her father.

'You told me that you never knew your father. That's sad. What happened, Bart?'

'He was an art student. He wanted to be a cartoonist. He and Mother were in school together. Then he got drafted into the navy during the Korean War. He and Mother were newlyweds, but he'd already got his draft notice, so they wouldn't defer him. Mother didn't even know she was pregnant. He got drafted and he was killed in the war.' He was looking at the white tablecloth, then felt her hand on his and looked at it, startled.

'Does this have something to do with that murder you were telling me about?'

'I don't know. Yes. I — ' He excused himself and went to the rest room. When he came back he changed the subject.

At the end of the meal they split the check. He said the evening had been great, and he asked if she'd go out with him again.

That was when she said, 'This Thai coffee is too sweet for me. I can make us some at my place that's much better.'

16

They had both parked in downtown Berkeley. He agreed to follow her home. She drove a glittering tan-and-cream Mustang. She parked on Oxford Street in north Berkeley. Lindsey pulled to the curb behind the Mustang and climbed from the Hyundai. Marvia was already standing beside her car.

'I like your car. It's a classic. Did you buy it on a cop's salary?'

'My little brother Tyrone gave it to me. He's the family moneymaker. It was pretty far gone when he got it. Worked on it for a year, and when it was ready to go, he gave it to me for my birthday.'

Her tenant apartment was in a huge Victorian house. They stood on the flagstone path while he looked at the exterior. Lindsey shivered. Like a Poe character he felt his senses tuned to an abnormal pitch. There were lights in a couple of windows in the house. A pointed turret reached upward from the building. Above it a handful of stars were intermittently visible through broken mist. The moon was covered by clouds but it made a bright patch in the darkness.

Lindsey felt his hand brush against hers. He took her hand, their fingers interlacing. A thrill raced from his finger-tips into his body. He turned toward Marvia and she turned toward him. He put his hands behind her shoulders, and pulled her gently toward himself. She did not pull away.

Her apartment was a single room on the top floor of the house. She took his coat and hung it in her closet. He looked around the tiny apartment. There was a bookcase stuffed with ragged textbooks on criminology, books on gaming and puzzle theory, books on mass culture and sociology.

She'd mentioned that she collected a few comic books herself, and they were displayed in mylar protectors on the walls. One called *All-Negro Comics*, dated June 1947, which he'd never even heard of.

Negro Heroes, Negro Romances, Roy Cam-panella — Baseball Hero.

'I was going to do a paper once, on the black image in comics. That was long ago, before I got out of school. Somebody beat me to it, but I kept my research materials.'

All Lindsey could say was, 'Nice.'

'We share a kitchen,' she said. 'Come on, let's have some coffee. But don't make too much noise, some of the neighbors complain.'

He sat at the kitchen table while she made the coffee.

'It's ready. You want something with it?'

He said, 'I'm pretty full.'

She led him back upstairs and they sat in her room. He took a sip of coffee, then asked, 'Ah, have you been a police officer for long, Marvia?'

'Not very. I was in the army for five years. In the MPs. When I got out I wanted to do something where I could use that experience.' She was sitting on a hard chair, facing him. Their knees almost touched.

'I'm not really a detective,' he said. 'But

in this case, I'm a kind of detective. And I was never mixed up in a murder before. I guess it's routine for you.'

She smiled. 'As a matter of fact it's my first. I don't know how far Yamura's going to let me run with it. What puzzles me,' she went on, 'is the reappearing comic books.'

He looked at her. 'I've seen stolen goods come back before. Sometimes in theft or embezzlement cases they offer restitution in exchange for a *nolle prosequi.*'

'Then why the killing? The killer must be the burglar. And when he was returning those comics, Patterson came out of the store, out the back way, and the burglar panicked and killed him. Find the burglar and you'll have the killer. Or vice versa.'

'But we haven't caught the burglar. Why would he return the comics when he was in no danger?'

She laughed. 'When I was in the army, in basic, they used to send out a squad of dumb recruits with shovels and have 'em start digging a ditch. A couple of hours later, after they'd got a good stretch dug and they're sweating away, sore and pissed, they'd send out another squad with shovels to fill it in.'

'You think the burglar changed his mind, maybe got scared of the loot? So he decided to return it? And it was just bad luck that he ran into Patterson and killed him?'

She shrugged. He drew in his breath at the movement of her body.

★ ★ ★

A motorcycle roared past during the night, waking Lindsey. He looked at Marvia, sleeping. He laid his fingertips against her cheek and she moved slightly but did not awaken. The clouds had cleared and moonlight angled into the room.

He watched her face, watched the printed quilt rise and fall with her breathing. It was a quilt she must have owned for a very long time. It was blue, with printed figures of Raggedy Ann and Andy. He couldn't put a name to his emotions. He put his face on the pillow, touching Marvia's.

* * *

At six a.m. the radio turned on to a newscast. Marvia was up and out of the room before he could even say good morning. A few minutes later she was back, dripping, from her shower. Lindsey sprang out of bed and pulled on his shorts, shirt, and trousers. He blushed.

She smiled, slipped out of her robe and toweled herself dry, laughing softly at Lindsey's embarrassment. 'You're so sweet,' she said.

He mumbled something unintelligible.

She was sliding her arms into the straps of a brassiere. She stood with her back to him and asked him to help with the hook in back. She said, 'You try to be so stuffy and dried up but you're not, you know.'

After a few fumbles he managed to get the hook closed.

'Was that your first time?' she asked.

He felt himself redden. He stammered.

'That's all right,' she said. 'In fact, I'm very flattered.'

He didn't know what to say.

'Meanwhile, I've got to report for duty.'

She peered around him at the clock radio. 'Okay, I'm on time. Look, I'm going to spend the morning following up on Patterson. The whole day, if I can get away with it.'

'You talked to ben Zinowicz?' Lindsey managed. He was sitting on the edge of the bed, putting on his shoes. His beard had never been very heavy; he could get away without shaving for a day. His clothing was neat enough to wear a second time.

'I told you about that. He couldn't possibly have done it. It was a nice idea, but he didn't do it.'

'What about Francis?'

She looked at him. 'Wife? Girlfriend?'

'Francis with an i. Very male. I met him once.' He demonstrated height and the width of shoulders with his hands.

She lifted her eyebrows. 'They gay?'

Lindsey shrugged. 'I think so but I don't know. Francis is a sort of live-in secretary and all-around major domo for ben Zinowicz.'

'Does he use a cane or walking stick?'

'I don't think so.'

'But you think he might have been returning those comic books for ben Zinowicz, and killed Terry.'

'Yes.'

'But then he would have brought the stick with him, and he didn't have a reason to do that unless he intended to kill Terry. Which messes up our accidental-encounter scenario.'

Lindsey said, 'Still . . . '

She asked for ben Zinowicz and Francis's address. He gave it to her. 'Richmond,' she said. 'Okay. I'll make a call up there and see what I can get. What are you going to do today?'

'I'm going back to Comic Cavalcade. Those stolen comic books weren't store stock. Not all, anyhow. There were consignors. I think if I can find the list of consignors, it might help. Terry Patterson had promised it to me, but I think I can find it at the store.'

She nodded. 'Sounds good. Get me a copy too.'

He agreed.

'Look,' she said. Now she put her hand on his. 'I don't know what Sergeant

Yamura or Lieutenant O'Hara said to you. I know you were talking to him the other day. He didn't like you a hell of a lot.'

'I got the same impression,' Lindsey told her.

'Just remember, you're not a cop, Bart. You're not even a private eye, right? You're an insurance man. You're after some valuable comic books. The murder part of this case is my business, mine and Yamura's. Try to stay out of it, and if you find yourself getting involved, get in touch with Dorothy or me. Don't try to be a hero.'

He nodded.

'I want to keep you safe, see?' From some hidden reservoir she brought out a Bogart drawl.

He held her against his chest. He could feel her snub-nosed revolver in its holster, pressing against his thigh.

* * *

Telegraph Avenue was changing into its morning character. Dirty-looking specimens wrapped in sleeping bags and quilts

225

were moving away from doorways and wandering toward whatever hope of breakfast they could find. Students were walking or bicycling toward the university campus, headed for early classes.

It was too early for Comic Cavalcade to open, so Lindsey got a café table once more, across the street from the shop. He sat watching for Jan Chiu or Linc Morris, but what he was thinking about was Marvia Plum. He knew that he could not have been Marvia's first man. But how many others had preceded him?

At length he saw two figures in quilted jackets and blue jeans halt in front of Comic Cavalcade. He watched Linc Morris tap the entry code into the keypad then unlock the front door and enter with Chiu close behind.

A gleaming white police cruiser rolled slowly past the restaurant. Lindsey turned his head to watch it, wondering who was inside. The cruiser sent a flare of reflected sunlight through the window where Lindsey sat. The morning was sparkling clear. He found himself grinning.

Was he the same person he had been a

few days ago? Was he living the same life? Was this the same world?

He'd have to speak with Ms. Wilbur, Mrs. Hernandez, Joanie Schorr. Make sure that Mother was all right. Keep International Surety informed, Harden and Johanssen off his back.

Had he ever before even been alive?

He finished his breakfast, paid the bill, and started across Telegraph Avenue.

17

Lindsey crossed in front of Comic Cavalcade in time to see Jan Chiu lock the door behind her. The store wasn't scheduled to open for another thirty minutes.

Jan turned back when Lindsey rapped on the glass. She recognized him and unlatched the door. 'Oh, Mr. Lindsey! The insurance man.'

She closed the door again, locking it behind him. Lindsey said, 'I'm still after the list of consignors of those stolen comics.'

From behind the counter Linc Morris said, 'I'm sorry, Mr. Lindsey. I looked for it yesterday but it didn't turn up.'

Lindsey said, 'I accidentally found one of the consignors. He showed me a receipt that Terry sent him for his comics. It looked like a computer printout. I think the information might be in your Circuitron.'

Morris waved a hand toward the store's computer. It stood on the counter near the cash register. 'We use standard software,' he said. 'Everything's here. You want to take a look?'

Lindsey breathed a prayer of thanks for Ms. Wilbur's help in learning to use the Circuitron. Comic Cavalcade had a hard-disk system, just like International Surety. He called up the correspondence files and looked for the letter Winston had shown him in Santa Barbara. If that was on the file then the others should be also.

An hour later he was finished. The computer printed out fresh copies of the receipt letters Patterson had sent to each consignor. He'd even sent one to himself, containing a list of the burgled comics that had come from store stock. The list of comics belonging to each consignor matched the master list of stolen merchandise.

There were five consignors. Two Lindsey already knew about: Patterson himself, and Sullivan Winston. Lindsey asked Linc Morris and Jan Chiu if they knew who any of the others were.

Morris pointed to a name on the list. 'He's the only one I know. Edvard Bjorklund. Edvard with a v and Bjorklund with a j.'

Lindsey said, 'Tell me about him.'

'Ah, he's . . . a middle-aged guy. Collector ever since he was a kid. He's more a friend of a friend of mine. I have a pal who runs a comics shop in Alameda. Bjorklund came to him to sell some comics from his collection. Some pretty valuable books, big-ticket stuff. My friend couldn't handle it so he sent Bjorklund to Comic Cavalcade. I really passed the guy along to Terry.'

'You know anything more? His profession? Background?'

'Yeah, well, the reason he wanted to sell his collection was his daughter. His wife is dead and he has this married daughter who lives someplace out of town. Up in the gold country, I think. She wants to buy a house, she and her husband, so Bjorklund wanted to sell the comics to help them with the down payment. That's all I know.'

Lindsey turned to Jan Chiu. 'Any of

these names mean anything?'

She studied the list. 'This one. Sojourner Strength. I know her from the radio. From KPFA. She does their radical lesbian show. I don't know where she lives; she uses the station for a mailing address.'

'Is everybody involved with comic books weird? I've never seen such a run of off-beat characters.'

'They're just ordinary folks, I think.' Chiu shrugged. 'Maybe they wouldn't fit in the insurance business, I guess.'

The euphoria Lindsey had felt earlier was fading. Sojourner Strength — surely that couldn't be her real name — had consigned the comics he had recovered from Helena Balter in Santa Barbara. Several more on the list were her property as well.

The last consignor — his comics completed the inventory — was a local resident: M. Martin Saxon of Claremont Boulevard, Berkeley. Lindsey whistled. Unless this was an amazing coincidence, the president of the company buying the comic books was also one of the sellers.

Lindsey put in a call to Ridge Technology Systems. He got as far as Saxon's administrative assistant, George Dunn. Dunn said, 'I didn't think your last visit here was particularly useful, Mr. Lindsey. Is this something we can handle by telephone — and quickly, I hope?'

'This concerns your boss, George, not you. Tell Saxon that there are some questions he's got to answer, and he can either answer them for International Surety right now or he can answer them for the cops a little later. It's up to him.'

Dunn said, 'Hold on, I'll check with him.'

At length George Dunn came back on the line. 'Mr. Saxon says he can see you in half an hour. There'll be a guest badge ready for you in the reception area.'

Lindsey hung up. The store had suddenly become a bustle of activity. Youngsters bargained for bubble-gum cards and recent comic books. An older collector had brought in a want list. Jan Chiu had squeezed past Lindsey to reach the cash register and was handling the sales.

Chiu broke away from a youthful customer to confront Lindsey. 'When do you think we'll have a settlement on the claim? Terry's parents were here, you know. They kept asking Linc and me, and we couldn't tell them.'

'Can't tell. Maybe we'll get 'em all back, and then there won't be any claim to worry about.'

Chiu looked serious. 'What about Terry? Anything on him?'

'That's up to the cops, not International Surety.'

In the time since he'd left Marvia's apartment on Oxford Street in the perfect morning air, clouds had crossed the bay from the Pacific and the temperature had dropped and the day had started to look like rain. Lindsey was starting to feel depressed. He left for RTS.

This time he didn't have to make an effort to get the attention of the receptionist. At his entrance she looked up and pressed a button on her desk. The connecting door opened and Dunn strode through wearing a gold-colored shirt and blue jeans. He was followed by a beefy uniformed security guard.

Dunn nodded to the receptionist who handed Lindsey a guest badge. He clipped it to his jacket. 'Come on,' Dunn said, and indicated the doorway.

Lindsey followed the path that he remembered, conscious of Dunn and the security man close behind him. The security man had a badge pinned to his shirt and a gun strapped to his belt.

In Dunn and Mabry's office, Selena Mabry was seated before her Circuitron 95. She wore a shirt that matched Dunn's in color and cut, and obviously nothing under it. She was running a graphics program on the computer's monitor, and blobs of pulsating color reflected on her skin.

Dunn ignored her. He pointed the security man to a chair and said, 'You wait here. I don't think you'll be needed but you'd better stand by anyway.' He pointed at Lindsey. 'Come on.' He tapped a code on a keypad next to Marty Saxon's door. The door opened with a soft shushing sound.

'Lindsey in, Dunn out,' a voice said.

Dunn scowled and let Lindsey pass him into Saxon's office.

Marty Saxon sat behind a huge scalloped table. In the room's odd lighting it was difficult to see him. A huge skylight covered the entire ceiling. The rest of the room seemed to be without walls.

Saxon stood up and walked around the table, extending a hand. He was shorter than Lindsey, but built like an athlete. 'You're from International Surety.' Lindsey nodded. 'I can see you're distracted. Sorry.' Saxon returned to his table and hit some switches on a pad built into its surface. 'Holograms,' he said.

The walls turned into redwood paneling, and the soft sound of crashing waves mingled with harp music came up.

'Let me show you something,' Saxon said. He punched some more keys. A door opened in the paneling and a second Marty Saxon strode into the room. He was wearing a three-piece suit and carrying a briefcase. He laid the briefcase on Saxon's worktable and turned toward Lindsey.

'I've come here to tell you about the newest member of the Ridge Technology Systems family of advanced desktop computers, the Ridge Circuitron 105. This system offers picosecond access time to a bubble memory with sixteen times the capacity of our previous high-end model without sacrificing full upward software compatibility and a new array of peripherals — '

Saxon hit a button on his keypad. The second Saxon and his briefcase winked out of existence. 'Holograms,' Saxon said. 'I love 'em. Got to show that to everybody who comes in. I'm not in business for money or for ego or for power. It's just so damned much fun. Now, what the hell do you want? What's this about Comic Cavalcade?'

Lindsey located a bent-metal chair, felt it to make sure it was real and sat down. 'Let me make sure of one thing. You are the same M. Martin Saxon who lives on Claremont Boulevard in Berkeley?'

Saxon grunted. 'Yeah, I'm the same M. Martin Saxon. Mather Martin Saxon. Descended from the infamous Cotton

Mather, believe it or not. Okay, shoot!'

'You know that Terry Patterson at Comic Cavalcade had completed the order for a comic book collection that your company had placed. And that there was a burglary at the store.'

'Yep.'

'And that Patterson was murdered.'

'I heard that on the car radio. You know, RTS fronted Patterson some bread for that order. Is he going to be able to deliver? The store, I mean? Otherwise I want my money back. I'll get the comics from Cape 'n' Dagger or one of the others. Or, what the heck, I'll buy Fillmore posters or Oakland Raiders memorabilia or find something else to do with the money. I've got to get rid of the stuff before the end of the year, my accountants are having fits.' He fixed Lindsey with a stare. 'I want to know why you're selling and buying the same comic books, Mr. Saxon. I've looked into the whole idea of your investing RTS cash in old comics as a tax shelter, and it seems legal enough. But why did you conceal the fact that you were one of the consignors of the comics your company is buying? Don't you realize that you open yourself to charges of a serious conflict of interest?'

'I might, but I'm not worried. I didn't make that list. Circuitron 95 did. Sheer coincidence that I had some of the comics on the list. I wanted to get rid of my collection anyhow. Just a bunch of 1960s Silver Age stuff. Kirby, Ditko, Kubert. It's nice enough for collectors but I'm not interested. Computers are more fun. Holograms. Digital analyzers. Robots. Satellite technology. Space probes. Going to send a robot to Mars in five years. Look here.' He leaned forward, prodding the surface of his table with a stubby finger. 'Russians are going to go to Mars. Fools in Washington can't make up their minds what to do, can't see beyond the next election. So I'm going to do it for them. Russians'll climb out of their Mars lander and Marty Saxon will walk up to them in a three-piece suit and shake hands in the name of all intelligent beings everywhere. Marty Saxon hologram operated by an on-site Marty Saxon robot, an

RTS computer, satellite-linked to RTS headquarters in Oakland, California. I'm going to do it! It's fun!

'That's why I sold my comic books. The Incredible Hulk can't compare with a Marty Saxon hologram walking around on Mars waiting for the Russians to arrive! You want anything else, Lindsey? I'm a busy man!

'Did I rob Comic Cavalcade? Not on your life. I want to get rid of this stupid money before the politicians take it away from me. I wouldn't queer my own deal there. Did I kill Patterson? Nope. I liked the kid. Besides, he was doing something for me, why should I want to off him? Look, you got any more questions, just let me know or give me a buzz any time, get my private number from Georgie out there. Don't let the door hit you in the ass as you leave.'

* * *

Before going to Point Richmond Lindsey had to make a brief stop in Walnut Creek, where he brought his domestic affairs up to date. Mother was doing all right. He had taken time to drive her down to the store and buy half a dozen old movies. The VCR was a big success.

Mrs. Hernandez and Joanie Schorr agreed to look after Mother while he continued the Comic Cavalcade investigation. He knew it was no long-term solution to his problem with Mother, but it would have to do for now.

Back at the office Lindsey and Harden hashed out the case. By the end of their phone conversation three of the five consignors were pretty well eliminated as suspects for the burglary as well as the murder.

Terry Patterson was obviously not the killer and Sullivan Winston was also out of the question — wheelchair bound as he was, and three hundred miles away from Berkeley.

Lindsey's interview with Marty Saxon had convinced him that Saxon was not the type to use the methods of burglary and crude murder to accomplish his ends. Lindsey wrote him off.

That left Sojourner Strength and Ed

Bjorklund. And then there were the Point Richmond two, Nathan ben Zinowicz and Francis. Sullivan Winston's story had almost convinced Lindsey that ben Zinowicz was responsible for his father's death.

Still, whether the events of 1953 connected with the Comic Cavalcade burglary and Terrence Patterson's murder three decades later or not, Lindsey wasn't going to let ben Zinowicz walk away untouched. To Lindsey, if not to the police, his father's death meant a hell of a lot more than Terry Patterson's.

He had to do something about it. But what? For all his fanciful role-playing as a hard-boiled dick, Hobart Lindsey wasn't really a tough guy. He couldn't see himself backing ben Zinowicz against a wall and beating a confession out of him, much less exacting vengeance, vigilante fashion, once he had that confession.

What was he going to do?

The least he could do was get out of his office and get moving.

★   ★   ★

Lindsey parked on Railroad Avenue again and started to make his way to the Baltic Restaurant. At the last moment he decided to avoid the Baltic. Francis might be there — or Margarita. He looked around Park Place and spotted another restaurant and saloon across the street. The Hotel Mac.

Once inside the Mac, Lindsey took his bearings. It was a fancier establishment than the Baltic, with the same motif of polished brass and restored brickwork.

Lindsey ordered a beer and set out to locate the pay phone while the bartender served it up. He dialed ben Zinowicz's home number and got Francis's voice on the tape. He hung up. The tape might mean that nobody was home, or simply that the prof didn't want to be disturbed.

Lindsey strolled back to the bar and picked up his beer. He felt a hand on his shoulder and looked in the back-bar mirror to see who it was.

Margarita. As if they'd had an appointment in the Hotel Mac.

Lindsey turned to face her.

'Bart Lindsey,' Margarita said. 'As I live

and breathe. Say, what's your sign?'

Lindsey tensed, then relaxed. Women were still strange and mysterious creatures, but they didn't frighten him the way they used to.

Margarita said, 'Come on over and chat. There's always room for one more.' She led the way to her table. 'Listen,' she said, 'if you won't bite on that one, how's about, do you come here often?'

'I just stopped in to use the phone. Look, the last time we met it all turned out very badly. I don't want anything to happen again.'

'Oh, you mean that little tiff on Railroad Avenue?'

'What do you know about that?'

'I'll swap you, one for one. What do you know about Franny and the professor?'

'Are they homosexuals?'

'I'm pretty sure they are, but I hope not, though. They'll give us a bad name.'

Lindsey reddened. 'Us?

'Never mind. You tell me what you know about them, okay?'

'Ben Zinowicz is a U.C. professor. Francis works for him. The professor is doing a consulting job for my company.'

'I don't suppose you know who slugged you outside the Baltic.'

'Do you?'

'Of course.' She downed her drink and signaled the waitress for another. 'You want anything?' she asked.

Lindsey still had half his beer. He shook his head.

'I've had my eye on Nathan and Francis for a while now,' Margarita resumed. 'The professor was a guest on my radio show one time. I just loved his political analysis of the contents of Little Annie Fanny and Mary Worth. He thinks he's so damn modern and enlightened, but all he spews out is typical patronizing patriarchal stereotypes. You know what that bastard did? On the way out of the studio he tried to cop a feel! Son of a bitch! It was obvious he was gay, but he thought he was flattering me by pretending! I could have killed him on the spot, but that would have jeopardized our FCC license.'

'I'm surprised you want to have anything to do with him after that.'

'I don't, really. But I've kept an eye on him and Mr. Muscles. We happen to live in the same town, and I have a creepy feeling about those two. They haven't done anything that I know of, like holding fascist cell meetings in their house or running guns to Nicaragua, but I wouldn't put it past 'em.'

'And you saw me get slugged when I left the Baltic? You followed me out and watched Francis hit me and leave me by the tracks?'

She laughed. 'He didn't leave you by the tracks, Bart. He left you *on* the tracks. If Mr. Muscle had stayed around to watch, you would have been hamburger meat by now.'

'But I woke up and saw the train coming.' He shook his head. 'I thought I was a goner, but I wasn't on the tracks. I was next to them, not on them.'

'Guess who dragged you off as soon as Francis climbed into his cute little BMW and puttered back up the hill.' She took a bow sitting down. She was wearing a low-cut dancer's top.

Her story about ben Zinowicz being a

guest on a radio show rung a bell in his mind. He said, 'What station do you work for?'

'KPFA, Berkeley.'

'Then you're — '

'Sojourner Strength,' she said. 'A.k.a. Margarita Horowitz. Somehow *A Chat with Margarita Horowitz* doesn't have quite the pizzazz of *The Sojourner Strength Liberation Hour*, does it?'

'Is Margarita Horowitz your real name, then?'

She swallowed part of her drink and smiled. 'My birth certificate actually says Naomi Ruth Horowitz. I just couldn't deal with that so I took Margarita as a kind of joke, but it stuck and I'm happy with it, in my private life. On the radio I'm Sojourner Strength.'

'Then you were one of the consignors. Some of the comic books stolen from Comic Cavalcade were yours!'

'You bet your flash panel they were! I was in the newsroom at the station when that burglary report came over the wire. Typical — it happened in Berkeley and we had to find out about it on a wire-service printer out of New York.'

'Look — not that it's any of my business, but why do you want to sell your comic books? From what I've always heard, collectors hate to part with their treasures.'

'I had those things from childhood,' Margarita said. 'I'm all grown up now. I've realized that there's no worth in such junk. Women have to be strong. Everyone has to be strong, but women have been the victims of history, and now we have to lead the liberation struggle. I don't look very strong to you, do I?'

Lindsey made a noncommittal sound.

'But just try something and you'll see what women can do! I've got my brown belt now, and I'm up for black in another month!'

'Okay,' Lindsey said. He didn't want to quarrel with a karate-chopping radical lesbian. 'If you saw Francis slug me and you pulled me off the tracks — uh, I appreciate what you did — why didn't you call the police? They might have caught Francis.'

'I don't like the police system in this

country. I don't want anything to do with it.'

'But the police did come, you know. When I came to I was trying to get my bearings; I climbed in my car and a police officer saw me. He thought I was drunk. Once he understood what really happened, he offered to help me. But he admitted there was no way he could find the man who hit me. But now we have a witness. We can pin this on Francis.'

'Forget it,' she said. She downed her drink and ordered still another. 'You're really nursing that beer,' she said. 'Look, I don't want anything to do with the cops.' She paid for her fresh drink. 'What are you going to do now? If you just came in here to pick up some meat, you're at the wrong table.'

Lindsey shook his head. 'I had the same feeling about the prof that you have. Even before Francis set me up and then you say tried to kill me. I saw ben Zinowicz after that. I've been to his home. I want to go there again. Tonight.'

She stared at him. 'Why?'

Lindsey shrugged. 'I don't know. I

don't even know if I can get inside the place. But there has to be something there that explains what ben Zinowicz is up to.'

She looked into his face. 'Are they out? There's usually one or the other at home, you know. There's not much happens in Point Richmond that I don't know about. Call it snooping or call it preventive surveillance. I don't trust Nathan and Francis. You think you can get into the house?'

'I dunno. I'm going to play it by ear.'

'I'll give you a ride up there. I live on the other side of Golden Gate. The refinery side, you know. With the rest of the poor folks.'

They left the Hotel Mac and she led the way to her car, a battered Volkswagen Bug. As Margarita started the engine, Lindsey said, 'Uh, can I ask you a question?'

'Sure.'

'All the things you're involved with. The *Liberation Hour* and all of that political stuff. I mean, you're an attractive young woman. You could have a home, a family, a career. And you could run for office if you want to do political work.'

Margarita snorted. 'Another fuzzy-minded liberal! You'll wake up someday.' She put the Bug in gear and pulled into the quiet street outside the Mac. 'Look, in the sixties I was a just a kid student at Berkeley High, but we went up to the campus when everything was happening at U.C. People's Park and all that. Where were you, Lindsey?'

'I'm younger than you, then. I was still a kid in Walnut Creek.'

'I learned the truth about the power structure in this society. We were trying to turn everything upside down. There were millions of us all over the country, do you realize that? If only the Vietnam War had gone on and Nixon hadn't resigned, we might have won. But they were our targets, they were our enemies. They were the thesis and we were the antithesis. Once they were gone, we lost our focus . . . Never mind. We can have the political lecture some other time.'

Climbing the steep hill behind the Hotel Mac, the Bug revved like a

Porsche. Lindsey made a comment and Margarita laughed. 'Right on the nose, brother. My roomie Susan customized it for me. If you ever need a hot mechanic, just get in touch.'

Margarita parked in a sheltered area underneath a cheese-box apartment house. 'It ain't much,' she muttered, 'but it's home sweet home.'

They climbed out of the Bug. Despite her low-cut top, Margarita was dressed warmly against the night. She'd retrieved a sweater from the pocket of her quilted jacket and pulled it over her head before she put on the jacket. Lindsey was shivering in a knitted pullover jacket and slacks.

She said, 'You know the way?' He jerked his head in the direction of San Francisco Bay.

They started walking down Marine Street. As they made their way down the darkened hillside, a lighthouse beacon flashed through the mist. The top of the Transamerica Pyramid was visible above the fog layer that filled the bay itself, obscuring San Francisco.

They reached Ocean Avenue and walked until they were opposite the professor's house. Lindsey recognized the familiar BMW parked in the driveway. 'That's it,' he whispered.

Lindsey said, 'I'll scout around. There must be some time when they're both away. Ben Zinowicz travels a lot. Francis can't just sit home like a guard dog when his boss is gone. I'll be right back.'

He slipped across the street and crouched down behind the BMW. He checked the license plate. It read NAT-PRO. What had happened to NBZ-PHD? Damn it, they had two cars, identical his-and-his BMWs. The first license plate Lindsey had seen obviously referred to the owner and his academic degree — a bit of tacky egotism but understandable enough.

But what did NAT-PRO mean? Okay, NAT was Nathan. And PRO? Maybe professor. Or maybe . . . what did the comic book collectors and dealers call the people who wrote and drew and edited the comics? Pros — professionals. Their world was divided into fans and pros, with the dealers living in a kind of twilight zone, one foot in each of those worlds.

It fitted with Sully Winston's recollection of the Lieutenant ben Zinowicz of three decades ago — desperately eager to become a pro, lacking the talent that it took and deadly envious of a younger man who did have the talent and had already achieved professional status. So he'd become a pro of a different sort. An academic. A scholar and critic.

Lindsey slipped around the side of the house and crept below the window line. A light was on in the living room. It flickered. Smoke was rising from the chimney. Nathan and/or Francis were probably sitting in front of the fire, brandy in hand, cozy and warm on a chilly night.

Lindsey crawled around to the backyard, where he could see a small boat tied to a dock. More role-playing. Nathan ben Zinowicz: the retired naval hero of a long-ago war.

Something flashed past Lindsey's face and caught him under the chin. He was jerked to his feet. Something was pressed against his neck, cutting off his breath.

'I ought to throw you right into the bay,' a voice whispered in his ear. It was unmistakably Francis's. A naked arm pressed against his cheek. It was hot, powerfully corded, and smelled of a sweet oil. It held him tight against a huge muscular body.

'Just come on along and don't make trouble and you'll stay alive for now. One sound and they'll fish you out of the bay.' He dragged Lindsey backwards, his feet pedaling to keep him from choking.

Francis pulled him through the back door of the house and into the brightly lit kitchen. With one foot he reached past Lindsey and kicked the door shut. He dropped the polished walking stick that had been pressed against Lindsey's Adam's apple and grabbed his arm. He twisted it up behind him, sending flashes of pain through Lindsey's head, and turned him around.

Together they marched through the house until they wound up in a luxurious bedroom. Nathan ben Zinowicz was sitting up in a gigantic, satin-sheeted bed.

He was wearing black silk pajamas decorated with gold piping and a shimmering gold-colored dressing gown. The costume had a vaguely naval look to it.

He shook his head sadly. 'Mr. Lindsey, you're becoming extremely bothersome. Are you that impatient for the report I've been preparing? It's all finished, you know. I was planning to submit the evaluations and my bill to your company tomorrow. I suppose I still can do that,' he mused. 'But tell me, what am I going to do with you?'

Francis released Lindsey, who was trying to rub his Adam's apple with one hand and his twisted shoulder with the other, all the while wondering where his ally Margarita Horowitz could be and what she was doing. Would she get suspicious and alert the police?

His first encounter with Francis had nearly cost him his life. What was in store for him now?

18

She didn't call the police. Nor did she try and break into ben Zinowicz's house and rescue him single-handedly. Margarita wasn't stupid.

Lindsey stood before Nathan ben Zinowicz's bed.

'What were you doing, Mr. Lindsey?' ben Zinowicz asked. 'Sneaking around my property late at night. You aren't a burglar, are you? You didn't pull off the Comic Cavalcade job, did you?'

'You're one to ask,' Lindsey snapped.

'What? You don't think I did it, do you? Look around you. You can see that I'm very well fixed.'

'And it takes a lot of money to maintain that lifestyle,' Lindsey countered.

Ben Zinowicz shook his head. 'Really, I am not in need, let me assure you.'

Lindsey noticed a polished walking stick leaning against his night table. He must own several of the things, which was how Francis had been able to use one as a come-along. It also meant that ben Zinowicz wasn't necessarily the person who had attacked Terry Patterson at Comic Cavalcade.

If ben Zinowicz had ordered Francis to return *Shock Illustrated* and *Science Fiction* to Comic Cavalcade, and Francis had been carrying one of the sticks with him — then he might have killed Terry. While ben Zinowicz was all the while teaching his early morning seminar. Then if Francis had brought the stick back it might be in the house right now, possibly with traces of Patterson's clothing and blood on the ferrule. Unless he had gotten rid of it — burned it in the fireplace here, or thrown it into the bay.

'Well, Mr. Lindsey, if you can't justify your presence here, I'm quite prepared to have Francis call the Richmond Police Department. Richmond doesn't want to drive out its few law-abiding, taxpaying residents. We get very good police service here on Ocean Avenue.'

'*Lewiston*,' Lindsey said.

Ben Zinowicz started. '*What* did you say?'

'I said *Lewiston*. Destroyer, United States Navy. Sea of Japan off Chongjin, North Korea, January 1953. I've done a little research. The war was already winding down. But the fighting was still going on. A flight of MiG jets had come in from their bases in Manchuria and attacked the fleet. You were a gunnery officer on the *Lewiston*. You had a rating named Sullivan Winston and an AB named Joseph Lindsey in your crew. Joey Lindsey was my father.'

Nathan ben Zinowicz lowered his face to his hands and sat unmoving for a long count. Finally he looked up, looked past Lindsey and said, 'Francis, please leave us. I'm sure Mr. Lindsey will behave himself. We really have to talk.' Lindsey heard the door shut as he left the room.

'Do sit down, Lindsey.'

Lindsey slumped into a satin-covered boudoir chair.

'What have you been told about the *Lewiston*?'

'I just got back from Santa Barbara. I

talked with Sully Winston. He told me about the MiG that crashed onto the deck of the *Lewiston*. He told me that you saved his life.'

Ben Zinowicz kept nodding with every few words Lindsey spoke. When Lindsey finished the sketchy story, ben Zinowicz said, 'So Winston told you that I was responsible for your father's death as well as his — Winston's — life.'

Lindsey nodded grimly.

'A pity. Poor Sully has been saying that for thirty years. Nobody wants to hear it anymore. The incident was fully investigated in 1953, Lindsey. Thirty-three years ago! The result of the inquiry was that I received the Navy Cross and the Purple Heart.'

'I saw them in your study.'

'Just so. And another souvenir.' He picked up his walking stick and jabbed through the blankets at his bad leg. 'I don't make a big fuss over this. In fact I was very lucky. Look at poor Sully! Look at Joseph Lindsey!'

'Yes,' Lindsey said, 'look at Joseph Lindsey! What about Sully's accusation?'

Ben Zinowicz said, 'Just what *exactly* did Winston tell you?'

Lindsey repeated the story as he'd got it in Sully Winston's motel room. He left out the part about Winston winding up in a mental ward.

When Lindsey finished, ben Zinowicz said, 'Well, that story is quite accurate, in terms of the physical actions Sully described. But who can know the contents of another man's mind? Poor Sully. His friend died. Joseph Lindsey was Winston's protégé, you know. Winston was an established cartoonist, and Joseph was the bright young talent. They were the closest of friends. The closest.'

He looked at Lindsey then. Lindsey looked back and waited.

'When that attack took place, everything was in chaos. Of course we had damage-control squads on the *Lewiston*, but when the MiG crashed on us there was sheer pandemonium. Some old-timers told me afterwards that it was like a kamikaze attack in World War Two. I grabbed a foam thrower. I was trying to save my men.

'They came at me like two sala-manders, two creatures of fire. I know they were trying to escape, trying to live, but all I could think was that they would claw at me, pull me down into that pit of flame. I wanted to save them but I had to defend myself, too, don't you see? I held one man off with my foot while I sprayed foam on the other. Then I turned back to try and help the first but it was too late to save him.

'I didn't even know who they were. Can you believe that, Lindsey?' The usu-ally composed ben Zinowicz had broken into a sweat. 'In the fire and smoke and noise, I didn't know that one was Sullivan Winston and the other was Joey Lindsey. All I saw was writhing salamanders, living flames trying to consume me.

'The investigators recommended me for the Navy Cross. You don't get that for murder, Lindsey, you get it for heroism. But I could never convince Winston of that. I visited him in sick bay, you know. He shouted accusations at me and started to become violent. I had to leave. I visited your mother before you were born.

Winston had already communicated with her. She became hysterical, just as Winston had. I never went back. What was the use? I'm no murderer, Hobart Lindsey, believe me.'

Lindsey put his head in his hands. He didn't know what to believe. 'What about the comic books?' he asked. 'You have to be the burglar. And Terry Patterson was killed with your walking stick.'

'But I was teaching when he was killed. I've already explained that to the police in Berkeley. A young black woman came to see me. All of my students can testify to where I was.'

'Then you had Francis return the magazines for you. Patterson came out the back door just at the wrong moment. He found Francis sneaking two of the stolen magazines back to the store and Francis knocked him down with one of your walking sticks and stabbed him where he lay. Stabbed him with the ferrule of the stick.'

Ben Zinowicz relaxed. 'Anybody can buy a walking stick, Hobart. Besides, why would Francis carry one? He has two perfectly good, lovely legs. Please, be sensible. Just stay where you are.'

He climbed out of the big bed. Leaning on his walking stick, he led Lindsey from the room and back to the study. He punched a series of numbers into an electronic pad to unlock his desk. He took out a manila file folder and placed it on his desk. 'You can take this with you if you wish. My bill is enclosed. Or I'll mail it to your office. As you prefer.'

Lindsey said, 'What are you talking about?'

Ben Zinowicz said, 'International Surety asked me to perform a task. I have performed that task. I have evaluated the stolen comic books, based on the descriptions you provided. This is my report. If you do not wish to take it with you, I will mail it. I just thought it would save time and effort if you take it with you tonight.' He handed the envelope to Lindsey.

'All right, then.' Ben Zinowicz pressed a button on his desk. 'Francis will show you out. I do not expect that we'll see each other again, Mr. Lindsey. I'm sorry about your father but I don't imagine you can feel much loss over a man you never met. I trust you can find your way back to the freeway without assistance.'

* * *

Lindsey turned and looked back at the house. Francis was just disappearing inside. So Lindsey had gone quietly, tail between his legs, and Francis hadn't even found it necessary to watch him get into his car and drive away. And that was a good thing, since Lindsey's car was still parked on Railroad Avenue behind the Baltic.

It would be a long, cold walk back to the Hyundai. Lindsey clamped an elbow down on the manila folder and started up Marine Street toward Golden Gate Avenue. His breath steamed in front of his face

Halfway up the hill he realized that there were two clouds of vaporized breath in the air. Margarita Horowitz was trudging beside him, and it was obvious from the way they climbed that she was in far better condition than he. Her karate training was paying off. 'How'd it come out?' she asked. 'I was watching.'

'They could have kept me prisoner in that house. They could have murdered me. They could have tied me up and thrown me off the dock and I'd be dead in ten minutes in that water. Why didn't you do anything?'

She snorted. 'I did. I kept to a safe distance and watched.'

'But why did you come along? I thought you were, uh, with me.'

'I came to watch. I told you that I think there's something fishy about those two, and I figured I might learn something useful. Not that I did.'

They were at the top of the hill. It had taken them ten minutes or so to climb from Ocean Avenue back to Golden Gate. Lindsey could see Margarita's souped-up Bug parked under her apartment. He said, 'Could you give me a ride back to my car? It's a long walk and it's awfully cold out here.'

Before she answered, a pair of fog beams swept up Marine Street behind them. Margarita yanked Lindsey into a clump of bushes. He felt Professor ben

Zinowicz's portfolio slip out of his grasp and scatter onto somebody's lawn.

The fog beams slithered past, cutting twin yellowish cones in the swirling vapor. At the corner they swung to the right and disappeared down Golden Gate Avenue.

Margarita was running ahead. Lindsey stopped to gather up the loose sheets of Professor ben Zinowicz's report. He stuffed them back into the manila folder and struggled up the last dozen yards to Golden Gate Avenue. Margarita was there, already sitting in her souped-up VW, the passenger door swung open, excitedly gesturing to him.

Lindsey jumped in and she started back toward Park Place, with its restaurants and bars, following the red eyes of the BMW's taillights far ahead of them. 'He's going slow,' Margarita said. 'That BMW can fly, but he's being careful. It's the fog.'

They came to Railroad Avenue. Lindsey's Hyundai was there but the Bug roared past.

'I think I know where he's headed,' Lindsey told Margarita. 'I think this is the big break. Stay after him.'

'I thought you knew where he was headed.'

'Probably I do. But there are a couple of possibilities. Do you think he knows we're after him?'

'No. He thinks you left before he did. I'm surprised he's driving so slowly, though, even with the fog. It's clearing up away from the bay here, and he's still taking it easy.'

'I think he's being extra careful because he doesn't want to get stopped by a cop. Not with what he's got in that BMW.'

'Spill it!'

'The Comic Cavalcade loot. The stolen books. He's been returning them by ones and twos, dropping them all over the state. He's dropped 'em in San Francisco, Berkeley, Sacramento, even Santa Barbara. But that's too slow. He's spooked now. I've been getting under his skin and he has to get rid of the rest of them fast.'

'Then where's he headed?'

'So far he's dropped them all off at comic book stores. That's where he's going.'

'He's headed for the San Rafael Bridge,' Margarita said. 'Hand me a dollar.'

Lindsey fished the money out of his trousers and shoved it toward her. At the toll plaza they caught up with the BMW. At this hour there was only one booth open, and they stood behind the BMW while the toll-taker made change for a big bill. Lindsey could read the license plate in front of Margarita's bug: NAT-PRO.

Francis didn't cop to anything. He got his change and headed onto the bridge. Margarita paid the dollar to the toll-taker and they were rolling again. 'Are there any comic book stores in Marin?'

'I don't know,' Lindsey said. 'But I don't think he'll head there anyhow. I think he'll head into the city, to Cape 'n' Dagger. On Twenty-fourth Street.'

They followed the BMW across the bridge. 'I don't think I like this,' Lindsey muttered. 'Maybe we should have rammed him. Got the highway patrol involved back there at the toll gate.'

Margarita laughed. 'Not this lady! Forget about that, bub!'

The BMW was approaching to the Golden Gate Bridge with Margarita's Bug following him at a distance. There wasn't much fog here, and Francis had to have noticed the VW's headlights in his rearview mirror. He decided to lose his pursuit. First he speeded up, trying to distance the Bug. He must have been astonished to see the VW match him in speed.

Then NAT-PRO was on the bridge itself, with the bug following 50 yards behind. The bridge wasn't exactly jammed up, but it was more crowded than the freeway had been. Cars that came cruising down through Marin had to slow on the bridge because of the thick mist.

The BMW was in the left lane, following a hippie in an old pickup truck. The hippie was crawling along; he didn't belong in the left lane. The BMW pulled even further left to try and pass, but a pair of oncoming headlights on the undivided roadway forced the BMW to the right to avoid sideswiping the camper.

But a huge Kawasaki motorcycle had pulled into the right lane, diagonally behind the camper. Obviously Francis hadn't seen it. As he swerved back into line between the camper and the modified Bug, Margarita pulled over to the right behind the Kawasaki. Francis slid into the right lane as well. If not for the motorcycle, he might have accelerated past the hippie van, hugging the safety rail, but instead the BMW plowed into the Kawasaki, sending it smashing into the rail.

The motorcycle driver was thrown clear, disappearing into the night mist. The BMW, its front end tangled with the Kawasaki, skidded against the guardrail and slowed.

Margarita hit the brake pedal with all her weight but the souped-up Bug paid no attention whatever. It smashed into the rear of the BMW. For a moment Lindsey was in a state of shock, then he realized that Margarita and he were unhurt — thanks to their seatbelts.

Lindsey climbed out of the Bug. Both its doors had flown open on impact. He staggered toward the BMW. The motorcycle driver was nowhere to be seen. Involuntarily, Lindsey conjured an image of the cyclist flying like Bulletman above the carnage on the USS *Lewiston*, and he muttered a prayer that the cyclist would somehow survive the accident.

Stumbling, Lindsey reached the rear of the BMW. The front of the Volkswagen had hit it tail-on. The BMW's trunk lid had sprung and was standing open. Lindsey peered inside. Even in his semi-dazed state he could see the beautifully tooled and metal-fitted oversize attaché case which was the only thing in the trunk.

He grabbed it and started to back away from the car.

The driver's-side door of the BMW opened and Francis stepped out into the orange lights illuminating the bridge. This time he was wearing shoes. And he carried one of Nathan ben Zinowicz's polished-wood walking sticks.

Without a word he raised it above his head and took a swing at Lindsey. Before the stick could make contact with its intended victim, Margarita Horowitz's foot appeared from nowhere and caught Francis on the wrist. The polished stick went flying.

Cars were pulling up all around the crash scene. All traffic was completely halted. Somewhere Lindsey could hear a siren and see the flashing lights of an approaching police car.

Francis seemed to forget about Lindsey and the attaché case. He lunged at Margarita.

She backed away from him, circling to stay out of his reach. She was making hostile noises. Francis lunged again. She backhanded him across the chops and dodged. Lindsey didn't know if that was orthodox aikido or whether she'd get twelve Hail Marys from her master for it, but it kept Francis off-guard and at a distance.

He lunged again and she kicked him in the face. He staggered and came at her again. This time he got past her defenses and put her into a bear hug. He backed her toward the bridge railing until her spine was pressed hard against the rail and Lindsey could almost hear her bones start to crack as the weight of his body pressed against her. Sirens were wailing closer and people from halted cars had formed a circle, but no one moved to interfere with the battle.

With a flash of hot shame Lindsey realized that that no one included him. He dropped Nathan ben Zinowicz's attaché case with its precious contents and attacked Francis, straining to pull him away from Margarita. Unable to budge Francis's arms, he grabbed two full fistfuls of hair and yanked with all his strength.

With Margarita still in his grip, Francis staggered back. The three of them crashed to the bridge deck. Margarita and Francis were up and at it again before Lindsey could even get to his feet.

Francis lunged after Margarita. She collided with the rail again and folded at the waist, rebounded and spun around. Francis made a final move toward her, attempting once more to get her in his bear hug, but she dropped into a crouch and caught his face with the edge of her hand. At the same time she kicked upward, dropping backwards onto her shoulders as she did so.

Francis went flying, his feet rising

above his head, making a perfect flip. He was silhouetted against the fog, illuminated by the bridge's orange magnesium lights.

For a long moment he was visible, spinning away from the bridge and downward toward the icy waters. Then he disappeared.

As the cops arrived, Lindsey was leaning over the railing, trying to find Francis, but he had disappeared into the fog. There wasn't even an audible splash when he hit.

19

The police escorted Margarita and Lindsey to a little holding room in the bridge maintenance shed. A highway patrol officer and a San Francisco cop did the questioning. They were sympathetic. No good-guy, bad-guy routine.

The motorcyclist from the Kawasaki had bounced off the railing and landed back on the roadway, the victim of three violent impacts. He'd been rushed to San Francisco General, miraculously still alive. The Coast Guard was already out dragging the bay for Francis. With the heavy tides running beneath the Golden Gate, he'd probably be swept out to sea before they could locate him.

The highway patrol cop turned to Margarita, smiling at her in admiration. 'You're lucky that Francis is gone and you're still alive, Ms. Horowitz. Where did you learn to fight like that? Witnesses say they've never seen anything like it.'

Margarita said, 'Women's Revolutionary Brigade, Dojo Number Three, Richmond.' The CHP cop looked stunned.

The San Francisco cop took over. 'We'll need complete statements from you both, but the prelims will do for now. Mr. Lindsey and Ms. Horowitz both checked out clean. So did Ms. Horowitz's vehicle. What's left of it.'

'Does that mean we can leave?' Lindsey asked. 'Can I have my attaché case?'

The city cop said, 'Are you sure that's yours, Mr. Lindsey? You've been through a serious automobile wreck and been involved in a fatal altercation. Maybe you're confused. You *are* Hobart Lindsey?'

'Oh, yes.'

'Your attaché case is embossed with the initials N.bZ. Is there some reason for that?'

'Actually, the attaché case itself isn't really mine,' he said, 'but what's in it is.'

He pushed the attaché case toward Lindsey across the table they were sitting at and asked, 'Would you mind opening it, then?'

Lindsey lifted one side of the case. He

could see that its two gold-plated clasps had combination locks. He repeated, 'The case itself isn't mine. I don't know the combination.'

'You wouldn't object if we open it, then?'

'Of course not.'

They had no intention of breaking the locks there in the bridge office, so the whole party piled into a couple of cruisers and drove through the city to the Hall of Justice. The cops were still very polite to Margarita and Lindsey.

On the way down to Fourth Street Margarita leaned over toward Lindsey in the back seat of the police cruiser. 'What is in there, anyhow?'

'Comic books.'

'Just pray it isn't drugs. If it is, you've really put your foot in it.'

Inside the gray, fortress-like building, Lindsey and Margarita were brought to a dingy office. They were given seats and the attaché case was laid on a desk.

The cop who'd brought them in from the bridge had stayed with them. A crew of others had wandered in and out and an evidence technician had carefully noted the description and condition of the case before opening it.

To Lindsey's surprise, it was X-rayed for booby traps. Then, holding a stethoscope on the locks, the technician proceeded to crack the combinations. The first lock took half a minute. The second went faster.

Their personal cop was still hovering, but a plainclothes dick had taken command of the scene. He said, 'What's this all about, Mr. Lindsey? Where was Francis One-Name going in such a hurry?'

Lindsey explained that he was an insurance adjuster pursuing the loot of the Comic Cavalcade burglary. 'International Surety,' he said. 'I work out of Walnut Creek but this account was in Berkeley. And the case seems to be wandering all over the State of California.'

The cop said, 'Oh, yeah. I heard about that burglary . . . You have credentials, Mr. Lindsey?'

Lindsey showed the officer his International Surety ID, then produced his copy of Terry Patterson's inventory, by now a little bit shopworn but otherwise clean. Lindsey told him what it was.

'Some of these have scribbles in the margin. 'SB, Sac, CC, SF.' What's that mean?'

'The loot seems to have been broken up. A few of the books have been recovered. Those are the cities where they were found. For some reason they were dumping the comics. Not selling them, just dumping them on to shops. Francis was moving the remaining books from his home in Richmond. I'd been closing in on them, and the burglars must have decided that the books were too hot to hold onto.'

'Okay.' The cop nodded. 'Let's check out the rest.'

The technician swung back the rich leather lid to reveal — two neat piles of comic books!

The comics were all carefully bagged and sealed. The evidence technician was wearing surgical gloves. She went over the contents of the attaché case carefully, comparing the comics with Patterson's list.

Everything checked out. Lindsey was starting to feel like a hero. International Surety was off the hook. At the cost of a few grand in buy-back money and a few hundred for expenses, he'd saved the company $250,000! And the insured — or his estate — would get back every comic book that he'd started with.

Except one.

What the hell, recovering thirty-four out of thirty-five wasn't bad. Especially when the thirty-four comics were worth $249,996.50, and the one left unaccounted for carried a guide price of $3.50.

They had everything except *Gangsters at War* number 27 — the 'extinct' issue.

The SFPD was getting more and more interested as the conversation went along. At one point the detective turned to Margarita and asked what her connection with all of this was.

'Some of the comic books belong to me,' she said. 'It was time to sell 'em at a fat profit and they were on consignment to the store when they were stolen.'

A uniformed officer, one of the cops

who'd wandered in and out while they talked, came back into the room. He handed the detective a slip of paper. 'Francis is his real name,' plainclothes said. 'Just Francis.' He shook his head.

'The car wasn't his, though. Registered to a Nathan ben Zinowicz, Ocean Avenue, Richmond. Huh . . . but Francis's license shows Ocean Avenue as his residence. What's your police contact on this, Lindsey? I hope you're not playing lone wolf.'

'Oh, no, Detective Sergeant Dorothy Yamura and Officer Plum, Berkeley Police Department. Sergeant Yamura's in charge of the case, but my day-to-day contact is Officer Marvia Plum.'

The dick said, 'Uh-huh.'

'And, ah, Yamura's boss. Lieutenant O'Hara.'

'We'll want to get in touch with the Richmond PD too. Okay, Mr. Lindsey, Ms. Horowitz. And we'll have to hold onto these comic books as evidence, but you can tell your insured that he'll get 'em all back eventually. We'll give the two of you a lift if you'd like. And you can expect to hear from us.'

'Of course,' Lindsey said.

Margarita Horowitz also assented but in a different tone of voice.

As they left, the plainclothes cop pulled Lindsey aside. 'Listen,' he said, 'you've been protecting your company's interests up to this point. That's great for you and for your company. But this is also a criminal matter, and now that you've got your comic books back, you can just butt out. Any questions, call your friends in Berkeley. Don't try and play Sam Spade, okay? Just a word of friendly advice from an old shamus.'

Lindsey said, 'Okay.'

But the cop didn't know anything about the *Lewiston*. No, Lindsey wasn't eager to play Sam Spade, but he wasn't ready to return to a life of processing claims and consoling widows either.

* * *

Back at Railroad Avenue, Lindsey offered Margarita a lift home and she accepted. He was reaching for his key when a new thought struck him. 'Look, the Baltic is still open. Let me buy you a drink.'

The female bartender eyed them curiously when they came in. She seemed surprised to see Margarita arriving shortly before closing time in the company of a male.

Margarita ordered her usual tequila concoction. Lindsey asked for a cup of coffee.

Margarita downed half her drink. She said, 'You going to follow that gumshoe's advice?'

'Why shouldn't I?'

'Because you're not satisfied. And neither am I.'

'You're without a pretty good car.'

'Don't worry. It's insured. With International Surety too. I hope your company takes a bath on the claim!' She laughed softly.

'Seems to me you'd be satisfied, then. Comic Cavalcade will get all the comics back. They'll complete their big sale and you and the other consignors will get your money. Incidentally, your comics turned up in Santa Barbara, they're not in the big batch. You'll be out of this and you're clean.'

'What about paying another visit to Ocean Avenue?'

'For god's sake, why?'

'Look here,' she said. 'One. Professor ben Zinowicz is already in this picture. He's an authority on old comic books, he's been a guest on my radio show, and he was a consultant to Terry Patterson on values.' She took a long sip of her drink. 'And ben Zinowicz has been working for you too. Seems to me there's a conflict of interest there, but never mind that. Two. Francis leaves ben Zinowicz's house, driving his car. In it is ben Zinowicz's attacheé case, containing most of the stolen comics.'

'Okay. Now what?'

'Three,' Margarita said. 'The cops are going to show up at the professor's house pronto and start asking him a lot of tough questions. Most likely, first thing in the a.m.'

'So what are you proposing?'

'We'll go to my place. I'll get my roommate Susan to join us, and we'll

284

head for ben Zinowicz's house. She can play lookout and you and I can beard the lion in his den. Before the police get there and money talks. Believe me, if we don't get there first, nothing will happen. Nothing! There's no way they're going to arrest that respectable hypocrite.'

Lindsey finished his coffee and checked his Timex. It was almost two o'clock. The last few drinkers were licking out the bottoms of their glasses.

Margarita and Lindsey left the Baltic together. As they hit the door, Lindsey caught a glimpse of the bartender reflected in the cut glass, staring after them.

They drove to Margarita's place in the Hyundai. She rousted her roommate out of bed. Susan looked like the mechanic she was: muscular body, short-cropped hair, blunt fingers with black rims. She gave Lindsey a hostile glance. Margarita filled her in on the events of the past few hours. When she came to the part about the fight on the bridge and Francis's final pinwheel to eternity, Susan jumped up and applauded.

The three of them drove to Ocean Avenue and Lindsey parked the Hyundai under a tree directly across the street from ben Zinowicz's house, ablaze with lights. Otherwise the street was dark. Beneath the tree, invisible inside the car, Susan waited as Lindsey and Margarita approached the house. Either ben Zinowicz was pacing like a worried papa, waiting for Francis's return — or he'd received word of what had happened and was bouncing off the walls in agitation and grief.

Lindsey pounded the polished knocker. Before the third knock the door opened and ben Zinowicz stood before them.

20

To Lindsey's surprise, ben Zinowicz calmly invited them in, sat them down side by side on a Louis XIV love seat in his living room, and insisted that they take refreshments. The fire had died down to embers, but ben Zinowicz added wood and poked the flames back up.

Ben Zinowicz didn't have a hair out of place, but his eyes looked watery and his nose red. He wore gray flannel slacks, an open-collared shirt with a soft cravat, and a belted smoking jacket. Nobody had dressed that way since Cary Grant, but ben Zinowicz was still doing it and making it work.

He brought out a bottle of brandy and three snifters, set them down on a low table and eased himself into an elegant armchair. He'd been leaning on his polished walking stick; now he leaned it against his chair. He gave Lindsey and Margarita a look of mildly offended innocence.

'Now, if I intended to poison you I wouldn't do this, would I?' He nodded toward the table. 'I'll pour for all three, then you can each choose your snifter and I'll drink from the third before either of you take yours. Is that fair enough?'

They went through the little ceremony. The brandy turned out to be terrific, and nobody keeled over, fatally poisoned.

Ben Zinowicz sat back with his snifter in his hands, warming the brandy and inhaling its fumes. After a while he said, 'They phoned me about Francis.'

Lindsey and Margarita Horowitz exchanged glances.

'I heard from the Golden Gate Bridge district office, the highway patrol, the San Francisco Police Department, the medical examiner's office, and finally from the Richmond police. Who's left? The FBI?' He managed to smile wryly, but his hands trembled.

'Maybe the DEA,' Margarita suggested.

'The Drug Enforcement Administration? Good heavens, why would they call me?' He paused, frowning. Then: 'Oh, I see! Oh, no, Miss — is it Strength? I recall now we spent a delightful witching hour together at that grubby little radio station of yours.'

'What was in the comic books, Zinowicz?' Margarita didn't want to play conversation games.

'You'll have them back soon enough. Look inside my attaché case.'

Lindsey snapped, 'Then you admit you stole them?'

He shrugged. 'Maybe it was someone else. Francis had them in the BMW. He won't be telling tales, so I suppose he might as well take the blame. It can't harm him now.'

Lindsey snapped: 'First the *Lewiston*. Now this. You don't turn a hair, do you?'

'If I did, Mr. Lindsey, I wouldn't be where I am today. 'Grace under pressure.' That's Hemingway, you know. Do you think I can get away with it still?'

'What do the police say?'

Ben Zinowicz smiled. 'I told you that the Richmond police give very good service to people like me — wealthy, respectable, white taxpayers who drive BMWs and live in carefully kept homes like this one. I'm very glad I have another BMW in the driveway.'

'You won't get away with it.'

'But why not? The police offered to send a man to see me, but I told them I'd be more than willing to come down to headquarters in the morning. They were grateful.'

'International Surety won't be so courteous.'

'But Mr. Lindsey, all the comics were recovered. The San Francisco police told me so.'

'What about the attacks on me and Terry Patterson? I don't suppose I can do anything about getting slugged, but there's a murder rap to deal with on Patterson.'

'Naughty Francis again. I'm very sorry, but you see, you seem to have run out of threats. I know you're very angry with me, but there's nothing left for you to do. So why don't you just leave quietly? I'm sure you know the way; you've been invited to leave here often enough. And I hope never to see you again. You or, ah, Miss Strength.'

Lindsey exchanged another look with Margarita. Was it over, just like that? Francis had been ben Zinowicz's companion and probably his lover, and now he, too, was dead, and all ben Zinowicz could say was that he felt relieved that there was a spare BMW in the driveway!

Lindsey stood up and started to circle the seat to head for the front door. Margarita rose and moved in the opposite direction.

Suddenly Lindsey saw the flash of a polished walking stick aimed at Margarita Horowitz.

Margarita had heard some slight sound — an intake of breath, or the faint swish of cloth on cloth as ben Zinowicz rose and moved. She reacted quickly. Instead of receiving the impact of the stick squarely on the back of her head, she was caught in the temple.

She collapsed, falling with a sudden and complete limpness that made Lindsey's stomach churn.

Using his one good leg, ben Zinowicz hopped around the love seat, grabbing the edge of it with his free hand. He flipped the walking stick end to end and brought its heavy head down a second time across Margarita's upper spine.

She twitched once, then seemed to settle onto the rug — her every muscle flaccid.

As Lindsey stood there, paralyzed, ben Zinowicz reached into his smoking jacket pocket and took out a gun.

'Wh-Why?' Lindsey stammered. 'You'd talked your way out of it. You were going to pin it all on Francis. Why didn't you just leave it?'

'I don't like having enemies. I don't like people sniffing around. Your mother is a harmless old woman wandering around in a past thirty years dead. And Sully Winston — well, he made a nuisance of himself for a while but now he's going to sit and rot in his little room. They represent no threat to me. But you two are another matter. Especially Miss Strength . . . All right, you're going to walk in front of me and do exactly as I tell you. First I want you to take your keys out of your pocket. Put them on the coffee table.'

Warily, Lindsey complied.

'Now turn to your right and walk very slowly through the alcove into the kitchen.'

Lindsey obeyed. He could hear the professor behind him, panting for breath.

'Now stand still,' he said. 'I'm going to direct you to a drawer in this room. You will open it slowly and carefully. You will find that it is full of tools and supplies. You will remove a long electrical cord and close the drawer again.'

Lindsey obeyed.

They went back to the living room, ben Zinowicz following Lindsey, gun in hand. Margarita Horowitz had not moved.

'Bind her wrists and her ankles,' ben Zinowicz ordered.

Lindsey estimated the distance between them and flung the electrical cord at ben Zinowicz. With two quick strides he hurled himself at the older man.

The heavy electrical cord flew past ben Zinowicz and bounced off the further wall as the professor ducked.

Lindsey saw ben Zinowicz point the gun and felt the hot blast of its explosion.

He waited for the impact of a bullet, wondering in a split second where he was hit. Then he saw the flash of ben Zinowicz's polished stick, felt its impact on the side of his head, saw the room twist crazily as he tumbled, dizzy and nauseous, to all fours.

Then he felt a terrific impact as ben Zinowicz pounded the head of the stick against his skull.

It was as if he'd been separated from his body. It was a distant robot and he was sending commands to it but somehow they weren't getting through and the robot just lay there.

Ben Zinowicz hobbled across the room and retrieved the electrical cord. Lindsey couldn't move his head. Ben Zinowicz crept across his field of vision. He could hear the professor talking but he could catch only a few of the words. He seemed to be talking to Francis.

Ben Zinowicz became visible again. He was on all fours, dragging the electrical cord. He was talking to Lindsey now, or seemed to be, or maybe he was referring to Joseph Lindsey. He kept saying he was sorry, he couldn't help it, he didn't mean it, he couldn't help it.

Lindsey felt ben Zinowicz roll him over and tug at his hands. He still couldn't move. He felt ben Zinowicz twisting the cord around his wrists.

He squirmed around on the carpet until he was crouching over Lindsey. 'Can't we make a separate peace?' ben Zinowicz asked. He looked into Lindsey's face pleadingly. Tears were coming from ben Zinowicz's eyes and rolling down onto his forehead. 'All right,' ben Zinowicz said. 'I can get rid of it. I've gotten rid of many things. Ernest said that. Something like that.'

He sat down on the carpet and grabbed Lindsey's wrists and started dragging him across the room. Lindsey could see and feel what ben Zinowicz was doing. He had been numb but sensation was returning and he could feel jolts and tingles in his extremities. While he couldn't move his fingers and toes yet, he detected the power of movement beginning to creep back into them.

Ben Zinowicz was sitting on the carpet with his legs in front of him. He would drag Lindsey a few inches, pulling with his arms and propelling himself by digging in the heel of his good leg and pushing. It took an eternity but they reached the rear door of the house. Ben Zinowicz struggled to his feet, opened the door, then retrieved his stick and bent over Lindsey, dragging him across the threshold into the backyard.

Susan was across the street in Lindsey's Hyundai. She wouldn't see! If only she saw them, she could come to the rescue, but she wouldn't see!

The professor left him on the rear lawn. Lindsey could see him limping back toward the house.

At length he heard ben Zinowicz again, gasping, muttering to himself, struggling as he dragged a weight from the house. The kitchen light illuminated the figure of ben Zinowicz hauling a limp human form across the lawn.

Lindsey could make out Margarita now. Her head hung at a floppy angle. Her limbs dragged. Ben Zinowicz would pull her a few feet at a time, then stop and rest.

A row of flagstones wandered from the kitchen door, across the rear lawn and down to ben Zinowicz's small wooden dock. Water lapped and splashed against the seawall. Ben Zinowicz's little power boat bobbed on its lines.

Ben Zinowicz limped back to Lindsey. He dragged him onto the little wooden dock and levered him over the edge with his walking stick. For a terrifying moment Lindsey thought the professor had dumped him into the bay, but instead he crashed down into the open cockpit of a power boat. He could feel strength and control seeping back into his body.

He lay unmoving, feeling the wire wrapped around his wrists.

With a thump Margarita Horowitz tumbled on top of him.

Ben Zinowicz clambered laboriously from the dock and started priming the boat's engine. Lindsey couldn't get at him. Margarita was too heavy to throw. And if he tried to dump her onto the deck the professor would probably shoot him before he could even make a move.

That was, if the professor still had his

gun. He'd fired once in the house, when Lindsey had flung the heavy electrical cord at him. The shot had missed — and the professor had done what with the pistol?

Ben Zinowicz turned as if sensing Lindsey's thoughts. He reached into his pocket and brandished the handgun once more.

Why didn't Susan get suspicious and look in the backyard and see them in the boat? She must have heard the shot ben Zinowicz had fired. She couldn't just abandon him and Margarita!

They pulled away from the dock. The bay was thick with fog. Remote foghorns sounded through the darkness, and dim lights shone feebly in the distance.

Far-off sounds came drifting through the night. The fog dampened some, carried others. Lindsey was drifting through a terrible dream. Why didn't he wake up? Why didn't Father get home from the war and make everything all right?

This man had killed him, that was why. Father would never come home from the war.

Lindsey started to cry for his father.

Ben Zinowicz said, 'Shut up! Oh, for heaven's sake, Lindsey, be a man!'

In silence they moved out into the bay. Lindsey decided to hold back, hoping that ben Zinowicz would think he was helpless and offer an opportunity — any opportunity — for him to escape, to survive.

The fog blocked out their view of San Francisco. Lindsey looked back at Point Richmond, where ben Zinowicz's home shrank rapidly until it became a doll's house, then a tiny color snapshot, then a single shining point. Then nothing.

The long Richmond Pier was before him, and beyond it the San Rafael Bridge. Ben Zinowicz was driving the boat almost parallel to the bridge, veering to the south, toward the Golden Gate.

He's going to dump us under the Golden Gate Bridge, Lindsey thought, *where fast-rushing tides will carry our bodies out to sea.*

He couldn't tell how long they rode. The spray coming over the gunwale felt like ice, stinging Lindsey's skin with each dip of the boat. Every so often ben Zinowicz would speak. To Lindsey or to Margarita, to Francis or to Sully Winston or to Joseph Lindsey, Lindsey did not know.

Finally ben Zinowicz cut the throttle to idle. He said, 'I'm going to let you and Miss Horowitz out of the boat now. I have this pistol trained on you, Lindsey.' He seemed to have regained his grasp on reality. 'I can still shoot you. No tricks. Can you move? I think you can move, Lindsey.'

Lindsey just sat there.

'Do as I say and you go into the water and you can swim for it. Even with your wrists tied. Maybe you can work them loose. You don't have much chance, but the other way you have none at all.'

Lindsey said, 'Why, ben Zinowicz? Just tell me that. Why did you steal the comic books? And then why did you give them back? What was in them? Drugs? Blueprints?'

Ben Zinowicz didn't seem surprised that he could speak again. 'There was nothing in them, Lindsey. I took them because I wanted them and I gave them back because I couldn't bring myself to destroy them. That's all. Now, let me see if you can climb to your feet. Apparently Miss Horowitz is really unable to help herself.'

Lindsey struggled to his knees. Leaning on the gunwale, he looked around. He could see the lights of the Golden Gate Bridge high above, and hear buoys clanking, a few distant engines, the slightest hint of the rush of traffic from the great bridge.

'Good,' ben Zinowicz broke in on his thoughts. 'Now, the rest of the way. Stand up. You can use your hands even though they're wired together.'

Lindsey said, 'Please. There must be something — '

'Over the side, Lindsey. Pretend you're in a pirate movie.'

Lindsey said, 'Wait. Look, this is going to get you the gas chamber. Head back to shore. Let us go. You can afford a good lawyer. You can get off with a prison term. You don't really want to kill us like this.' As long as he talked, as long as ben

Zinowicz listened, Lindsey and Margarita stayed alive. Even if it was only a few extra minutes, a few extra breaths.

He saw a couple of points of light in the distance, through the fog. Small boats, fishermen returning late from an expedition or starting long before dawn to reach some secret spot where the big ones ran. He even saw a light high above. He heard a distant buzzing.

The electrical cord was cold and slippery. In the dimness he was able to work on it, work to untie his wrists. Ben Zinowicz hadn't knotted the cord, and in the gloom Lindsey was finally able to free his hands unseen.

He looked over his shoulder. Even in the darkness Margarita's face was visible, as pale as death. But her dark hair had fallen across her open mouth, and it fluttered with her every breath. He felt something catch in his chest. Then a light in the darkness caught Lindsey's eye. Where was it coming from? He looked up and saw a light swirling and shifting.

'Now!' ben Zinowicz ordered.

Lindsey moved. He pushed himself

upward and forward, lunging at ben Zinowicz like a cartoon hero flying at a villain.

Ben Zinowicz raised his pistol and a flash of flame burst from its muzzle. There was a crash as the bullet tore into the seat Lindsey had just left. Ben Zinowicz got off a second shot, and this time Lindsey felt a solid impact. His left foot went numb.

But Lindsey was already in the air, moving with the force of his lunge. He smashed into ben Zinowicz like a football tackler.

The pistol clattered behind Lindsey and he felt himself and Nathan ben Zinowicz tumble over the bow of the boat and plunge into the icy bay.

Lindsey struggled against the shock of the chilling water, confused, turning in circles and trying to locate the boat. Ben Zinowicz grabbed him from behind. He plunged Lindsey beneath the surface but he couldn't maintain his grip and Lindsey struggled away, shoving against ben Zinowicz and twisting around, searching for the boat.

The light from overhead was now brighter, closer. Lindsey was disoriented. He swallowed a mouthful of cold brine. Ben Zinowicz grabbed him by the hair and tugged him backwards.

Lindsey swung a backhand blow at ben Zinowicz. His whole body still tingled from the impacts it had received. And he was starting to grow numb from the icy water. The professor was wiry but he was thirty years older than Lindsey and his strength, too, was being sapped by the cold water. He released his hold on Lindsey's hair and started to swim away.

The light was coming closer. An amplified voice called down from above. The voice was issuing instructions.

Lindsey tried to obey the voice.

Something surged alongside Lindsey. Someone threw him a lifeline. It had a ring on the end of it. Lindsey got one arm through it and clung for his life. High above he could see something hovering, shining its bright spotlight on Nathan ben Zinowicz's power boat. Half blinded, Lindsey thought he could see the form of the professor, struggling unsuccessfully to pull himself back into the boat.

Then Lindsey was hauled on deck and put on a stretcher. There was a confused scurrying and shouting. Lindsey kept shouting that Margarita Horowitz was in the boat, they had to rescue her from the boat. Then they were carrying him inside, inside where it was warm and dry and safe.

21

Lindsey was lying in a hospital bed, suffering from mild shock and exposure. They kept him warm and dry and they fed him. In a few hours he'd be able to check out and get back to work, as good as new.

Except that he didn't feel he'd ever be good as new. The side of his head was heavily bandaged. Touching it, he felt nothing. How many blows had Zinowicz landed with his stick?

Lindsey glanced toward the bottom of his bed. His wriggled his right foot toes and felt them rubbing against the crisp sheet. But his left foot was numb. His brain sent the signals, but his toes didn't pay any attention.

He managed to sit up, and reached for his left foot. A wave of pain swept upward from the foot and he thumped back against the pillow.

He remembered now. He'd been shot

in the foot, and then he and ben Zinowicz had gone overboard, leaving Margarita behind. He'd been rescued by the Coast Guard helicopter that hovered overhead. Uniformed men had dragged him from the water. But what about the others?

The door swung open and his room filled with visitors. A Coast Guard commander. The San Francisco plainclothes detective he and Margarita had talked with earlier that night. A Richmond police officer with a lot of braid and metal on his uniform. An assortment of colors and sexes in medical baggies.

And a vaguely familiar Oriental woman in civvies — Sergeant Dorothy Yamura. And behind her, in uniform once again, Marvia Plum. Marvia smiled at him, and he felt a tightness in his throat.

The Coast Guard commander said, 'The medics tell me that you're going to be all right, Mr. Lindsey.'

'Is Margarita okay?' Lindsey had no trouble talking. 'Did that bastard kill her? What happened to him? And how did you know we were there?'

The commander said, 'They're both

here. You owe a vote of thanks to Miss Susan Gerber. She's with Miss Horowitz now.'

'Is she all right?'

The commander looked at one of the medical types.

'She's holding her own. I don't think she's in imminent danger. But we'll have to see about loss of function.'

The commander said, 'What happened to her, Mr. Lindsey? She seems to have suffered a severe beating.'

Lindsey thought, *I saved her by attacking ben Zinowicz*. But he didn't feel as if he'd done her a great favor if she was going to spend the rest of her life in a back ward hooked up to tubes.

Lindsey asked again, 'How did you . . . ?'

'My people were on the bay looking for Mr. Francis. He may not have been swept out to sea — yet.' The commander passed the ball to the Richmond brass.

'Miss Gerber called us. She said she'd seen you and Miss Horowitz go into Professor ben Zinowicz's house. She thought she heard a shot, and when you didn't come back out she went looking for you.

She banged on the door, but no one answered, so she ran to the back of the house, where the door was open. She went inside and found no one, so she telephoned us.'

Lindsey muttered, 'Then what?'

'We dispatched a car. Even before they got there, Miss Gerber had found the furrows in the backyard. Someone had dragged Miss Horowitz and yourself from the house to the dock. Is that correct?'

Lindsey said, 'Ben Zinowicz did it. He smashed Margarita with his stick from behind. He shot at me and missed, but he got me with the stick.'

'It fits,' the cop said. 'We'll look for the bullet in his house. Maybe you can help us. We were the ones who called the Coast Guard.'

The commander took over the narrative. 'And since we already had a copter up and cruisers out looking for Francis, we alerted them to look for your power boat. You were lucky that the professor headed toward the Golden Gate.'

'The gun,' Lindsey said. 'Where is it?'

'It was in the boat. We have it.'

Lindsey said, 'Where's the professor?'

The Richmond brass said, 'He tried to swim away. He'd have died before he reached land. The Coast Guard guys got him. He's on this same floor. Handcuffed to his bed. He's got a long, hard time ahead of him.'

'Enough, now. Everybody will have a chance to sort things out,' the chief medic in charge spoke decisively. He shooed the others from the room. Marvia got to Lindsey's bedside for a moment before leaving. She touched his hand, he grabbed hers, and then she was gone.

The San Francisco detective stayed behind when the others left. He pulled a chair over to the bed, turned it around and straddled it. 'I warned you not to play Sam Spade, he said sourly.

'I flushed that rat out of his hole, didn't I?

'Sure,' said the cop. 'And nearly got yourself killed for your trouble. People think they can get shot and just heal up. They don't think about severed arteries and bleeding to death or shattered bones and winding up crippled. And you got that poor girl beaten within an inch of her life. She may die yet. Have you thought about that, Mr. Hero?'

'I'm sorry about that. But it was her idea to go back to the house — we couldn't just let it slide. But was it worth . . . what happened to her?'

'You'll have to work that out for yourself, fella. But it's over now, right?'

Lindsey said, 'I'm awfully tired. Please. I need to rest.'

'For god's sake, if you think you have to keep meddling, at least promise you'll work with the cops. Whatever town you're in. You've already got so goddamn many jurisdictions in here, it looks like an interagency summit conference. This is going to take a building full of lawyers to straighten out.'

'Okay,' Lindsey whispered. He suddenly couldn't keep his eyes open. He fell asleep with the San Francisco dick still sitting by his bed.

The next day his doctor brought the good news that his foot was healed enough for him to leave the hospital — the cast he wore and the crutches he used would be cumbersome but necessary. Although his right eye was black, his face discolored, it looked worse than it felt.

Before checking out of the hospital he called Marvia at the Berkeley police number. The operator told him it was her day off, so he tried her at home. Marvia was happy to hear from him and offered to drive him home from the hospital. He accepted.

Then he called Ms. Wilbur. He briefed her on the situation, emphasizing the recovery of all but one minor item among the stolen comics. He asked Ms. Wilbur to pass along the information to Harden at Regional and to ask him if he wanted to inform Johanssen at National or have Ms. Wilbur do it directly.

'Don't you want to talk to them, Hobart?' Ms. Wilbur asked.

Lindsey said, 'Not yet. I will, but not yet. Let them wait.'

Ms. Wilbur said, 'Well, all right!' He could hear the grin in her voice. He had the fleeting thought that he'd misjudged Ms. Wilbur; there was no way she was a mole working for Harden.

Next, Lindsey called his home. Mrs.

Hernandez answered. Mother was all right. Mrs. Hernandez and Joanie Schorr were keeping things under control. Mother had decided that her little Hobo was at scout camp. She was happy watching black and white TV shows and old movies on video tapes.

Then he picked up an Oakland telephone directory, which included the City of Alameda. He found a number and address for Edvard Bjorklund. The last remaining consignor.

By now it was obvious to Lindsey that ben Zinowicz was responsible for the burglary and the attacks on himself and Terry Patterson. How the police would sort out ben Zinowicz's actions from Francis's remained to be seen, and Lindsey had a creepy feeling that the professor would escape every accusation except those resulting from the beatings and shooting of Margarita and himself. Ben Zinowicz would be ruined in academic circles and would probably spend a long time in prison.

But what lay behind the whole sequence of burglary and reverse burglaries of the comic books? And what was the connection between the events of the past few days and the tragedy aboard the *Lewiston* more than thirty years ago?

Lindsey dialed Bjorklund's number, but the phone had been disconnected and no new number was listed.

The case was winding down and almost everything was settled. But the now changed Hobart Lindsey wasn't satisfied. He'd been through a lot, he'd learned a lot, and he wasn't ready for business as usual.

By the time Marvia arrived at the hospital he was sitting in the lobby, in a wheelchair per regulations, his wounded foot elevated, his crutches across his lap. The hospital had sent his clothing out for a quick clean-and-press job. He wore only one shoe. There was no way he could have got the other one on, and the law in its thoroughness had taken it as evidence and furnished him with a receipt.

One leather shoe, left foot, water-logged, with bullet hole and blood. The bullet hole was only in the shoe's upper, and they'd made a second entry on the receipt, for the bullet removed from his foot!

Marvia ran to Lindsey's wheelchair, knelt beside him and put her arms around him, pressing her cheek against his. His heart jumped.

Once she'd wheeled him outside, he stood on his crutches and she handed control of the chair back to an orderly. She helped Lindsey into the passenger seat and started the Mustang's engine. 'Your place or mine?'

He said, with a rush of guilt, 'I didn't even stop to see Margarita!'

'Wouldn't have done any good. I asked. No visitors. Guarded condition. It doesn't sound encouraging.'

'That son of a bitch,' he whispered. 'What will happen to her? What will happen to Susan?'

There was no answer.

'Marvia, I want to go to Alameda. You can drop me in Richmond and I'll take my own car. It's an automatic, and it's my left foot. I'll drive with the right one.'

She shook her head. 'I'll drive you. But why Alameda?'

He told her about his visits to the consignors. Edvard Bjorklund was the

315

only consignor Lindsey hadn't inter-
viewed. Maybe he would provide the
missing pieces of the puzzle.

22

Marvia got on the freeway headed toward the island city of Alameda, once a resort area where rich San Franciscans maintained summer homes. It had been a struggle to get Lindsey's injured leg into the car. But once they were rolling, the trip was easy.

In recent decades Alameda had become the site of a huge naval air station where giant carriers had their home port. Lindsey had visited Alameda before, on business for International Surety. It was the kind of old-fashioned town that he liked.

Marvia hit the glove compartment and Lindsey extracted a map of Alameda. Bjorklund lived on Clinton Avenue, a street lined with perfectly preserved Victorian houses and immaculately tended lawns and flowerbeds.

Edvard Bjorklund's house was closed up. A sign posted on the lawn said it was for sale. Lindsey jotted down the name, address, and phone number of the realtor.

'Let's find a pay phone and try the realtor. Unless you think you ought to check in with the local police first,' he said.

'Not yet. This is your show. But if we need 'em, you can be sure I'll let 'em know I'm here.'

A folksy woman who could have come straight from the old Ma Perkins radio show answered the phone at the realty office. 'I'm interested in the Bjorklund house on Clinton,' Lindsey told her.

'That's a brand-new listing. You're the very first person to enquire. Have you seen the house? It's a lovely Victorian. And in wonderful shape! Would you like to come in and get the details, Mister . . . ?'

'Lindsey. Hobart Lindsey.'

'Well, if you'd like to stop by our office, then we can ride out there together. You're bound to fall in love with it!'

He climbed gingerly back into the Mustang, relayed his conversation with Ma Perkins and gave directions to the realty office.

318

As they drove, Marvia said, 'You might have done better to handle that entirely by phone. Maybe you'll want to talk to her alone.'

Lindsey asked, 'Why?'

Marvia said softly, 'You'll see.'

At the real estate office Marvia helped him out of the Mustang and they found his contact, the only person present in the office. She looked up as they entered and watched coldly while Lindsey swung toward her desk on his crutches. Marvia stayed close.

Lindsey gave his name. 'I phoned you about the Bjorklund house a few minutes ago. Actually, we've already been out there and looked it over. It looks perfect.'

The realtor said, 'I'm terribly sorry you came all the way out here. The house was just sold. I no sooner hung up after talking to you than I had an offer. It's gone now. I'm afraid it was the only listing we had that you'd be interested in, Mr. and Mrs. Lindsey. I really don't know when we'll have another Victorian. In fact, Alameda is a dreadfully tight housing market just now. With the navy and all.

Have you considered looking in Oakland?'

'Look, it's important that I get in touch with Mr. Bjorklund. Even if the house is gone.'

Ma Perkins brightened a little, although the chill she had projected still hung in the air. 'You know the family, then, Mr. Lindsey?'

'Only slightly.'

'Then you didn't hear the terrible thing that happened.' Ma Perkins clucked. 'You know, some people wouldn't even want a house just because of what happened there.'

'Exactly what did happen? Ed didn't tell me.'

'I'll say he didn't! How could he, the poor soul?'

Lindsey was starting to get a sinking feeling. He waited her out. By now he realized that she'd assumed he and Marvia were an interracial couple, and had been horrified at the thought of selling them the Bjorklund house. But talking was another matter.

'Such a nice man,' she said. 'A

decorated war veteran, played Santa for the Christmas party at the navy base every year. He was a widower. Still an attractive man too. And then murdered like that.' She clucked.

'Murdered — how?'

'Oh, the police said it was a burglary. Poor Mr. Bjorklund must have woke up in the middle of the night and surprised a burglar in his house. Shot him dead, he did. One shot. Right through the heart. At point-blank range too.'

Lindsey sat frozen, staring at her, feeling ice in his belly.

'The police said there was nothing missing. The house was ransacked, as if the burglar was looking for something. But Mr. Bjorklund's daughter came in from out of town and said she couldn't find anything missing. And the police never did get a clue. Nobody reported hearing the shot, but that doesn't mean anything. The houses on Clinton are big and far apart.'

Lindsey asked, 'When did all this happen?'

Ma Perkins said, 'Why, just after

Thanksgiving, it was.'

Just before the Comic Cavalcade burglary and the whole rest of the sequence of events had begun. Everybody else connected with this case might be satisfied, but Lindsey was only starting to get excited!

He swung toward the exit on his crutches. Marvia moved ahead of him and opened the door. Behind him he heard Ma Perkins sniff and mutter, 'I declare, what you see these days.'

Inside the Mustang he turned toward Marvia. 'I'm sorry,' he said. 'I didn't realize — I wouldn't have put you through that. I mean, I thought that was all a thing of the past.' He was trembling with unexpected rage.

She put her hand on his. 'She doesn't know any better.'

'Even so. Damn it, what if we were married? What business is it of that stupid old biddy!' He breathed deeply. 'I think I need a drink.'

She found a coffee shop, parked the Mustang, and helped him inside. After they ordered, he pulled himself upright, swung onto his crutches and made his way to the pay phone. He fished some coins out of his pocket and looked up the number of Comic Cavalcade in his pocket organizer. The pocket organizer was a mess after its dunking in San Francisco Bay, but it would have to do until he could replace it.

Jan Chiu answered the phone. 'We heard about what happened,' she said. 'We're all so grateful, Mr. Lindsey — Terry's parents, and Linc and I. We think we can keep the business going, now that you got back the comics and everything. You're a real hero. All we need now is to get the comics back from the police, is that right?'

'That's right. You'll have to be patient, but you'll get them before too long.'

'It was Professor ben Zinowicz, right from the start!' Jan Chiu said angrily. 'And we thought he was Terry's friend.' Lindsey detected a sob in her voice.

'Listen,' he resumed, 'I need some more information. About Ed Bjorklund.'

'I — I don't know much. Terry dealt with him. I think he was just in the store once; some friend of Linc's sent him here. Maybe Linc can put you in touch with him.'

'Hardly,' Lindsey said. 'He was murdered.'

Chiu made a shocked, incoherent noise.

Lindsey said, 'Maybe you'd better put Linc on. He can tell me some more about Bjorklund — I hope.'

Linc Morris's voice came over the line. 'I'm sorry, Mr. Lindsey. I don't think I can tell you much more than I did the other day.'

'Look, you told me that another dealer sent Bjorklund to Patterson. What was his name?'

'Uh, Billy Clausen. He and I used to go to conventions together.'

'What's the name of his store?'

'Alameda Funnies.'

'Which comics did he bring in to Comic Cavalcade?' Lindsey scanned the now illegible list in his organizer and jotted down some notes as Morris spoke.

'Mr. Bjorklund brought in some good comics,' Morris said. 'There were two early *Captain Americas*, I remember, one with a Simon and Kirby cover and one with a Schomburg. And there were a couple of war comics, and some undergrounds.'

'You remember which war comics?' Lindsey asked. The blood rushed in his ears as he waited for Morris's reply.

'Nothing valuable, but very rare. *Gangsters at War* 26 and 27. That's a strange one too — the burglar took *Gangsters at War* 27 but he left 26. They weren't part of the RTS order, but Mr. Bjorklund was selling the whole batch, so Terry took them even though those *Gangsters at Wars* aren't really worth anything. The burglar — the professor . . . why would he do that?'

Lindsey said, 'Are you going to be at the store all day?'

Linc Morris said, 'I . . . uh, y-yes. Jan and I think we should hire a couple more people to keep up the staff, but we didn't want to ask Terry's parents about that. Not yet. So, uh, I'll be here all day. But . . . why? I thought everything was all over.'

'There's something else. I'll be there in

a few hours. Don't let anything happen to you.'

Lindsey headed back toward the table where Marvia was waiting. She stood up and helped him with his crutches. The warmth of her hands still went through him every time they touched.

She said, 'What's all the mystery? Why are you trying to dig up this murder in Alameda?'

'The burglary isn't quite over. And I don't think the murder of Terry Patterson was the first in this case. I think Edvard Bjorklund was killed over those same comic books.'

'You're out to pull everything together, aren't you? The thing in Korea in 1953 and Ed Bjorklund and the Comic Cavalcade burglary and Terry Patterson's murder.'

'That's right.'

'For god's sake, Bart, what if Comic Cavalcade had given their insurance business to some other company? You're only in this thing by happenstance!'

'I know Dorothy Yamura doesn't like coincidences, but they happen. Anyhow,

I'm in it, and I'm not getting out till it's over.'

'Okay,' Marvia said placatingly.

'Do me a favor,' Lindsey said. 'Would you look up Alameda Funnies in the phone book, then find it on the map and get us there?' She gave him an oblique look but agreed.

Alameda Funnies was on another of the town's few shopping streets. The kid who ran it could have been Terry Patterson's clone. He looked like an overgrown junior high school class brain. At least he didn't seem shocked or offended to see a white man and a black woman walk into his store together.

'Are you Linc Morris's friend Billy Clausen?' Lindsey asked. 'You sent Edvard Bjorklund to Comic Cavalcade?'

'Yes, right. Say, what's this about?'

'You know that Linc's boss Patterson was murdered and his store robbed?'

'I know. I heard.'

'Okay. I'm investigating the case for International Surety. Officer Plum is with the Berkeley Police Department.' Clausen blanched. 'Tell me what you know, son.'

Lindsey gave the kid an encouraging smile.

'Yes sir. Ma'am. Mr. Bjorklund wanted to sell me some good comics. Expensive items. But I don't go in for the big-ticket collectibles. Maybe someday, but not now.'

'Uh-huh. And Bjorklund was raising cash?'

'Uh, actually Mr. Bjorklund said he wouldn't mind leaving his comics on consignment.'

'You'll have to help me, Billy. If he was willing to leave them on consignment — leave them until you sold them and then got his cash — why did he have to take his books all the way to Berkeley, to Comic Cavalcade?'

'Wouldn't have worked. My customers know my stock. They know what I carry and what they won't find here. I did try and buy a few of Ed's books. He had a couple of old *Gangsters at Wars* that I could have used; they're only worth a few bucks apiece, but they're curiosities. A town like this, lots of sailors around, they like comics with navy stories in 'em. All war comics, in fact, but especially navy stories.'

'And *Gangsters at War* had navy stories?' Lindsey asked.

The kid said, 'All the services. Army, marines, air corps, and navy stories.'

'But Bjorklund wouldn't leave *Gangsters at War* on consignment?'

'He wouldn't split up his collection, even to sell it. So I sent him to Linc Morris. I really feel rotten about that, mister. Ed Bjorklund's comics were part of the batch the burglars got from Terry's store, weren't they?'

'Don't blame yourself,' Lindsey told the kid. His version of the events wasn't quite accurate, but it was close enough. 'Those weren't the comics the burglar was after.'

But actually they were, Lindsey told himself. He was convinced that the burglary was all about *Gangsters at War*.

23

Back in Marvia's Mustang they started once more toward Oakland. Marvia said, 'Okay, mystery man. You want to tell me what you have in mind?'

'I want to follow up those two comic books. *Gangsters at War* 26 and 27. My father served on the *Lewiston* with Sully Winston and then-Lieutenant ben Zinowicz. He drew at least one cover for *Gangsters at War*. He died in a battle that left Sully in a wheelchair and ben Zinowicz walking with a cane. And Sully claims that ben Zinowicz was directly responsible for my father's death.'

Marvia nodded and kept driving.

'And Ed Bjorklund was a retired navy man too. Maybe he served on the *Lewiston* in 1953 . . . Either that or he knew ben Zinowicz or Sully Winston after they left Korea.' He took a deep breath. 'Bjorklund turned his copies of *Gangsters at War* over to Terry Patterson. He didn't need those *Gangsters at War* but he took them both because Bjorklund was selling his collection as a package. Later the whole RTS collection was stolen from Comic Cavalcade, and *Gangsters at War* 27 went with the collection. You'd almost think that the burglar grabbed it by mistake. Anyway, still later, all the comics were returned except for *Gangsters at War* 27.' He shifted in his seat, wincing as a sharp pain shot through his injured foot. 'Do you think the coincidences will make Sergeant Yamura happy?'

Marvia said, 'I doubt it! Bart, I think I'll detour by Oxford Street and get into my police uniform. Sometimes it helps to show your colors.'

★ ★ ★

Minutes later they arrived at Comic Cavalcade. Lindsey asked Linc Morris for a fresh copy of the inventory of stolen comics. Together they crossed the street to Cody's Café for an informal conference.

The pair created quite a stir when they

all walked in. They appropriated a commodious booth and ordered coffee and rolls. Lindsey spread his fresh copy of the inventory on the table. He said, 'Now, look this over for me, Linc. I want you to confirm that this is the correct list of the books that were taken.' Linc Morris and Marvia Plum both looked at Lindsey as if they thought this was a strange request.

Morris slid the list in front of him and studied it. Finally he said, 'Absolutely correct. I can see every one of those comics in my mind's eye. Just the way Terry arranged them for Ridge Technology — in order by value. You know, the most expensive book came first and the least expensive came last.'

'You're sure?'

'Absolutely!'

'How about *Gangsters at War*? I saw number 26 still in your store.'

'That's right. None of those issues are worth much. They were part of Ed Bjorklund's consignment.'

Marvia said, 'Go on, Mr. Morris. What about those comics?'

'Well, it made sense for the burglar to

take the RTS order. He wouldn't want *Gangsters at War* in particular, but I guess Terry left it with the RTS collection because it was part of Ed Bjorklund's consignment, I suppose. I thought it was really strange that he only took 27. 26 was right there too, and he left that one.'

Marvia said, 'They weren't part of the RTS order — we have their list, and *Gangsters at War* isn't on it — and that was what he took — except for that one comic book, number 27. That damned number 27 is too elusive, I wonder if it was ever there to start with?'

'It was there, all right.' Morris closed his eyes in concentration. 'Cover by Alex Schomburg,' he said. 'Picture of an American paratrooper coming through the window of a room where Nazis have an old man and a gorgeous French-woman tied up. Lead story was called 'These Gams for Goering.' Second story was 'Dead Man's Revenge.' There were just the two stories. Oh, and they had this neat feature; they published collectors' cards on the back cover — portraits of famous gangsters. Number 27 had Al

Capone's brother Salvatore and Bonnie and Clyde, just like in the movie.'

This guy was amazing!

'The usual ads,' Morris continued, 'and a text story, and a letter column. I remember that comic very well. I know it's gone. The prof must have taken it with the rest. And now you tell me that we're getting everything back except for *Gangsters at War* 27. That's okay; it's worthless really.'

Lindsey smiled, 'Thanks, Linc. You've been a real help. Now I guess you'll want to get back to the store. Otherwise, Jan is going to be swamped.'

Morris said, 'Okay, Mr. Lindsey. Officer Plum. You'll keep me posted, about getting back the comics?'

'You bet.'

Morris left.

'Can you get a search warrant for ben Zinowicz?' Lindsey asked Marvia.

'The Richmond police have already got one. His house was absolutely clean.'

'What about his office at Wheeler Hall?'

'There too. We got the warrant for his office. Academic files, dull as dishwater. I was there myself. What did you think we'd find?' Marvia asked.

'*Gangsters at War* number 27.'

Marvia finished her coffee and reached for the bill. 'Well, I don't need a new search warrant to take another look. We can go up there right now.'

* * *

Marvia checked in with the campus cops and one of them kept her and Lindsey company while they went through the professor's office. There was a yellow police ribbon sealing the office, and the two cops — one city, one campus — circled each other like dogs from rival packs.

Lindsey said, 'Look, I have a feeling I know where he'd keep it. Check his files and see if there's one for a paper for the Proceedings of the Institute for the Study of Mass Culture. It'll be on the subject of 'extinction'.'

Marvia gave him a disbelieving look but she went to ben Zinowicz's locked file cabinet. The lock had already been expertly picked. Marvia whistled. 'Here it is.'

She carried the neat manila folder over to ben Zinowicz's antique desk and laid it down. She opened it, the campus cop and Hobart Lindsey watching over her shoulders.

There were the notes for ben Zinowicz's article, a set of fan-folded word processor printouts of the manuscript, a set of galley proofs — maybe the same ones Lindsey had seen him working with at his home. And Ed Bjorklund's copy of *Gangsters at War* number 27.

They stood there like a living tableau, slowly turning the pages of the thirty-three-year-old comic book, meticulously studying each story.

Linc Morris's recollection had been perfect. 'These Gams for Goering' was a World War II story, naturally. Chicago gun moll gets out of a prison term by volunteering for military service and winds up parachuting into Nazi-occupied France and rescuing a scientist who's designing a super airplane. At the end of the story she gets a medal from General

Eisenhower himself — a nice touch for 1953!

'Dead Man's Revenge' was a different kind of story. A minor thug gets recruited from pre-quake San Francisco and winds up in an interplanetary war somewhere in outer space. He sacrifices his life to blow up a whole alien planet.

The stories were pretty much the same, variations on a theme. Some kind of criminal gets caught in a war, faces a moment of truth, undergoes moral regeneration in the face of mortal danger, and winds up a hero. At least the gun moll in 'These Gams for Goering' got to enjoy her new status. The poor dub in 'Dead Man's Revenge' had to die to make his point.

But nothing here seemed to contain the needed clue.

They even read the readers' letters. Mostly they contained technical nitpicks over the way the artists drew weapons and uniforms. Some of the readers praised the artwork in back issues. There was a little black-bordered box that announced the death of Joseph Lindsey, the sailor-artist who had done the cover for *Gangsters at*

War number 26, while serving with the navy in Korea.

They were just about ready to give up when Marvia said, 'What about the text story?' She flipped the comic book until it fell open to two pages where a story was printed over a yellow background in microscopic type. It looked almost like two pages out of a real book, except that the columns of type were narrower and set side by side. This was the last hope, and a feeble one at that. As all the comics dealers had told Lindsey, nobody ever read those little text pieces.

They started through the story together.

THE SNOWS OF FUJIYAMA
by Nat Benson

'Really, it doesn't hurt a lot.'

'And right here — when I push?'

'It did hurt a lot at first. But I passed out after the first few seconds, didn't I?'

'That happens. It's really for the best, sometimes.'

'Sure.'

That was all they had to say just then. He thought back over his life, thought about his childhood. How he had always wanted to draw. He copied covers from *Collier's* and *The American Legion Magazine*. Was he ever any good? Certainly not as a kid.

Of course, kids aren't expected to do good work. Opper hadn't been great as a kid. Herriman hadn't been great as a kid. Refining your craft. That was what it was all about.

'You ought to eat some soup.' The ward orderly, a Chinese POW, Mao Lo, was pestering him.

'Bring me a seven-and-seven,' he said. 'I'm dying, ain't I?'

'No booze, sir,' Mao Lo said. 'Ship's rules.'

Art student days. He drifted off. Sitting in cafés late at night, watching sailors on leave getting picked up by bar girls. Drinking with other students. Studying by day and drinking by night and always looking for love.

But had he ever done anything really good? He was always going to do something good. Always going to do it. But had he ever done it?

Slowly, Death pedaled by his cot on a Schwinn two-wheeler.

Overhead he could hear the hospital ship's routine. It proceeded day and night, in calm or storm. It didn't matter whether he lived or died.

Later he awakened, remembering how he had got here. Doing his job, he'd been doing his job. Not drawing. He was always going to draw, but now he was doing other things.

Until his first sale it hadn't mattered. He was just another tyro, an amateur. His best friend was a big man in the field, but until he made his first sale himself, he was a nobody.

Then the check had come, and in a few months he'd have his work on the cover of the magazine. Everybody would see it.

'Eat this, sailor, sir.' Mao Lo was back.

'Leave me alone. Get seven-and-seven.'

'You must try. You mustn't die,

sailor, sir. If you don't give up, you won't die.'

He didn't believe that.

Standing on deck, manning the guns. Remembering it all. Knowing that he'd be back home soon. Knowing that the war was nearly over.

Beneath the gray skies of the Sea of Japan, keeping his eyes on the horizon, waiting to see the MiGs that he knew were coming. All the sky's faint colors: mauve, lavender, ecru.

'On guard, men,' the lieutenant said. He shook his head like a lion shaking its mane.

Big lieutenant, big officer. The gunner knew that the lieutenant was an artist himself. And he had no talent. The gunner knew that the lieutenant had no talent.

Until he'd summoned the gunner and his friend, the older artist, to his compartment, he hadn't known.

Then he saw the lieutenant's drawings.

A little technique, a lot of hard work, but hardly any talent. About as much as you could balance on the head of a pin.

The older man had tried to let the lieutenant down easy. But the younger one had been more honest, more courageous. He'd face a fact and say it was so.

Or maybe he was just stupider.

Now he lay on his cot in the bay of the hospital ship. Dying, dying. And how was it to die? Easy!

When he got home he'd resume his career. He would be the protégé of the older artist. He would be one of the good ones. With luck, he might be one of the great ones! That he knew.

'We'd better move this man, and fast!' Big deal, he thought. What care I?

'Let Mao Lo help,' the faithful Chinese orderly pleaded. 'Get stretcher. Can pull.'

Splendid fellow that he was. But the artist knew there was no use to it. He was dying. That was all.

Entering the ward he saw Death

again, walking his Schwinn now. It was a shiny red bike. He'd had one like it long ago.

'Very soon,' Death seemed to whisper. He leaned his bike up against the artist's cot.

'Easiest ride you ever had.' Death turned and pointed and grinned. 'It's a bicycle built for two.'

'Ride with you?' the artist muttered in reply.

'Make sure he stays warm,' the medic said to Mao Lo. 'And keep him flat on his back.'

Not that it mattered. That was certain.

Soon, over the Sea of Japan, though, he started to feel better. They had got him into a helicopter. The chopper rose through the icy gray sky. The MiGs had come and he had tried to do his job and he had done it well along with the rest of the gun crew and the MiG had exploded and thrown flaming jet fuel on him and on the older cartoonist but they had tried to crawl to safety and the lieutenant was there and he had looked at them and had seen the cartoonist who had spoken kindly of his clumsy attempts and he saved him by coating him with a foam thrower but the young artist who had been honest with him, brutally accurate and honest, he kicked, with one blow of his booted foot he had sent the artist back into the flames where he writhed and screamed until he passed out and they came and took him away and transferred him to a hospital ship and tried to save him but it didn't matter he was dying anyway and he looked through the copter's Plexiglass windows and saw the sun shining on the conical snow-peaked Fujiyama and the clouds surrounding it too.

Soon he stopped breathing and his arm dropped off the edge of the cot. Then they knew he was dead and they took away his corpse and put it in the ship's morgue down below.

Lindsey looked at Marvia. Marvia looked at Lindsey. Suddenly the campus cop burst out laughing.

'What's so funny?' Lindsey asked him.

'The story's a Hemingway parody. It's really terrible, but it's very funny, too. This is 'The Snows of Kilimanjaro'. When did he write this?'

Marvia turned the comic over to expose the date on the cover. The campus cop said, 'That fits. The movie came out in '53. They get advance releases in the military; I know we did when I was in the service.

'Benson must have seen *The Snows of Kilimanjaro* and gone scurrying to the library for the original story and written 'The Snows of Fujiyama' as his absurd attempt at homage. I love it!'

Lindsey said, 'I think this case is solved. This is the last piece of the puzzle. Marvia, you know what this is? *It's ben Zinowicz's confession.* It jibes with Sully Winston's story — that ben Zinowicz has denied for thirty years! The murderer was Nathan ben Zinowicz, alias Lieutenant ben Zinowicz. Alias Nat Benson, the author of this story!'

Marvia studied the old comic book for

a long time. She stared at the pages of 'The Snows of Fujiyama' in silence, slowly nodding to herself.

Then she took a pencil and paper out of her pocket. She printed two columns of block letters, running vertically down the page, switching back and forth between *Gangsters at War* and her worksheet. She studied her handiwork, then drew a line through the first four letters in the left-hand column, drew another line across the page, then crossed out the next five letters in the right-hand column. She continued that way, alternately crossing out groups of letters and drawing lines across the page. When she finished she turned the paper around. 'Talk about chutzpah!'

Lindsey read the block letters that remained on Marvia's sheet. 'Good God!' he whispered. 'Like a little kid playing secret agent.'

Marvia nodded. 'Come on, Bart. Let's go see Sergeant Yamura.'

24

The campus cop witnessed Marvia's signature on the evidence bag. They sealed ben Zinowicz's office again, then Marvia and Lindsey headed for Berkeley police headquarters.

Sergeant Yamura wasn't there. They wound up outside Lieutenant O'Hara's office, where the lieutenant flexed his bureaucratic muscles by making them wait.

Lindsey wandered down the hall and located a pay phone. Jack Glessner would more likely be at home than at Cape 'n' Dagger.

Alvin Olsen answered the ring. When Lindsey identified himself, Olsen told him that Glessner had died during the night. Olsen was now the acting general manager of the Cape 'n' Dagger chain, pending reorganization of the business.

After an embarrassed silence Lindsey told Olsen that all the Comic Cavalcade loot was now recovered. He had just wanted to thank Jack for his help. Olsen thanked him for calling.

Lindsey then phoned his office. 'The phone's been ringing like crazy,' Ms. Wilbur said. 'Mr. Harden called three times. He says would Mr. Lindsey *please* return his call. Imagine that! And Ms. Johanssen at National. She wants you to call her back. She called between Mr. Harden's second call and his third. Somehow he found out, and he says please return his call before you return Ms. Johanssen's.'

Lindsey said, 'Some fun.'

Ms. Wilbur said, 'Mr. Coffman, the lawyer, says he wants to buy you a drink at Maxi's first chance you get. Bart, you're the golden boy of International Surety, you know. There's even a squib in today's *Wall Street Journal* about the takeover and what the improvement in International Surety's field operation can mean.'

'Do me a favor, Ms. Wilbur. Call Harden and Johanssen and tell them I'm tied up and I'll get back to them as soon as I can. And call Eric Coffman and tell him he's on and I'll bring a friend. I'll get back to him about a day and time.'

'I'll be delighted,' Ms. Wilbur said.

Lindsey called the hospital to ask about Margarita Horowitz. They put him through to her room. Margarita's roommate Susan Gerber answered.

'The doctors don't want to say,' she told him, 'but I don't think there's going to be any change, God damn it!'

Lindsey went back to O'Hara's office. Marvia Plum was sitting on a hard-backed chair working on a report. She looked up and gave him a smile.

O'Hara's door finally opened and a red-faced uniformed cop came out. From inside the office O'Hara shouted, 'Okay, Plum, get in here and bring that insurance guy with you.'

Once in O'Hara's office, Marvia stood respectfully at attention. O'Hara growled, 'Siddown.'

Lindsey hadn't waited for the invitation, he had already sat down.

'Okay,' O'Hara said, 'I understand you got all your comic books back, Mr. Lindsey.'

'Lieutenant, there's a lot more to this

than stolen comics.'

'Yeah, that little storekeeper kid that got whammed. That was a pity. And I know about your little boat ride with the professor. He's been booked by a U.S. commissioner. We'll need you for testimony — whoever tries the case will. I guess you could bring a civil action too. Looks like the prof has a bundle. You might as well go after it. You and Miss Horowitz, the poor thing.'

Marvia Plum spoke up. 'Lieutenant O'Hara, there was also the whole matter of that car chase, the incident on the Golden Gate Bridge, Professor ben Zinowicz's friend Francis.'

O'Hara said, 'I know about all that. City of Richmond, highway patrol, Coast Guard, City and County of San Francisco — none of it happened in Berkeley. Not my problem. You got something else? Otherwise I got other things to take care of. You belong on your post, Plum, not playing helper to this insurance boy.'

Lindsey started to intervene but Marvia pressed him back into his chair. 'Lieutenant, the Bjorklund killing in Alameda — '

'Never heard of it. I don't solve crimes in Alameda and Alameda don't solve crimes in Berkeley. Anything else, Plum?'

Calmly, Marvia said, 'Lieutenant, Mr. Lindsey has reason to believe that Professor ben Zinowicz was involved in a murder that took place many years ago. Edvard Bjorklund also knew about it. In fact he was probably a witness to the incident. There was another survivor, now living in Santa Barbara,' Lindsey added. 'Professor ben Zinowicz had written a short story based on the incident. His confession — or maybe his boast. It was published in a minor comic book in 1953. Nobody paid any attention to the story back then, and it was completely forgotten. It was one of those little text stories they used to put in comics. They did it to meet some nutty postal regulation. He was a fool to allow it to be published, but he felt safe.'

O'Hara nodded. 'Yeah, I read comics when I was a kid. Nobody I knew ever read one of those dopey stories.'

'Except that Ed Bjorklund read this one!' Lindsey resumed. 'I don't know what went on between him and the professor. I have a feeling that Bjorklund may have blackmailed ben Zinowicz. For thirty years! Then there was some kind of final confrontation. Bjorklund had a grown-up daughter. She needed money. Bjorklund tried to hit ben Zinowicz for a big lump payment — that's only my guess, but I think that's what happened. Ben Zinowicz refused to pay. Bjorklund was a comic book collector; he'd been saving comics for thirty-odd years. He took his comics to a dealer in Alameda and tried to raise the money for his daughter. The dealer sent him to Terry Patterson in Berkeley and he left the comics with Patterson on consignment.'

Lindsey felt like Angela Lansbury explaining a convoluted murder scheme to Tom Bosley on TV.

'Ben Zinowicz went to see Bjorklund. He wanted the comic book that his confession was printed in. *Gangsters at War* number 27. Bjorklund told him he couldn't have it; he'd decided to sell his collection and the comics were in Berkeley.'

O'Hara said, 'Hold it. This Bjorklund had this confession of the prof's for thirty years? And for all that time ben Zinowicz paid him off. And then when Bjorklund goes for the big pot, ben Zinowicz stonewalls. So Bjorklund takes the comic book down to a store and sells it for peanuts. Are you kidding?'

'That's weird,' Lindsey admitted. 'But what was he going to do if ben Zinowicz just refused to pay? Sully Winston had been yelling about the *Lewiston* incident for years and nobody believed him. The first time around, the navy had investigated, and ben Zinowicz came away with a medal! All Bjorklund had was a thirty-three-year-old comic book. There wasn't really anything he could do, but he and ben Zinowicz were so tied up in their relationship that neither of them realized it. Until the end, I guess. It was really sick. A blackmailer and a murderer, feeding off each other's needs. Ben Zinowicz's guilt and pride. Bjorklund's greed.'

O'Hara was listening with more respect now. He said, 'Then if you're right, ben Zinowicz finally went to Alameda and killed Bjorklund. I still have problems with that.'

Lindsey said, 'I don't know whether ben Zinowicz believed Bjorklund about having sold the comic book and then acted in rage, or didn't believe him and acted to keep him from ever telling what he knew. Maybe he thought the book was still in Bjorklund's house and went there to get it away from him. I'd guess that Bjorklund and Sullivan Winston didn't know about each other. If they had, they could have hung ben Zinowicz. Separately, nobody believed Winston, and Bjorklund had found it more profitable to take money from the prof than to speak up. By the time Bjorklund tried for the main chance and ben Zinowicz called his bluff, poor Bjorklund had put himself out on a limb. If he blew the whistle on ben Zinowicz he'd also reveal himself as an extortionist. But when the final showdown came, ben Zinowicz killed Bjorklund. And then he ransacked Bjorklund's house — either searching for the comics or trying to simulate a burglary. Whichever.'

Marvia said, 'Maybe it was Francis who did the killing.'

'Okay,' O'Hara said. 'We can get the

ballistics report on the bullet that killed Bjorklund. We have the one that ben Zinowicz shot at Lindsey. If they match, we've got a possible case. But once ben Zinowicz had killed Bjorklund — if he did — what comes next?'

'He followed up Bjorklund's story,' Lindsey said. 'He discovered that the comics really were in Terry Patterson's store.'

'This is all a wonderful theory, Mr. Lindsey.' O'Hara frowned. 'But why didn't the good professor just buy the cheap comic book from Terry Patterson?'

Lindsey shrugged. 'Patterson was such a compulsive scholar in his field, ben Zinowicz must have been afraid to direct his attention to that particular comic book and its text story. There was just one thing that kept Patterson — or some other fan — from reading ben Zinowicz's confession years ago.'

'Yeah — what?'

' 'Nobody ever reads the text stories,' ' Lindsey quoted. In a way, that made ben Zinowicz's whole series of crimes unnecessary, but he didn't see it like that. There was his confession in print, in what was almost certainly the only surviving copy of a very obscure comic book. Ben Zinowicz had written a learned paper himself about 'extinct' publications, and had used *Gangsters at War* number 27 as an example!'

'So the prof tried to burn down the store,' O'Hara jibed, 'to destroy that one comic book.'

'You're not far off. He started a fire for just that purpose, but then he ran up against his own scholarly compulsions. He started the fire, then he realized that he was going to destroy all that precious accumulation of popular culture.'

'Comic books?' O'Hara roared.

'Yes. To him they're the stuff of modern mass culture. He couldn't bring himself to destroy them. So he put the fire out himself and decided to steal the comics instead. To steal the whole Ridge Technology collection and take *Gangsters at War* with it. The big burglary, taking the RTS books, was just a red herring. But once he'd stolen the valuable comics, he had to get rid of them.'

'And everything that followed, including two deaths and the beating of Miss Horowitz and shooting you, was part of returning the unwanted comics. Even though he'd successfully stolen them and they were worth a quarter of a million bucks.' O'Hara's voice dripped sarcasm.

Lindsey said, 'An old insurance scam. Steal or destroy or even kill a whole group of victims to conceal the fact that you're out to get just one of them. He stole thirty-five comic books with a cumulative value of a quarter-million dollars. Thirty-four of them were worth hundreds or thousands of dollars apiece. One was worth $3.50. That was the only one he really wanted.'

Marvia said, 'Here's the comic book with his confession.' She handed O'Hara the manila evidence envelope with the comic.

They waited in silence while he read the story by Nat Benson. Finally he looked at Marvia. 'You got anything else?' he asked.

She showed him the note transcribed from the initials in the story. 'The left column, Lieutenant, is the first letters of each paragraph. The right column is the last letters of each column.'

'I heard about you and crosswords, Plum.'

'Yes sir. The way you decode it, you start down each column. One will be gibberish, the other will spell a word. When you come to the end of the word, you draw a line across the paper and switch to the other column.'

O'Hara dropped the scrap of paper onto the comic book. 'Uh-huh. So the left column starts out R-A-I-T. That's nothing. But the right column is T-H-I-S.'

'Correct. Then you switch columns.'

'Yeah. The left column is S-T-O-R-Y, and the right is junk. Then the right says I-S. Then the left says, uh, A-B-S-O-L-U-T-E-L-Y and the right says T-R-U-E. Holy shit! I can't believe this! A professor, hey?'

'It's all right there, Lieutenant.'

O'Hara grabbed his telephone. 'Operator? Call the Alameda County Prosecutor's office and have 'em send an assistant D.A. up here, *fast*. And get Dorothy Yamura in.

I don't care where she is!' He frowned at a sudden thought. 'But look, once he had stolen those valuable books, why did he try to smuggle 'em back into the stores? Why not sell 'em — or keep 'em for himself?'

Marvia Plum answered that. 'If he tried to sell them, they'd be identified at once. And he couldn't keep them — they were too dangerous. Thirty-five time bombs waiting to explode.'

O'Hara tried one more. 'Why not just burn 'em?'

Marvia shook her head. 'As Mr. Lindsey said, he may have been a murderer and a thief, but he was a scholar and a collector, too. He'd rather die than destroy those comic books.'

'Then why didn't he destroy the one comic book that was dangerous to him?'

Marvia said, 'The creative ego, Lieutenant. All that warped soul had ever wanted in life was to be a comics professional. To draw or at least to write a story for the comics. That one lousy story, 'The Snows of Fujiyama,' was the only thing he'd done in his life that he was really proud of. To let the single surviving copy of that comic book be destroyed — to become extinct, in his words — was simply unthinkable.'

The door opened to admit Sergeant Yamura. Five minutes later the assistant D.A. arrived. O'Hara led Plum and Lindsey through the whole story again. When they finished the Assistant D.A. nodded and smiled. 'The whole story hinges on ben Zinowicz's alleged visit to Alameda, to Edvard Bjorklund's house. I don't expect he'll help us much in that regard. We'll check his class schedules and out-of-town business and hope we can show he was in the area that night, and that there's no alibi.'

'It looks to me as if Francis really did kill Patterson,' Lindsey said. 'Suppose ben Zinowicz tries to alibi for the night Bjorklund was killed and lays that on Francis too?'

'That will be tough. Always easy to dump guilt into a grave. It's going to be exceedingly difficult to get him for that murder anyway. But he definitely shot you in the boat, and he attacked Ms

Horowitz. One way or another I'll hang his ass!' She didn't even blush when she said that. 'Where is he now?'

Lindsey gave her the hospital where he and Margarita and Nathan ben Zinowicz had all been taken.

She picked up the telephone.

Five minutes and three calls later she hung up, looking grim. 'He's out on his own recognizance. Can you believe that? Academic community, homeowner, war hero — they O.R.'d him! I'll get a fresh warrant for him — we'll have a pickup order in an hour.'

Marvia drove Lindsey back to Point Richmond to pick up his Hyundai. 'You sure you can handle it, Bart?'

He said, 'I'll be okay.'

Marvia kissed him on the lips.

He climbed into his Hyundai, wrestled his crutches into the back seat, and cautiously started the engine.

Marvia follow him in her Mustang until he lost sight of her on the freeway. He would be back in Walnut Creek in no time.

25

Lindsey nearly rammed the car sitting in his driveway. It was getting dark and he was exhausted and didn't expect to find a vehicle parked outside the one-car garage.

He extracted his crutches from the back seat and leaned on them as he locked up the car. His headache had subsided somewhat, but now his wounded foot was giving him gyp.

As he approached the car blocking the driveway he saw the personalized license plate — NBZ-PHD!

What was that son of a bitch doing here? Lindsey was rocked by waves of emotion passing through him: first shock, then rage, then fear.

Who was in the house with ben Zinowicz? Joanie Schorr? Mrs. Hernandez? Or only Mother?

A few strides carried him to the front door. He fitted his key in the lock, shoved the door open, and maneuvered himself inside on his crutches.

The only sound was the loud rock beat of Bill Haley coming from the TV.

Mother was wearing a cardigan sweater and plaid skirt. She sat in her favorite easy chair, a fixed smile on her face and a dazed expression in her eyes.

Behind her Nathan ben Zinowicz leaned on the back of the chair, his weight balanced on his good leg. His polished walking stick was drawn across Mother's throat. With one quick tug ben Zinowicz could cut off her breath.

Lindsey stared. 'Haven't you done enough? Haven't you — ' He ran out of words.

Ben Zinowicz said, 'You know, your mother and I were acquainted many years ago. I've simply returned to pay a social call.'

'Lieutenant ben Zinowicz is your father's friend,' Mother said. Watching the TV, she seemed oblivious to the stick drawn across her throat. 'He came to visit us. We have to be hospitable, Hobo.'

She looked at Lindsey and ben Zinowicz. 'You've both hurt yourselves,' she said. 'You have to be careful, you know.'

Lindsey ignored her. 'What do you want, ben Zinowicz?'

Ben Zinowicz said nothing.

Mother said, 'Nathan is a fan of your father's, Hobo. He came to look at Joey's work. You know those comic books that Joey draws for. But I can't remember where I put them. Do you remember where I put them?'

Lindsey stared at ben Zinowicz. 'Is that it? You think we have more copies of *Gangsters at War*, the famous extinct comic book? I guess you're not as crazy as I thought.'

Ben Zinowicz said, 'You've given me reason to hate you, Lindsey. An emotion of which I had purged myself. Or so I thought. Perhaps another purgation will succeed.'

Lindsey had no idea what ben Zinowicz was driving at.

Ben Zinowicz lowered his walking stick from Mother's throat and made his way to the couch, leaning on the stick. 'You've dredged up unhappy memories, raked the coals of a fire that I thought dead and cold thirty years ago. You should have left me alone. I would have returned the favor.'

'Leave you alone? After what you've done?' Lindsey placed his hand against his bandaged face, shifting his weight on one crutch to free the hand.

Ben Zinowicz said, 'You do not understand the pain you've caused me. That awful day on the deck of the *Lewiston*. Hobart, what do you understand of pain? Of guilt? Don't you know that Sullivan Winston told me his dreadful story a hundred times — the same story he told you? About his dreams, about my saving him from the flaming holocaust and kicking Joseph Lindsey back into the fire?'

He dropped his gaze to his own crippled leg and shook his head slowly. 'Did I fight Lindsey off because he was going to pull me into the flames? Was it because we would all have died — Winston, Lindsey, and myself? Did I cause one death to avert two others?'

He exhaled slowly as Lindsey stood

fascinated, his half-mad mother and his wounded foot equally forgotten.

'I'd convinced myself. Winston kept gouging me. Bjorklund kept gouging me too. But even so, I'd managed to put aside my guilt. Managed to believe that I kicked your father then to save Winston and myself. Not because I wanted Joseph Lindsey dead. Not because I hated him for having the talent that I lacked, for having the success that I had failed to attain. Not for the cruel truth that he spoke about my work.'

Lindsey felt sweat on his face.

From the couch ben Zinowicz continued. 'Do you know what it is to live with such a burden? To live with that guilt, with the self-loathing and pain that it brings with it, for thirty-three years? Yet I had succeeded in suppressing it, Hobart. It would come back sometimes in the night and Francis would hold me while I wept. You've taken him from me and you've stirred up the coals and brought back all the shame that I thought I had rid myself of forever. I hate myself now, Hobart. And you've done that to me.'

Somewhere in the house the telephone rang, again and again. To Mother it was just background noise, her attention fixed on the TV. Ben Zinowicz spoke over the ringing, ignoring it, and Lindsey listened only to the professor.

'And now,' ben Zinowicz said, 'I'm ruined as an academic. I don't mind prison — that isn't what devastates me. It's who I am. Your damned father showed me that I'd never be a comics professional. And you and your friend Sojourner Strength took away Francis.

'What can I take from you, Lindsey? You're so pitiful, you don't even have anything to lose. Except your mother! I'm going to take her from you. I'm going to kill her, right here, before your eyes. Then I'll call the police, or you can do it for me. And they can do what they will with me. I won't mind.'

The telephone had stopped ringing.

Lindsey said, 'You killed my dad, and you killed Ed Bjorklund, and you killed Terry Patterson. But I don't believe you'd kill Mother!'

Ben Zinowicz said, 'Francis killed them

both. I sent him to Alameda to get the comic from Bjorklund. Bjorklund said he didn't have it anymore. He extorted money from me for thirty years. Then he sold his comics. He's the crazy one, not me. I'd have paid forever. But he had to make a big killing, and I sent Francis to buy the comic book back from him. I'd tried to bluff him out, but when I saw I couldn't, Francis went to pay him off for me and Bjorklund said he'd sold the comics, and Francis killed him.'

He extracted a handkerchief from his blazer pocket and wiped his eyes. 'I loved Francis, Hobart. He wasn't very bright, and he was sometimes violent, but he had a good heart. But he killed Bjorklund. And he killed Patterson.'

'You're still a murderer,' Lindsey said. 'You killed my father and you tried to kill Margarita Horowitz and you tried to kill me. Margarita may yet die.'

'Not my fault,' ben Zinowicz muttered. He pushed himself upright, leaning heavily on his walking stick. '*You* made me do those things, Hobart. If you'd just left me alone, everything would be all right.' He started forward.

Lindsey blocked his way, balancing on his crutches and his good foot like a three-legged beast.

'I am a commissioned officer in the United States Navy,' ben Zinowicz said. 'Step aside, Lindsey. I am a tenured professor at the University of California. I'm a professional! Don't you know I'm a pro? Didn't you see my story in *Gangsters at War?* Step aside!'

He balanced on his good leg, raised his walking stick, and swung it viciously at Lindsey. 'You'll get this, and then she will,' he grunted.

The stick rebounded from Lindsey's instinctively raised crutch, flew across the room and clanked against the side of the TV.

Ben Zinowicz hopped forward and Lindsey hit him hard with his shoulder. The older man tumbled to the floor. Lindsey watched him struggle back to his feet.

Ben Zinowicz stood with most of his weight on his good leg, looking around for his stick. He spotted it and started to hobble toward it.

Lindsey dropped his crutches, hopping forward on his good foot. Waves of pain pounded upward from his wounded foot. He reached the stick before ben Zinowicz and almost toppled over. Ben Zinowicz caught up with him. He delivered the bandaged side of Lindsey's head a back-handed smash. The impact was like a grenade going off inside Lindsey's skull.

He flexed his good leg and threw everything he had into a punch aimed at ben Zinowicz's face. He landed off target, a glancing blow that sent the two men tumbling to the floor.

Ben Zinowicz scrabbled frantically after his stick. Lindsey grabbed ben Zinowicz's wrist to keep him from swinging the stick again. Two cripples struggled on the carpet.

Someone was pounding on the door. 'I'll go,' Mother said cheerily. 'If you children can't behave, you won't be able to play together. Do you want little Nathan to have to go home, Hobo?' She swung the door open.

Three uniformed figures poured through

the foyer into the living room. Marvia Plum ran forward. Next to her was a Walnut Creek patrolman. The officer grabbed Lindsey and pulled him away from ben Zinowicz. Marvia shouted at the officer, who responded by letting go of Lindsey and wrestling the stick away from ben Zinowicz. He tossed it across the room and clamped a pair of handcuffs onto the professor's wrists.

Marvia knelt on the floor and took Lindsey in her arms. Over her shoulder he could see the third officer, a sergeant, standing with drawn revolver, pointing the weapon at ben Zinowicz. Leaning on Marvia, Lindsey climbed painfully to his feet.

Mother had scurried back to her easy chair. She sat cross-legged on the cushion, hands to her temples like a pair of horse blinders, concentrating on the black and white TV images.

Ben Zinowicz was leaning against the wall, staring from one to another, his face ashen.

Mother smiled at Marvia. 'You must be the new girl,' she said. 'I try to keep up with the house but it's such a problem with a little one underfoot and my husband away at war. It's hard to get a good colored girl to clean up. I hope you'll work out better than the last one we had.'

Lindsey asked the sergeant, 'How did you know he was here?' He jerked his head, indicating ben Zinowicz.

'We didn't know,' the sergeant said. 'Officer Plum was worried about you. She tried to phone here a few minutes ago, but nobody answered. So she drove past and saw the cars. We were cruising by and she flagged us down.'

Marvia said, 'I was worried about you, Bart, so I followed you out here. You lost me for a while, then I spotted your car again. And the BMW.'

Lindsey didn't care about that. He held Marvia and whispered, 'I'm sorry about Mother.'

Marvia smiled sadly. 'She still thinks it's 1953, Bart. I guess that's her excuse. It's better than most.'

'Does it ever stop hurting?' he asked her.

'Never. But you learn to cope with it,' she told him. 'You have to.'

'I will,' he said.

THE END

We do hope that you have enjoyed reading this large print book.

Did you know that all of our titles are available for purchase?

We publish a wide range of high quality large print books including:
Romances, Mysteries, Classics
General Fiction
Non Fiction and Westerns

Special interest titles available in large print are:
The Little Oxford Dictionary
Music Book, Song Book
Hymn Book, Service Book

Also available from us courtesy of Oxford University Press:
Young Readers' Dictionary
(large print edition)
Young Readers' Thesaurus
(large print edition)

For further information or a free brochure, please contact us at:
Ulverscroft Large Print Books Ltd.,
The Green, Bradgate Road, Anstey,
Leicester, LE7 7FU, England.
Tel: (00 44) **0116 236 4325**
Fax: (00 44) **0116 234 0205**

Other titles in the
Linford Mystery Library:

THE DARK CORNERS & OTHER STORIES

Robert J. Tilley

A schoolboy disappears — but the missing child may not be all he seemed . . . A mortician and his family find their new neighbours disturbingly interested in their affairs . . . Quiet Mr. Wooller finds himself the only man ready to take down the Devil . . . An escaped convict stumbles upon an apparently idyllic holiday cottage . . . A spouses' golf game ends in murder . . . In an outwardly perfect marriage, one partner is making dark dealings . . . A young man is subjected to a bizarre hostage-taking . . . Seven unsettling stories from the pen of Robert J. Tilley.

THE SYMBOL SEEKERS

A. A. Glynn

In 1867 a box treasured by a distin-guished American exile in England is stolen. Three battle-hardened ex-Southern soldiers from the recently ended Ameri-can Civil War arrive on an unusual mission: two go on a hectic pursuit of the box in Liverpool and London, whilst third takes a path that could lead to the gallows. Detective Septimus Dacers and Roberta Van Trask, the daughter of an American diplomat, risk their lives as they attempt to foil a grotesque scheme that could cause war between Britain and the United States . . .

SONS OF THE SPHINX

Norman Firth

'We have read of your intended expedition to Egypt, to the Pyramid of Khufu . . . Only death can be your lot if you embark upon this journey. The Sons of the Sphinx.' So reads the sinister message in fine Arabic script mailed to a Hollywood movie producer. But the filming goes ahead — and the body of his chief cameraman is found with his throat cut . . . While in *Corpses Don't Care*, the grand opening of a luxury hotel is ruined by a series of six corpses turning up in the most inconvenient places!

THE LION'S GATE

V. J. Banis

On holiday with her wayward sister Allison at a lakeside town, Peggy Conners is perplexed when Allison packs her bags and vanishes overnight, without explanation. Believing her sister to be in great danger, Peggy eventually traces and confronts her, now living on an island at the Lions family mansion. But then Allison asserts that her name is actually Melissa Lions — and that she has never seen Peggy before in her life!